PENGUIN BOOKS

No Way to Say Goodbye

To Mom
I remember the days when the power in your legs and arms had gone, all hope for a bright future was lost and you in a home with your radio playing on.
I remember your face and the smile in your eyes.
I remember your faith and the lesson that hope never dies.

To my godchildren, Conor O'Shea and Laura Kerins. For you I wish the best this world has to offer but when the shit hits the fan, and it will, Bannie will be there.

# 1. Only twenty miles

It was a rainy afternoon in south Kerry – driving rain reminiscent of the opening credits of a Hollywood action or end-of-the-world movie when, if given to fantasy, one might have expected a muscular, sinewy and scantily dressed male to power through the deluge with a damp and distressed girl in his arms and a gun in his back pocket. What he would do with the girl or the gun, and what the girl and the gun had to do with the rain, would be left up to the imagination of the fantasist. Still, Mary thought, there's nothing like the image of a wet man with a purpose to brighten up an otherwise boring indoor day.

She sat on the window-seat and pulled back the curtains to watch water hit water and slide from the decks of the boats bobbing fiercely by the pier. Mr Monkels, her large yellow Labrador, lay with his head on her lap. He was peeved because rain meant no walk and he loved his walks, even though his advanced years meant that they were little more than a series of rests. Mary smiled at her hefty old friend. "It's not the end of the world, Mr Monkels – there's always tomorrow."

Mr Monkels was unimpressed. He sighed, and the sigh turned to a grunt, which was followed by the low wheezing that often made Mary wonder whether he had a form of dog asthma. Then again, as his age in dog years was the equivalent to eighty-one in humans, it was a miracle that he could breathe unaided, never mind go for a walk. Mary stroked his left ear, which, although deaf, still retained sensitivity to touch – the right, although in perfect working order, had been partly missing since a nasty fishing accident some years before.

Mary's father had given her Mr Monkels, and he had been only two months old at the time of the accident, running around the deck of her uncle's boat while she had concentrated on taking a black-and-white photo of a dead mackerel. Her cousin Ivan was practising casting. Accidentally and inexplicably the hook had found itself embedded in Mr Monkels's ear. Mr Monkels yelped and Mary raised her head in time to see her puppy sail through the air like a furry missile. Ivan shouted, "Jesus on a jet-ski! Watch him go!" before the pup plummeted paws first into the water. He rose to the surface quickly, splashing and yelping. Ivan rescued him. Unfortunately, a large part of his ear had become what Ivan would later term "a casualty of the sea".

Now she stroked his good ear, smiling at the memory of her puppy wagging his tail despite his near-death experience. She had thought back then that he either possessed Herculean bravery, or was Daffy-Duck stupid, and as it turned out, it was a little of both. She lost herself in his big brown cloudy eyes for a minute or two. His nose was dryer than she'd like. She picked up his head and moved it onto a waiting pillow. Mr Monkels moaned a little and briefly she wondered if, in promising him "tomorrow", she'd led him up the proverbial garden path.

The cottage was old and quaint, well insulated and warm, with a homely smell of log fires and home cooking. This had been her primary reason for buying it. She liked its feel.

The kitchen had been refurbished two years ago to Mary's taste but in keeping with its old-worldliness. She liked pottery and had indulged herself with lamps, vases, plates and cups.

The walls were painted a deep purple but the colour was only partially visible under the multitude of black-framed photographs that lined them. As a teenager Mary had been consumed by photography, taking workshops after school and saving for a decent camera and darkroom equipment. Initially, she had shown a flair for black-and-white shots, injecting even the most mundane subject with mystique and beauty. In her late teens she had turned to portraits and hounded her friends for their faces and time. It had been her son who had inspired her to use colour, with his jet-black hair, pink cheeks and blue, blue eyes. A boy like Ben just didn't belong in black-and-white.

Mary's sitting room was like a gallery, with photos of the objects and people in her life, living and dead, on all sides. Her favourite image, for no particular reason, was of a crystal bowl in front of a window with light streaming through it, but there were others, too, of which she was fond: her father bent forward in deep concentration, his glasses on the tip of his nose and the paper in his hand; her auntie Sheila, apron on, hair pinned back, stirring a stew with a grin on her face that suggested she'd just heard a dirty joke; her cousin Ivan, tanned, lean and boyish in shorts and an old fishing cap, casting his line; her old boyfriend Robert, with his shining black hair and smiling eyes, linking arms with Ivan, who was pulling her friend Penny's blonde hair; and Adam, Penny's giant footballer boyfriend, laughing. Mary liked the photo of a black cart laden with freshly cut white lilies because it reminded her of the day that she and Robert, her first and perhaps only love, had gatecrashed a gypsy funeral to get drunk on generosity and free beer. These were only some of the photos she surrounded herself with.

Ben had a wall to himself. It wasn't a shrine but a gallery of her son's laughter, his tears, tantrums, joy and sadness, all captured in twelve eight-by-ten photos that represented the five years of his life.

There were only two bedrooms, but Mary didn't need any more. She lived alone and had done so for five years. She gazed now at her son grasping a wriggling Mr Monkels, and smiled at him, now dead as long as he had lived. He beamed back at her, for ever a five-year-old, and for ever smiling.

She checked the time, realized that the hair dye had been on for well over half an hour – it smelt like shit in sunshine, and she wasn't sure if it was that or the onset of glaucoma that was bringing tears to Mr Monkels's right eye – and went upstairs to wash it out. Later she combed her hair in front of the bathroom mirror, slapped moisturizer on her face and tried fruitlessly to rub out the black rings around her eyes. *Great – I look like a red-haired panda.* She had been dyeing it red since she was fifteen, and few remembered her natural mousy-brown: fire-engine fake set off her pale skin and emerald eyes, even when they were tired and betrayed her twenty-nine years.

Mary emptied the fridge of the food that had gone off during the four days she had been sequestered in her room with a migraine. The rain continued to pour, rattling the windows. Rain always reminded her of Ben – not because he had liked it or any great memories featured it. Perhaps it was just that a lazy indoor day allowed her the time to remember him. Or maybe it was the sound – as though the world was weeping – or the way it crept down the window like tears.

She went into the sitting room, intending to play some music, but instead found herself staring at a framed black-and-white photo of Robert, then a sixteen-year-old boy, standing by a lake holding up a large fish and grinning, his eyes so like his son's. Now as she looked at him she felt more like his mother than his teenage girlfriend. She often wondered what he would have been like if he had lived past seventeen.

"Cheer up, Panda Face," she said, when she glimpsed herself in the mirror.

Mr Monkels groaned. She laughed a little and put on the Scissor Sisters. "After all, Mr M, no one does happy like homos!" She chuckled at her joke but her dog didn't share either her sense of humour or her taste in music, because he buried his head under his big paws, reminding her that she needed to get his claws clipped.

Mary went back into the kitchen and boiled the kettle to make a pot of tea, then pulled out the biscuit tin. It was definitely a day for tea and biscuits. Ivan had dropped in a DVD earlier and she was looking forward to a pleasant evening in front of the TV. But first she'd empty the wash-ing-machine, despite encroaching exhaustion. Mary hadn't slept well the previous night – she'd been woken by a strange dream in which a teenage boy, with a hood pulled tight and covering his face, had been running. She had heard his feet pounding the street and watched his pursuers coming around a corner. His feet moved faster and faster but his steps became shorter and shorter until he was running to stand still. She had woken with a start, her heart racing. Morphine hangover, she'd thought, which made sense: the severe migraine had necessitated two morphine injections each day for four days.

After a shower, a glass of water and a gargle with mouthwash, she had returned to bed with an uneasy feeling that had guaranteed she would lie awake. She often had "feelings" and sometimes they had forecast something terrible but mostly they came to nothing. Around three thirty, weary yet alert, she wondered if the cryptic dream had foretold something bad, as when she had dreamed of Tina "The Hill" Murphy, trapped inside a large, angry-looking egg. At the time she had dismissed it as nothing more than her own propensity for weirdness, but the following week Tina had collapsed at WeightWatchers with a ruptured ovary. Or, indeed, when she had dreamed of Jimmy Jaw frantically searching for something in what appeared to be a large medical wastebin: later that week he'd lost his little finger in a freak sawing accident. And there had been the time when she'd woken to an image of Sheena Shaw's cat, Johnson, on a flying carpet, passing through clouds in the company of a sickly miniature pig, only to hear the very next day that he had been throwing up bacon. The cat had survived but Sheena's six-month-old carpet stank to high heaven and required replacing.

Mary began listing some of the endless possibilities. Was the hooded boy a metaphor for a death? *Poor Mr Monkels!* She worried about her dog until approximately three fifty

6

at which time, having accepted that the link between a hooded boy and an ancient dog was tenuous, she considered whether or not the dream might have related to Penny's disastrous love life. Then again, this disaster was on-going. *That might explain the running. Poor Penny!* But the kid was definitely a boy, not a girl, and after all, Penny's love life might not have been the stuff of fairytales but at least she had one. It was just after four fifteen when she had begun to contemplate why she was alone. *Am I frigid? No, I like to get laid just as much as the next person. It's very relaxing. Am I scared? Yes? No? Maybe. OK, this is getting too heavy. Change the subject. Am I a lunatic? Has grief driven me to the edge of sanity?* She smiled – in her head she was humming "She's A Maniac".

Although her ramblings distracted her, they had no effect on her elevated pulse or sense of dread so she refocused. Her dad had just had his heart checked and was healthier than a fourteen-year-old. Ivan seemed happy and healthy, although he was still adjusting to life after an acrimonious separation. It had been more than a year ago, but he hadn't even attempted to find himself a girlfriend. It seemed a great waste to Mary as her cousin was kind, loving and not an ugly man. At around five she vowed to watch over him, knowing that he wasn't built to be alone.

At six she was still uneasy. Maybe it was down to the rain that had started to fall just after she had woken from the dream. The pier had flooded last year and some of the cottages had been badly damaged. She had miraculously escaped for no other reason than sheer luck and there was no way she would be lucky twice. It was extraordinary that she'd been lucky once. Maybe fear of flooding was niggling in her. *Yeah, it must be that.*

Despite her outward appearance, which suggested a calm, cool nature to those who loved her, and possibly an impenetrable, cold one to others, Mary often worried about things that most people didn't. She would often daydream about terrible events that she would undoubtedly survive while those around her didn't. The end of the world was her recurring nightmare – she'd be left to stand in the centre of the universe alone, with nothing but thousands of miles of bodies and destruction around her. She wasn't depressive or paranoid; she wasn't insane or morbid. She was just aware that bad things happened and that they could and did happen to her. She didn't have the comfort of viewing death and disaster as some faraway notion to be skipped over in favour of a conversation about shoes.

It was a belief long held by Mary and many of the townspeople of Kenmare that she was a curse to those who loved her. She had long ago become used to being called "Mary of the Sorrows". Of course, it was used mostly behind her back but sometimes an individual slipped and more often than not she responded to the truncated version: "Mary of the . . .".

People around her had died – her mother, her boyfriend and her son – and she had long ago accepted that her place in the world would be apart from the crowd. Her father had often attempted to disprove her theory – after all, he had survived – and she would smile at him, but it didn't help that she would most likely survive him too, and that one day he would be a picture for her to lose herself in on a rainy day.

Mary put a basket of neatly folded clean clothes under the stairs: a four-day headache culminating in a sleepless night meant she was too jaded to iron. The phone rang and she considered ignoring it but curiosity was her downfall.

"Hello?" she said.

"Jesus, have you seen the rain?" It was Penny.

"Yeah," she agreed, relieved to hear her friend's voice. "Mr Monkels is like a pig."

"Mr Monkels smells like a pig," Penny retorted, and Mary laughed because she was right – his farts brought tears to your eyes.

"Are you better?" Penny asked.

"Yeah."

"No blind spots, facial paralysis or partial blindness?"

"Nope, I'm back in black."

"Excellent," her friend noted. "Why don't we celebrate and head over to Killarney to see a movie?"

Mary looked out of the window again. "It's horrible out there. I was planning on a night in with a DVD, the rain at the window, the dog on my lap and a pot of tea at my elbow."

Penny's heart was set on the new George Clooney film. "I swear you're such an old lady, Mary – how the hell are you ever going to meet someone if your idea of a great night is sitting in with a dog?"

"Oh, and going to the Killarney Cineplex is a great way to meet men?" Mary countered. "Besides, there's a lot to be said for staying in," she continued, while attempting to remove a chocolate stain from her cardigan, armed with saliva and her thumb. At the same time she realized that the cardigan gave Penny's previous statement some credence so she took it off. She might be unwilling to look for love in a Cineplex but she wasn't inclined to turn into Miss Marple. "Why don't you come over?" she asked.

"Hmmm, let me see . . . George Clooney or you and a dog?"

"What's the movie?" Mary asked.

"Who cares? I just want to look at something pretty," Penny answered, true to form.

"And I'm supposed to be the sad one!" Mary shook her head in mock-despair.

"Yeah, well, 'Penny of the Sorrows' doesn't have the same ring to it. Besides, there's nothing sad about wanting to watch that sexy bastard get up to a few tricks."

"I used to love him in *ER*. He was so great with kids . . ."

"Yeah, that's what's so appealing!" Penny giggled.

Silence followed – they had reached an impasse. Mary wanted to stay within her four walls and Penny to break free of hers.

"Come on, I have a deep need to be shallow and a desperate need of distraction. If you drive, I can have a drink," Penny pleaded.

Mary thought about it. "You always need distracting."

Penny would have pushed, but she knew how Mary felt about crossing the mountain in the rain and also that, despite what Mary had said, her head probably felt like it had just been kicked.

"I have a bottle of wine in the fridge," Mary said, knowing that would be the deciding factor in whether her friend chose her over a movie star.

"All right," Penny conceded. "What's the DVD?"

Mary grabbed it from the coffee-table. "*What's Eating Gilbert Grape?*" she read off the label.

"What's eating what?"

"It's directed by Lasse Hallstrom." She knew her friend hadn't a clue or a care as to who he was.

"What?"

"He directed *Once Around*," she read on.

Penny remained unimpressed.

"Which was a Sundance favourite apparently," Mary continued pathetically.

"Sundance means worthy and worthy means complete crap." Penny's capacity to imbue her voice with disdain was quite theatrical.

Mary smiled. "Yeah, well, this one mentions nothing about Sundance, it's about . . ." She read on silently.

Penny was busy weighing up her options. "An eating movie directed by a man who sounds like a weather system or George Clooney?" It was an unfair contest – but she didn't feel like facing the mountain alone either and she had to get out of the house. Still, she needed more information before she committed to a night in – after all, she could always go to the pub.

Mary hadn't noticed the actors' names and, when at last she did, she knew the deal was sealed. "Hah! Starring Johnny Depp and Leonardo DiCaprio!" She heard Penny stand up.

"Open the wine, I'm on my way."

# 2. Who is who?

Penny pulled a bottle of wine from the rack, reminding herself to replenish the dwindling supply. She was pulling on her coat when the phone rang and, thinking it would be Mary, attempting to put in a post-migraine chocolate order, she picked it up.

"Penn." It was Adam.

*Oh, God, no – go away.* "What do you want?" she asked, pissed off that he'd caught her off guard.

"You," he said, and she sensed his sheepish grin. She wanted to punch his face in.

"Is that what you told your wife?" she said, her voice dripping with sarcasm and just a hint of bitterness.

"Don't." He sighed, and she wanted to cry.

She remained silent. There was nothing left to say. He'd said it all the night before. He had to end it. He could never leave his wife. And, in fact, she had known this. Although she loved him – and she truly did – he wasn't hers. He had three kids and ran his father-in-law's business. He belonged to his wife. She'd earned him – at least, that was how he'd put it when he'd broken off their affair for the last time. It didn't matter that Adam was her first love or that Penny was his passion. It didn't matter that they had loved one another for more than half their lives. It didn't matter that he had married his wife on the rebound. It didn't matter that he didn't love the woman. It didn't even matter that they had turned into some soap-opera cliché. He was married to someone else and that meant Penny was leftovers and destined to remain on the periphery in the shadow of another woman's marriage. But no more. She was well and truly sick of it.

"You were right to end it. I don't want to be alone any more, Adam," she said, tears tumbling again, much to her chagrin.

"I don't want that for you either. I . . . I . . ." Clearly he didn't know what to say – there was nothing to say.

She could hear him breaking down and now she wanted to hug him but she couldn't. She was determined to be strong. "I have to go," she said.

"Don't," he begged.

She hung up and sank to the floor, crying for the fifth time that day. She was going to cancel the stupid DVD evening, but then she became terrified that Adam would turn up at her door, and if he did, she would most certainly let him in, and once he was inside she wouldn't be able to say no. But first she'd have a drink, just to settle her nerves.

Afternoon had passed into late evening and then to night. The town was silent, with few venturing out. Penny drove past the pubs, restaurants and shops, all brightly painted and featuring window-boxes, whose colourful contents absorbed the falling water thirstily. She had stopped crying, instead allowing the rain that coursed down the windscreen to do it for her. Sinéad O'Connor's rendition of "Nothing Compares To You" had been playing on the radio and she'd broken a fingernail in her hasty attempt to change the station. Still, everything was fine now. She would go to Mary's and they'd watch a DVD and she'd talk rubbish and forget about the sad, sorry, pathetic mess that was her world. Although she had often worried that her friend had given up on love, it was days like these that made her wonder if Mary was right. She wouldn't admit it, though, not yet – she might be heartbroken but she still had hope.

At the window Mr Monkels stood up and barked hello to Mossy Leary from number three who had stopped to help Penny – she was battling to open her umbrella although she had to walk just ten paces from her car to the door. Mossy was in his late thirties with long dark hair in a pony-tail. He was skinnier than Kate Moss and had saucer eyes that Penny often joked made him look like a cartoon character. He was a part-time fisherman, part-time house-painter, part-time sculptor and full-time stoner.

Mary opened the door and waved at him. He gave her the thumbs-up, then headed off towards town on a quest for a few free pints. She smiled at her friend, who was cursing the umbrella and attempting to shield her head with a hand.

Mary had woken to Penny's knock. Her watch revealed that hours had passed since her friend had agreed to come over. "I thought you were on your way?"

"I'm here, am I not?" Penny asked, with a playful grin.

"You live ten minutes not six hours away."

"Sorry." Penny pushed past her. "I got held up." She didn't elaborate.

Mary poured a glass of white wine from the bottle she'd had chilling in the fridge. Penny drank, then turned off Simon and Garfunkel's ode to the sound of silence, which had been on repeat for most of the evening. "What's wrong?" she asked.

"Nothing."

"Are you maudlin?" Penny narrowed her eyes and adopted the pose of interrogator.

"No," Mary said.

"Liar. Still, at least it wasn't Radiohead. I swear I'd have left."

Mary smiled. "I'm fine." She topped up Penny's glass.

"Good. I can't do depressing tonight," Penny said, as she slumped into a chair. She wrinkled her nose as Mary disappeared into the kitchen. "What's that smell?"

"Shit in sunshine," Mary said, returning. She handed Penny a plate of brown bread and smoked salmon. She had mouthed "shit" rather than saying it aloud – she had stopped swearing soon after she became a mother.

"Dyeing your hair?"

Mary nodded.

"Nice job." Penny put her feet up on the sofa and made herself comfortable, with the plate on her lap.

Mary disappeared into the kitchen again.

"Hey!" Penny shouted.

"Yeah?"

"Mossy mentioned that Lucy Thomas was in next door earlier."

Mary came back with some chilli nuts, which she placed on the table. "Oh, yeah?" she said.

Penny knew her too well to be fooled by her nonchalance. "I wonder if you're due a new neighbour." She smiled as she sipped and began to read the blurb on the DVD box.

Meanwhile Mary struggled with the curtains. "No way," she mumbled, more to herself than to her friend. "She's probably just checking the house for flooding."

Penny was grinning. "She's come all the way from Mallow to check for flooding? Yeah, that must be it."

Mary looked out of the window at the boat that had docked earlier that week, slapping against the pier wall. "What's it like in town?"

"Wet, windy, ghostly." Penny was reading the back of the DVD with an expression of confusion on her face. "'A prisoner of his dysfunctional family's broken dreams in tiny Endora, Gilbert (Depp)' – I love him! – 'serves as breadwinner and caretaker for his mother and siblings following his father's suicide, his older brother's defection . . . Momma (Darlene Cates)' – who's she? – 'is a morbidly obese shut-in' – Oh, my God! – 'who hasn't left the house in seven years and her children include retarded Arnie . . .' Wait a minute – DiCaprio's retarded? You *are* taking the piss!"

Mary couldn't help but enjoy Penny's disgust. "Ivan said it was funny in parts," she said.

"Funny? Yeah, it really sounds hilarious!" And then it dawned on Penny. "Jesus, it was filmed in 1993! DiCaprio's retarded and his balls hadn't even dropped! What am I supposed to do with this?" She was holding the DVD in the air like a demonstrator in a supermarket.

"I don't know – what would you have done with it if DiCaprio *wasn't* retarded and his balls *had* dropped?" Mary grinned.

"Good point," Penny agreed. "Still, this does not sound remotely shallow." She sighed, laying the DVD on the coffee-table.

"Are you OK?" Mary asked, concerned. She seemed OK but she was a master in the art of masking. Mary had often thought what a great actor she would have made, but Penny had joined an acting class one summer and hated it, calling those around her a bunch of jumped-up talent-free tossers. Then she had made what could only have been described as a grand exit. Now she was smiling but Mary sensed a problem. *Maybe the dream* was *about Penny*.

"I'm fine. It's just the endless rain," Penny lied. She wasn't ready to admit that she and Adam had ended their relationship, first because she wanted to forget but also because she wasn't sure that either of them would be able to stick to their guns. After all, they had broken up many times before. "Just put the film on and pass the bottle."

Mary was suspicious but she didn't say anything. When Penny was ready to share her problem, she'd be there to listen. She knew what it was like to have people stick their noses in.

They were halfway through the film and Penny was finishing off the wine. Mary seemed to be enjoying the sad tale. Crispin Glover as the undertaker made her laugh and Darlene Cates prompted an "Aaah!"

By contrast Penny mumbled, "Kill me!" several times while she downed her wine and played with her broken fingernail.

"If I didn't know DiCaprio was an actor I'd believe he was retarded," said Mary. "He's really pulled it off."

"Yeah, it's great," Penny said.

"Like that Down's syndrome kid – you know, the one on that TV show with the blonde girl who did *Romeo and Juliet* with DiCaprio. What's his name?"

"Corky," Penny said, perking up.

"Yeah, Corky. He was great."

"He was. Wrong girl, though – you're thinking of the blonde who went out with the HIV-infected teenager." Penny was looking for the corkscrew.

"Rob Lowe's brother?"

"Yes."

"I thought she went on to play Juliet?" Mary said.

"No, that was the redhead from that other show. She was in love with the dyslexic rebel and had a gay best friend."

"Funny – I could have sworn Juliet was Corky's sister," Mary said.

"The guy who played her boyfriend is a lead singer with a rock band now," Penny said, still searching for the corkscrew.

"Rob Lowe's brother?"

"No, the dyslexic rebel."

"Oh. Any good?"

"Haven't a clue," she said, finally locating it. She opened the second bottle and poured a glassful.

Meanwhile, on screen, DiCaprio was being left to freeze to death in a cold bath overnight, forgotten by Depp, his horny brother.

"Kill me!" Penny repeated.

"We can turn it off," Mary offered, battling the urge to cry for the boy, shaking and blue-lipped, on the screen.

"No. It's fine. Seriously, it's not that bad," Penny conceded, but then Depp ended his affair with the married Mary Steenburgen, and Penny broke down in tears.

"Do you need a break?" Mary asked, and Penny nodded, unable to speak.

"OK." Mary switched off the TV.

Penny wiped her eyes, mumbling something about how pathetic she was.

"Do you want some coffee?" Mary asked.

"No. I'll finish my wine."

"Do you want a hug?"

"That would be lovely."

They hugged.

"I'm such a sap," Penny said. "But, Mare?"

"Yeah?" Mary pulled away while Penny composed herself.

"Do you think it's better to be alone?" Penny asked.

"No." Mary shook her head. "But possibly safer."

"Yeah, I suppose you're right."

"So you're fine?" Mary asked, with a raised eyebrow, while Penny blew her nose.

"I will be."

Mary leaned over and kissed her forehead to comfort her, much as she'd once comforted her son. "Yes, you will," she said. *Once a mother, always a mother.*

Penny was too drunk to drive home so Mary fixed up the spare bedroom when the film finally ended. She wasn't usually a crier, unlike Mary, for whom hiding emotion was a constant battle. Mary wasn't sure if her friend had ended her affair with the only man she had ever loved and she didn't know how desperately heartbroken she was – but she didn't know much when it came to love. She didn't have a clue what it was like to feel anything other than ambivalence towards the men who had crossed her path since Robert had died. She had little understanding of Penny's heartbreak.

And yet Penny believed that she understood Mary's lethargy towards love. To her mind, Robert had been Mary's first and only love. Even now she couldn't forget the one who had tied her up in knots, as she faced her thirties.

Mary's first love had died, leaving her a son who had followed his dad. Of course, Penny thought that Mary couldn't let herself fall in love because love had only brought her suffering. But Penny's view of Mary's pain was simplistic. Penny was a diehard romantic. She liked to think that Robert was the Romeo to Mary's Juliet. In reality, Mary's reasons for being alone were far more mundane than that.

That night Mary tucked Penny in, while Penny made a drunken, silent pact to be more like her friend. She vowed to close off, to shut out the world and all its rubbish. It occurred to her that maybe then she'd have half a chance of being happy.

Mary stood at the bedroom door, watching Penny who was stirring. "You need to go to the loo again, don't you?" She wondered what the hell was going through her friend's mind.

"I can go myself," Penny slurred.

"I know," Mary said, hoisting her from the bed.

And as they walked to the bathroom arm in arm, Penny asked her why life was so hard.

"Because God is a spoilt child and this world is just a game He plays to amuse Himself."

"We're prawns," Penny agreed.

"Pawns."

"That's what I said – prawns."

Mary helped her to sit on the loo, Penny's pants around her ankles, not shy – they had been sharing toilet stalls since they were in their early teens.

"Mare?"

"Yeah."

"He loves me."

"I know." Mary steadied her on the seat. She might not have been sure what was going on inside her friend's head but she knew she was suffering. She'd watched her suffer for years, the victim of love.

Penny and Adam had fallen for one another at fourteen, six months before Mary and Robert had become an official couple. Back then, everything had been possible, and love, rich and fulfilling though it was, was deemed puppy-like. Deep down, they all knew that there would be life after their pubescent passion. It was a pity for Robert that he wouldn't live past secondary school and it was a pity for Adam that Penny would move on to a college in Dublin to study journalism while he stayed at home and worked in his dad's restaurant. After her first year, Penny had yearned for city life and he was a content country boy. Initially he had felt left behind but he was young and as keen as she was to explore other loves. Besides, he'd never wanted to be anything other than a restaurateur and there was no better place for that than Kenmare. It was a beautiful place to live, and profitable.

The father of the woman who would later become his wife was a Dutch millionaire and had spotted the town's potential on a visit in the late eighties. He had invested in a small seaside hotel on the outskirts and, while Penny worked as a journalist in Dublin, her first love found a new life as husband, father and hotel manager at a quaint manor house. It was just a shame for Penny that the reality of city living didn't match the fantasy – worse still that no other man could replace Adam in her heart. She had believed that love would come again but it didn't and she was left empty and rattled. As for Adam, it was a shame that in losing Penny he had lost his belief in romance. Maybe it had ensured that he would rush into a relationship of convenience. But the greatest calamity was that, in the end, when Penny came home, it was too late.

As for Mary, well, she suffered the loss of her first love, showing great strength, and her shock pregnancy was proclaimed a miracle. Even the parish priest agreed that the child was meant to be, despite her youth and the lack of a wedding ring. Then again, less than six years later when her son was so cruelly taken, that same priest would have probably thought of her baby's death as some sort of moral lesson. Not that any priests dared to call upon her with their views after she had punched the Archbishop in the face less than a month after her child had died.

Mary settled Penny back into bed, pulling the blankets up to her chin. Penny was out of it. "It'll be OK," she whispered. "Whatever's going on, you'll get over it."

"I won't," Penny slurred – she was in fact still half awake.

"You will," Mary told her drunken friend.

"I shouldn't have come back!"

"Don't be silly!"

"I don't want to end up like you," Penny mumbled clearly, despite her encroaching stupor.

Mary stood up. Hurt, she backed away. "No. I suppose you don't," she said, and closed the door. Penny would never have set out to hurt her, and if she remembered the conversation the following morning she would apologize.

Mary went to her room, upset, but Penny had a point. Mary hadn't had a proper relationship with a man since her son had died. Before that there had been a few men but none had lasted longer than a few months. She undressed, pulled on a T-shirt and crawled into bed. Mr Monkels resented having to move over to his side of the bed and Mary knew it was ridiculous that her dog had a side of her bed, but he did.

For hours Mary lay anxious and awake. *What the hell is wrong with me?* Mr Monkels was wheezing, but the rain had stopped, which was good. *No need for sandbags.* When she looked out of her window the water seemed calm – the boat was no longer slapping against the pier wall. Still her eyes refused to close.

Despite another night with little sleep, Mary was the first to wake. She showered and dressed while Penny and Mr Monkels slept on. She laid out the dog's breakfast and started to cook something for Penny. She broke some eggs and the bell rang. She left them to sizzle in the pan while she opened the door. Jerry Letter grinned at her. "Soft day," he said, handing her two bills from his postbag.

"Coffee?"

"No. I'm running a bit late and I promised Maura I'd take her to Killarney to get her ingrown toenail sorted out."

"Too much information, Jerry!"

"You think that's bad, you should see her arse!" He winked at her, and gave his familiar gummy smile. "I hear Lucy was in next door last night?"

Mary grinned. "You don't miss a trick."

"Well?"

"Well, what?"

"So you're getting a new neighbour?"

"You tell me."

"I hear it's soon," he said, winking.

Ivan walked up behind him. "Jerry!" He clapped the postman on the back.

"Ivan," Jerry said. "That was a fair old game on Saturday. Damn near close to losing."

Ivan laughed. "Ah, sure, almost losing is better than almost winning."

Mary waved at Jerry, who was already halfway down the road, then followed her cousin in and closed the door.

"Just in time for breakfast. Jesus, I'm a mighty man for timing!" He handed her his newspaper and sat down.

"I watched the film," she said, while she broke some more eggs.

"Did you cry?" he inquired, making coffee.

"No." She chuckled. Ivan knew her better than anyone, including Penny.

"Liar! You cried when a Fraggle stole the Gorg's tomato in *Fraggle Rock*." He laughed at the memory.

"OK, Ivan, we both know that the tomato was Junior Gorg's only friend. Not to mention the fact that I was a child."

"You were sixteen," he said, sitting down.

"All right, I might have squeezed out a tear or two over DiCaprio last night but Penny did most of the crying."

"Penny was here?" he asked.

"Still is. Why?"

"It's over with Adam."

"I guessed," she said. "How is he?"

"Devastated but it's for the best. How's Penn?"

"Not really talking. She got drunk and went to bed."

Ivan nodded. "It's for the best," he repeated.

"Yeah, I know."

24

Penny appeared in the door, hung-over, with her head in her hands. "And just when you think things can't get any worse you succumb to the hangover from a place they call hell."

Mary went to her medicine press and handed her friend two painkillers, while Ivan poured her a glass of water.

"You know?" Penny asked Ivan.

"I do."

She looked at Mary. "Did I tell you?" she asked, embarrassed by the gap in her memory.

"Not in so many words. I'm sorry, Penn." She served the eggs.

"Thanks," Penny said, welling up.

Ivan hugged her. "It's for the best," he reiterated.

They sat down together, Mary and Ivan eating eggs and Penny chasing hers around the plate.

"What's the situation with next door?" Ivan asked his cousin.

"New neighbours?" Penny asked, attempting to perk up.

"Yes," Mary said. "Three days and counting."

Ivan knew she hated to be bothered and secretly hoped that whoever moved in next door would do just that.

"Stop grinning!" She shook her fork at him.

"Let's hope they're interesting." Penny sighed.

"Well, just as long as they can speak English," Ivan said.

"Jesus, there's nothing worse than having to deal with people through sign language and a shagging phrase book," she said.

"Oh, sweet God!" Mary moaned, while Ivan and Penny grinned at one another.

# 3. The new neighbour

Four days had passed since Sam Sullivan had emerged from rehab and made a call that would hopefully change the course of his life. It had been a long flight, New York to Dublin, followed by another shorter and more uncomfortable flight, Dublin to Kerry, followed by a thirty-mile drive to Kenmare.

The man at Avis had given him a map, which would take him onto the Cork road rather than over the mountain pass. "Safer," he'd advised. "The mountain on a night like this is a killer, especially for you tourists. Sure you're not able for it at all!" He chuckled.

Sam thanked him and left. He should have asked some questions because a mixture of confusion, exhaustion and a bad map meant he ended up on the mountain. The rain continued and the road was turning into a stream. He crawled along but the water was rising and the large potholes and dips in the road were becoming more and more waterlogged and dangerous. The locals were obviously using the Cork road because he was alone.

Despite the weather, though, he couldn't help but stop to absorb the surrounding bleak beauty. He had never been a picture-postcard kind of person, and couldn't remember having been touched by a beautiful beach or a field of flowers but now, on this cold and miserable evening, he looked out onto the jagged grey rock above the winding road, which wove through drenched and dripping woods, and it captivated him.

Even so, after two hours' jolting through potholes the scenery was getting old.

When he arrived into the town it was after seven and the rain kept coming down. A small black-and-white signpost revealed that he had reached his destination and he sighed with relief. The cliff-top twists and turns had been an unexpected challenge and he felt he'd run and survived Nature's gauntlet. The town opened up before him, and even through the endless drizzle he found its quaint charm, coloured walls and jagged stone alluring. Despite his exhaustion, and because he had no idea where he was going, he circled the town twice, driving slowly so as to soak it all in. Large windows revealed warm rooms with candles placed on tables, the flicker of log fires in open bars, restaurants with low lighting, a chef and waitress sitting opposite one another, a bottle of wine between them.

He reached the top of the town for the second time and flagged down the only man on the street, handed him the address on a page printed from the Internet and asked for directions. The other grinned widely, showing his gums, and before Sam knew it, he was sitting in the car beside him. "You're nearly there now – I'll take a ride with you. I've a boat to check on," he said, and put out his hand. "Jerry Letter."

"Sam Sullivan," he replied, shaking the man's hand.

"Then we're both Sullivans!"

"I thought you said your name was Letter?" Sam was confused.

"I did, and it is and it isn't," he answered.

"OK," Sam agreed, and drove in the direction that Jerry was pointing.

Jerry laughed to himself. He liked Americans. They were a lot better to banter with than the Germans. Germans never seemed to have much time for Jerry. "I'm the postman," he said, after a moment or two.

"Excuse me?"

"Jerry Letter – I'm the postman."

"Oh. OK. That should make sense."

"Ah, but it does. You see, you and me, we're not the only Sullivans in this town. There's plenty more. In fact, the place is full of us, and as for first names you couldn't throw a pint in any direction without hitting a Jerry, a John, a Jimmy, a Robert, a Peter, a Frank or a Francie. So, you see, to tell one Jerry Sullivan from another, we just call each other by what we do or what we wear or what we're into."

Sam laughed.

"Take the right." Jerry nodded.

Sam took the right and looked to his left at the boats wrestling with the high tide. Hills rose behind the dark blue water, the heather casting a purple hue on the sky, and to his right he saw a line of little cottages built of rock, standing firm against the battering wind. "That's you." Jerry gestured.

Sam stopped the car directly in front of the cottage. "Looks good," he said, supremely glad to have arrived.

"It may look good but the place has been empty for a year. I hope to Christ she's not damp."

Before Sam could respond Jerry was helping him remove his bags from the boot and waiting for him to produce the house keys.

Once inside, Jerry took a good look around. "She seems fine. Lucy's been taking good care of her."

Sam just shook his head – as entertaining as Jerry Letter was, he wanted him gone.

Jerry was no fool, and once his American friend was settled and he'd ascertained the man was a New Yorker, unmarried, some sort of executive, and had travelled alone, he took his leave. "Well, we'll see each other around so, Uncle Sam." He tipped his hat and walked out into the rain, as relaxed as though it was a fine day.

Sam scratched his head. *Holy shit, that guy should work for the CIA!*

Without stopping to assimilate the ground floor of his new home he went straight upstairs, stripped off and got into the large brass bed that was waiting to envelop him. His head hit the pillow and he was asleep. Even the rain beating against the window couldn't wake him.

He didn't wake in the morning either, even though the sun broke through the clouds and glinted on his window-pane. He slept on as the chirping birds taunted Mr Monkels, barked as he attempted to run up and down the back garden, while they perched on their feeding table, snacking comfortably, savvy enough to know that unless the mutt grew wings he was no threat. Sam would spend his first full day in a foreign country asleep – as a lifelong insomniac, he'd have thought it impossible. During the next day he woke once or twice, but for just long enough to remember where he was and that he was free.

While he was asleep, Sam didn't have to think or worry about the commotion he'd left behind. The past four days since his release had been eventful. On day one he had planned his escape hastily from the back of a limo. He had spent day two in the office with Leland, who had been shouting, waving his finger and actually spitting, as he roared about his *protégé*'s ingratitude, disloyalty and betrayal. "What the hell are we supposed to do with those goddamn British pretty-boys?" he had screamed, referring to their latest signing, his neck reddening and a vein pulsing in his temple.

"You do what you do best, Leland, you promote them," Sam said, as calmly as he could.

"You're not leaving!" Leland had threatened.

"Yes, Leland, I am," Sam had responded, steadfast despite his mentor's menacing demeanour.

"If I'd known you were just going to disappear, I'd have left you to rot!" Leland ground out, once he'd realized that Sam was not to be intimidated.

"I'm glad you didn't. By the way, did I thank you for picking up the bill?"

Leland glowered.

Sam turned to leave.

"You'll never work in the record business again!" Leland said predictably.

"I hope not." Sam smiled. "See you around, Leland." He closed the door behind him and a part of his spirit soared.

Walking through the office, he felt like Jerry Maguire without the embarrassing fall, the stolen fish or a girl called Dorothy – but his head was held as high and his dream of a different kind of future was just as real. Those around him had said hasty goodbyes, caring no more about him than he did about them. He took the lift to the lobby, saluted the latest doorman and promised he'd never enter the building again.

The saliva shower aside, his second day out of rehab had been a good one.

On day three he had visited his mother, despite his reservations and the barring order. She had cried when she saw him, pulling him in from the street quickly so the neighbours wouldn't see. His dad was out, as Sam had known he would be. She'd brushed the hair from his face and sighed. "You look good for a corpse," she said, attempting to smile.

"I'm OK now, Mom," he said.

"It's over?" she said.

"I promise." He begged himself silently not to mess up.

His mother sobbed while she made coffee, and he looked around the kitchen he hadn't seen since he was last caught shooting up in his brother's bedroom on Christmas Day last year. That day he had punched his dad, breaking his nose, called his mother a whore and refused to leave until his brother threatened him with the police.

"I'm sorry, Mom," he said, biting back the emotion that, as a man, he'd learned to conceal.

She held on to his hand across the counter. "I'm just glad you're back," she said, tears tumbling.

"I won't let you down again," he promised.

"You said that before."

"This time is different. I've left work."

"You have?" She was comforted by that although she knew his job was only one of his problems. Long ago she had let him down when he'd needed her most.

"I'm leaving."

31

"Where are you going?"

"Ireland."

His mother was taken aback. "Ireland?" she'd repeated, shocked.

"I always promised Gran I'd go. So I'm going."

"Wow!" was all she could say. Still, she was beaming. She'd never been to her mother's homeland but she was happy that her son was to visit the country her mother had loved. "When?"

"Tomorrow morning."

"And your dad?"

"Tell him I'm sorry about his nose. Tell him I'm well and it's going to be OK."

"You're sure?" she asked.

"I am," he lied.

"You were always your grandmother's favourite," said his mother. "She'd be proud."

Sam had no doubt that, if she had been alive, she would have kicked his ass. Still, he was glad he'd seen his mother and, as hard as it was when she hugged him, he hugged her back. Perhaps his shrink had been right when he had simply advised: "Whatever it is, just let it go, man!" He desperately wanted to.

Later that night he had dinner with Mia in her favourite restaurant.

As soon as he had extended the invitation she'd known he was ending their relationship, yet she'd agreed that he could pick her up at eight. There had been technical problems with the video shoot and it had run on so she had just spent the fourth day in a row dancing on set for seven hours. Her ankle needed to be strapped and she'd have to take painkillers for her back. She'd left the studio with the set beautician, who would ensure that her hair and makeup were perfect. If she was going to be dumped by the love of her life, at least she'd look good while he was doing it.

Sam arrived outside her building at eight sharp. Building security escorted her to the limo. Sam kissed her cheek and they sat in silence until they reached the restaurant. Outside, paparazzi bulbs flashed as she made her exit from the car, careful that they didn't get a shot between her legs. Sam walked in ahead, knowing they were only interested in a name. She felt like a lamb being led to slaughter, not that she showed it. She was used to facing the flashes alone, so what was different about tonight? She turned it on. She smiled and paraded, winked and waved, and when they'd got what they were looking for she joined Sam, who was ready to order. They discussed the problems with the shoot, the recording of her third album and the inevitable tour but he waited until they had ordered coffee instead of dessert to talk properly.

"I have to leave," he said simply.

She nodded and asked him to pass the milk.

"Did you hear what I said?" he asked.

"You're leaving."

"You're not surprised."

"Well, if you're going to break up with Leland the day before you break up with me, what do you expect?" she asked, even-toned.

"I didn't think," he admitted.

"You never do." She forced a smile and waved at a fellow limelighter who was passing and reeked of Dior – they'd be forced to smell her long after she had left.

"I'm sorry," he apologized, for the umpteenth time that day.

"You are," she agreed. She was playing it tough but the façade was crumbling. "So are we really over?"

"I don't know," he said, unable to be honest with either of them.

"You don't know?" she repeated, tears welling and all pretence gone.

"I just need time," he said, and now she was crying openly.

"It's not over," she begged. *Please don't leave me!*

"No, it's not." He backed down. *Coward!* "Do you want to go home?" he asked, concerned that people would notice her unravelling.

"Yes," she agreed. *Hold it together.*

"Waiter!"

And suddenly she broke down completely, even though they were in public and in a place where every waiter was on the razzis' payroll. Sam found her loud sobbing deeply disturbing – the reason he'd taken her there was to avoid a scene.

Mia couldn't help it because, as bad as he was, she couldn't bear to lose him. The waiter dropped the bill and grinned, knowing he was going to earn some extra cash. She attempted to compose herself and Sam told her how amazing she was, how talented, beautiful, graceful and elegant. He sounded like a fan.

"You're incredible," he said.

"And yet you're leaving."

"I have to."

She snorted, her pain turning to anger. "Take me with you," she pleaded, as she picked up her handbag.

34

"I can't," he said, and watched her bottom lip tremble.

"So take me home," she said, standing up. Her makeup was streaked.

"Do you want to wash your face?" he asked, aware that every cameraman in Manhattan would be outside, waiting.

"No," she said, striding towards the door. "It doesn't matter."

He followed her out, but this time when the bulbs flashed into her bleary eyes, he stood right beside her as the vultures descended.

# 4. New town, new man?

The rain had stopped, the sky was bright blue and Mary was in work for eleven o'clock. She sat up at the bar while her dad, whose name was Jack, poured coffee. Pierre the French chef breezed past and grunted hello. Mary gave him the fingers.

"Oh, yes, Marie, so very sexy of you!"

"I try to please."

"Well, try harder!" He gave her a prod, and her dad laughed.

Pierre was soon safely ensconced in the back kitchen blasting out MC Solaar. Mary's dad sighed to illustrate his distaste of French rap, which was one step too far up the musical ladder for him. Mary liked Solaar, not that she would have admitted it to Pierre.

Her dad pulled up a stool. "I hear he's American," he said.

She returned his smile. "Who is?"

"Your new neighbour."

"How the hell –" She didn't bother to finish – very little happened in Kenmare without her father hearing about it.

"I know things," he said, tapping his nose. "Have you met him?"

"No," she said.

"He has money," he told her, watching her from the corner of his eye.

"Really," she said, in a tone that suggested disinterest.

"Unmarried." She ignored him. "He's alone."

"Aren't we all?" she said, becoming irritated.

"So it's all to play for," he concluded.

"How do you know so much about this American?" she asked.

"Mattie Moore was in first thing this morning. It seems Jerry Letter took a lift with the American last night. Mattie says he was quiet enough."

"Jerry or the American?" She got up to wash her cup, turning her back to signify that the conversation was nearing its end.

"You know well enough. Jerry will lead the rosary at his own funeral." He was resigned to his daughter's ways but secretly wished she'd show some interest in anything other than work and that feckin' dribbling dog.

Lunchtime was hectic. They ran out of leeks – Jessie, waitress and general factotum, had forgotten to reorder them. Mrs Lennon waited fifteen minutes for an omelette, then received one smothered in tomatoes, which she'd specifically asked them to leave out: an allergy made her head swell to the size of a small country. Fiona, their latest part-timer, dropped a trayful of monkfish, causing near-hysteria in Pierre, who tore a strip off her. She burst into tears and ran out of the kitchen mumbling something about the money not being worth it.

When Pierre attempted to give Jessie shit, she roared, "I forgot the leeks, so I forgot them! Live with it!" As a fifty-year-old mother of four she wasn't about to have some jumped-up tourist tell her what was what.

"Jessie, he didn't mean anything," said Mary, acting as peacemaker for the second time that day.

"Marie, she can't forget – the ticks are there to show her!"

"Is he calling me thick?" Jessie asked, knowing that he was referring to the ingredients tick-box, which had been designed especially so that she wouldn't forget key ingredients.

Mary was annoyed now. "Jessie, get a grip."

Jessie backed down, and Mary walked out before they could start another argument.

It was shaping up to be one of those days. Her dad wasn't much help, having abandoned his post in favour of joining his friends Patty Winslow and Con Moriarty – the latter had received his starter with his main course. He'd been eating there for twenty-five years so he ate it as a side dish, suggesting he could start a trend. Patty was reading aloud about an incident in the House of Lords and was clearly annoyed – she was banging her fist off the table every few minutes and mumbling about "injustice". Although she had retired to Kenmare fifteen years ago and had never returned to her home town in Kent, she only ever read the English papers, followed English politics with ferocity and had had the BBC before anyone else in town.

Mary's dad and Con were far too busy enjoying their old friend's frustration to notice or care about the chaos around them.

It was after seven when she got home, glad that she wasn't working the bar that night and praying for sleep. A flashy red sports car was parked outside. This irked her for no reason other than it reminded her of her unwanted neighbour. Although the rain had finally stopped it was cold, so she lit a fire and looked through her music collection, searching for something she could disappear into. Nirvana seemed to suit her mood. She lined up their albums. She'd start with the MTV unplugged session before moving on to *Nevermind* followed by *In Utero*. She turned the sound up so that she could hear it in the kitchen and was cooking when the doorbell rang. Cobain was singing loudly about a dirty bird and she was absorbed in the melody as she chopped an onion. It was Mr Monkels's bark and his steady pacing at the door that alerted her to a visitor. She wished whoever it was would go away.

Penny stood outside, shivering and jumping on the spot.

"Hey, you," Mary greeted her, when she opened the door. She was always happy to see her – being with Penny was as easy as being alone.

"Can I come in?" Penny asked, as though she needed to, and followed Mary to the kitchen. "You're cooking," she said, stating the obvious, and grabbed a beer from the fridge.

"Shepherd's pie – are you hungry?"

"No food. I'm on day five of the heartbreak diet and I'm starting to see results." Penny sipped from the can.

Even in crisis Mary found her friend amusing. As she cooked they talked about their day. Mary filled Penny in on the histrionics at the bar and Penny told Mary about her trip to Tralee to report on a local man who had won millions on the Euro lottery. By the time dinner was ready she had drunk three cans. Mary tried to insist that she ate by putting a plate of food in front of her. Penny was afraid to go home in case Adam was there and wondered if she should go away for a week or two, but Mary pointed out that she'd done that before in an attempt to end their affair and it hadn't worked. In fact, as soon as she'd got home he'd turned up at her door and she was right back where she'd started except for her tan. She was subdued over dinner and Mary knew what was going through her friend's mind: they'd been down this road too many times for her not to. So they sat, and while Mary ate, Penny drank and Kurt Cobain beseeched someone unknown to rape him.

Penny looked towards the stereo. "Rape me?" she repeated. "Bloody weirdo!"

"It's a metaphor for self-loathing," Mary said.

"How is it that I'm the one who went to Trinity yet you're the one full of shit?"

"It's a mystery." She was glad Penny had come over.

Just then Mr Monkels began to bark and head-butt the window.

"Who the hell is that?" Mary said.

Penny sat up, alarmed that Adam might have followed her to her friend's home. She stayed in the kitchen while Mary went to the door.

"There's no one here," Mary called.

"Are you sure?"

"All clear!" It wouldn't be like Adam to come after Penny, as much as Mary knew he would want to. *Poor Adam, he really did make a mess of everything.*

Sam had woken just after seven p.m. He was hungry but not enough to get dressed and venture into the town. However, there was no food in the house and he'd never make it to morning without eating something. He went to the car to find his cell phone. The dog next door had barked, panted and slobbered some sort of welcome and he wondered if he should introduce himself to the occupants of the house – maybe they had a local takeaway menu he could borrow – but he decided against it. He was in a robe, after all, and he wasn't hungry enough for introductions. Upstairs he took a long hot shower, then pulled on a pair of jeans and a plain T-shirt and went downstairs to the sitting room.

He looked around his new and alien environment for the first time. The cottage was cute. The kitchen could stand to be bigger but the sitting room had great character, with its wide fireplace made out of grey rock, blackened in places by many log fires. A ridiculously comfortable sofa was positioned directly in front of it, and to his left, a large window looked out at the grey hills and black sea. *Funny – the hills were kinda purple and the sea was definitely navy last night.* It was then he noticed that the house came without a TV. *Weird.* The shelf under the coffee-table contained a number of books. He sank into the sofa and began leafing through them.

*The Bourne Identity* by Robert Ludlum. *Saw the movie, and the mini series. Matt Damon did a fine job. I never did like Richard Chamberlain.* His mind rambled on, as he debated which book he'd lose himself in. *Birdsong* maybe, although war was depressing and, since he was alone in a foreign nation and had just come off heroin, it might be wiser to choose something more uplifting. He picked up a rather thick book entitled *The Deptford Trilogy* by Robertson Davies. *Hmmm, three for the price of one.* The blurb was interesting: myth, magic, saints, Satan, illusion, reality. It all sounded like his past year. He decided, in the absence of a TV, that he would dedicate himself to reading his first book since high school. But before that he had to eat – his appetite had returned halfway through his marathon shower. He searched the house for leaflets from takeaways, came up empty-handed and knew he had no choice but to venture next door.

Mary was sitting on the sofa. Mr Monkels was sprawled at her feet on his bed in front of the fire. She was drinking a glass of wine Penny had poured for her – she had found a stray bottle of red under the stairs once she'd consumed all the beer. Penny was sitting in the window nursing her drink, watching the white street-lights dance on the black water and absentmindedly swirling the contents of her glass. Nirvana had been replaced by James Taylor, and each girl was adrift in a world of her own until Penny's voice broke the mood.

"There's a man out there," she said, suddenly alert, peering through the curtain. "It must be your neighbour. It looks like he's going to his car."

"Fascinating," Mary said.

"Oh, my God!" Penny said, dropping the curtain and sinking to the floor. "He's coming to the door and he's a total ride!"

Mary laughed, thinking she was messing around, but then the doorbell rang and her heart skipped and she felt like a bold child on the verge of being caught. "Get up," she whispered to Penny.

Penny did so slowly, and slunk across the room to stand in the doorway between the kitchen and the sitting room.

Mary viewed the front door, feeling a little panicked. This man had been her neighbour for just twenty-four hours and already he was knocking on her door. *Knickers!* The knock came again so Mary opened it.

Penny sighed audibly. She couldn't believe it – her best

friend's neighbour was a Calvin Klein billboard underwear model, a box-office-breaking movie star, a chiselled god with pretty hair surrounding a beautiful face. Mary heard the sigh and didn't share her friend's opinion: instead she saw a bloody annoyance. But there was something about him that even his gorgeous face couldn't distract her from. It made her anxious yet she couldn't put her finger on why.

He spoke. "Hi. I'm Sam Sullivan."

"OK," she responded. She didn't mean to sound rude but that had been all she could muster.

He put out his hand. "From next door."

"Hi." She shook it awkwardly, wishing he'd leave. She opened the door wider so that her old friend could say hello to her new neighbour but she wasn't asking him in.

"I was just looking for a menu for a place that delivers," he said, realizing that his neighbour wasn't as welcoming as they'd said Irish people were in the Aer Lingus brochure.

The other girl laughed. "Nowhere delivers," she said.

"You're kidding," he said, looking over the first's shoulder.

She shook her head, smiling coyly with one leg behind the other and one arm hanging casually as if she was a teenager on dope or attempting an impression of Bono singing "Maggie's Farm" at Self Aid.

"I didn't see that coming." He was disturbed by this news.

"You can eat here," the second girl offered. "We have loads. Don't we, Mare?" She moved towards him and put out her hand for him to shake. "I'm Penny Walsh," she smiled a winsome smile, "and this is my friend Mary Mackey. She's friendlier than she first appears. She'd love you to stay."

Mary smiled, teeth gritted, at the stranger while silently wishing a nasty case of the clap on her friend. "Of course."

"No, thanks. I'm really tired and not much company," he said truthfully. Sam was no more interested in making new friends than his reluctant neighbour was.

Mary felt bad. "I could pack it up for you. It's still hot and you could drop the plate back tomorrow," she said, moving away from the door. "Just leave it outside, it'll be fine."

Sam was starving now and the smell of cooking was killing him. "That would be great, thanks."

Penny flirted with him while Mary plated the remaining shepherd's pie and checked the fridge for some sort of dessert. She had a cheesecake but it had been there since the previous Tuesday. "What's today's date?" she called.

"The nineteenth," Sam told her, battling Mr Monkels who seemed fascinated with his balls, which Penny pointed out, to Sam's embarrassment.

Mary screamed at her dog from the kitchen and, sulkily, he took to his bed in front of the fire, groaning like a cheeky teenager. She emerged from the kitchen with the plate. He thanked her; she told him it wasn't a problem with her hand on the open door. He left and she closed it quickly.

Penny was shaking her head.

"Don't," Mary warned.

"He might be the prettiest man I've ever seen in real life. Maybe even a little too pretty. I didn't have time to make up my mind." Penny was a little put out that her friend had done everything to get rid of him but push him out of the door. She plonked herself down on the window-seat again, flicking at the curtain for one last glimpse, but he was gone.

Mary remained silent, the American already past tense. *How could I forget?* she asked herself. *How is it possible that I could forget? How could I not know what date it is?*

44

Penny was still talking but her voice seemed far away. No wonder she couldn't sleep. The past week was starting to make sense. She needed to be alone. She got up. "I'm taking you home," she said.

"What?" Penny exclaimed, swirling her wine.

"I'm tired," Mary lied.

"OK, but I can drive myself." Penny got up, but after the beers and half a bottle of wine she wasn't going to be allowed to drive anywhere.

Mary dropped Penny at her house. It was set on a hill overlooking a sweeping valley littered with sheep interspersed with the odd cow, and spotted with clusters of wild flowers. The latter couldn't be seen at night, of course, but a hint of their perfume hung in the air. Her neighbours were having a party and the music wafted into her garden. She had the key in the door when Adam called to her. She braced herself before turning. "What are you doing here?" she asked.

"I'm not here, I'm next door – Neil asked us." He pointed towards her neighbour's home.

"Alina's with you?" She almost cried.

"No, she's with her dad in Cork. He's not well." He approached her, his hands in his pockets. "I wouldn't have come but I wanted to see you."

"We're not getting back together," she warned.

"I know." He made it to the steps. "We're leaving." He couldn't look at her.

"I don't understand." But her voice shook, suggesting she did.

"Alina knows."

"What does she know?"

"About us."

Penny's legs felt as if they would fail her. "Five years we've been together. We finish and now she knows?" She couldn't believe it.

"She found out a week ago. It was why I had to end it."

That didn't make any sense. "Why didn't you tell me?"

"She didn't want me to." His eyes rested on his feet.

"She didn't want you to?" Penny repeated, the combination of confusion and abandonment becoming a little too much for her.

"She wants us to start afresh. There's a business opportunity in Cork. Her dad's there and she has some friends."

"She didn't *want* you to!" Penny repeated.

"Did you hear what I said? I'm moving to Cork!"

"You hate Cork." She heard herself sounding childish.

"It's not a choice. She's going to take the kids. If we don't make a go of it, she says she'll go back to Holland. I can't lose my kids. I'm so sorry."

"You're weak," Penny said, with a trace of anger.

"Yes."

"You make me weak," she said, softening.

"I'm sorry."

"It's really over."

"Yes, it is," he said.

*Oh, God.* She closed her eyes. Sinéad O'Connor's version of Elton John's "Sacrifice" played around them; she hadn't been able to escape Sinéad lately.

And suddenly they were dancing, holding each other tight under a half-moon, moving in circles that symbolized their relationship, both afraid to let go, both willing the song to continue while silently their insides tore.

46

When the song ended Adam reluctantly returned to the party, leaving Penny to get into her bed with a bottle of vodka.

It was after midnight when Mary found herself in the part of the forest she rarely visited. Just once a year, on 19 March, and that was enough. She'd brought a teddy she'd picked up two weeks previously before she'd allowed herself to lose track of time. She carried Ben's favourite cloth, and a flashlight to navigate her way through the darkness. The tree stood tall and strong, aside from the broken limb, which had been amputated long ago. She took out the cloth and began to wipe the plaque bearing the name of her son, in the place he had died but, more importantly, the place where he had lived, laughing on the makeshift swing. A swing that every child in town had swung on at one time or another, until 19 March 1999 when the limb had given way, catapulting Mary's baby high into the air before gravity pulled him back to earth in such a way that he'd landed on his neck, snapping it instantly. She laid the teddy by the flowers her father had put there earlier that day. *At least he could rely on you, Dad.*

She touched the clean plaque tenderly, then looked around to make sure she was alone. It was cold enough for the mud beneath her to crystallize and she could see her breath forming a trail in the night air. She stood with a hand up each opposite sleeve, shivering despite her many layers of clothing. "I can't believe it's been six years," she said.

"It seems like only yesterday," came a whispered reply from the darkness.

Mary weed herself a little. "Hello?" she asked, in a voice that suggested mild hysteria.

"Is that you, Mary?"

The voice was muffled but more distinct and coming from behind her. She turned quickly and pointed her flashlight in a take-charge-while-shitting-it manner that reminded her of Dana Scully in *The X-Files* circa 1993 before Dana'd lost the weight and was still a sceptic.

"Hello?" she said again, scanning the foliage with her flashlight, which was of little use because her eyes were closed.

"Mary, girl, if you don't help me up I might freeze to death." The voice was suddenly familiar.

"Tom?"

"I can't get up," he said, from the ditch that hid itself behind a large rhododendron.

Mary parted the bush to reveal Tom on his back, much like an upturned turtle, too drunk to negotiate his way onto his feet. She sat him up. "Jesus, Tom, you nearly killed me with the fright!"

"Sorry, pet," he said sheepishly. "I just thought I'd call upon our boy on the way home and mistook that bush for a chair and the rest, as they say, is history." His skin was frozen.

"How long have you been out here?" she asked, worried that her son's paternal grandfather would fall victim to pneumonia.

"Not long," he said, patting her shoulder.

"I'll take you home," she said.

"In a minute," he said.

"OK."

She'd always been fond of Robert's father, and he and his wife had been good to her and Ben. For a while they had even felt like family, but when Ben had died, Tom's wife,

Monica, couldn't bear to stay in the town that had robbed her of so much. They had moved to Spain where they spent most of their time, only visiting Kenmare once or twice a year. It had been five years now since they'd gone and in that time Mary and her child's grandparents had drifted apart.

Tom wasn't a drinker. In fact, he had been a Pioneer of Total Abstinence up until Robert had died. After that he took a drink each year in his memory and when Ben joined Robert he did the same. So, twice a year Tom drank and even then he could only manage three pints before he was helpless.

He stood in front of the plaque, with his hands knotted in prayer. Mary stood back and allowed him his moment.

"Mary," he said, swaying.

"Tom," she responded.

"Do you think he ever looks down?" he asked, eyes brimming.

"I know he does," she said kindly.

"You do?" he said, perking up.

"They all do," she said, taking his arm and guiding him down the path that would lead him home.

"Do you really believe that?"

"I do."

"Do you see them?" he asked conspiratorially – he knew about her cryptic dreams.

"No," she admitted, "but sometimes I feel them around me."

He nearly stumbled on a root but she caught him in time and steadied him.

"I don't," he confessed, and a tear escaped. "I'd love to," his voice shook, "one last time – just to see them both one last time." He tried to collect himself.

"You'll see them again." She smiled sadly. "I know they're waiting."

He wiped a tear from her cheek. She hadn't even noticed she was crying. "Some say you're a bit of a weird one," he said, smiling at her, "but I've always thought you were lovely, just lovely."

She laughed at his honesty.

He squeezed her arm and they walked on together.

It hadn't been the visit she'd expected: it had been nicer.


Sam enjoyed a late meal courtesy of his reluctant neighbour and then, by the light of a log fire and a small reading lamp, he opened the book that led him to a place called Deptford. There, he basked in magic, murder and intrigue, and he didn't have to think about the mess he'd made of his life. He didn't worry about the people he'd trodden on or the lives he'd had a hand in ruining. Most importantly, sitting in the half-light, lost in another man's world, he didn't have to address what he'd done and why he'd done it. He could pretend that his life to date had been one long accident and that he was better now. The ghosts that had haunted him were silenced — at least for the time being.

# 5. Looking down

It had been a long, hard night and, if Mary was right and those who had left this world sometimes looked down from the skies above, they must have seen that respite was necessary. From a distance these five souls would have seemed wretched in their own quiet way, and looking down, they would have wept to see what had become of the children the five had once been: Sam, the American boy who had been so full of promise, now hiding terrible secrets that would hold him hostage, clean or not; Penny, alone and covered with vomit, hugging a bottle instead of the man she had lost to unfulfilled ambition; Ivan, the cheeky chap, a father of two at twenty-four and terribly alone in his thirties; Adam, the boy who had dreamed of being a hero only to mess it all up; and Mary, born unlucky, once luminous but now dulled by pain.

In this world, Mary had been tested more than most, born to a dead mother, her father wailing and traumatized. He hadn't picked her up for six months but once he did she would be loved like any other child by a doting father. And although she'd felt her mother's absence, it was mostly in her teenage years, and her auntie Sheila was always on hand to provide the necessary feminine influence. Auntie Sheila was her father's brother's wife and Ivan's mother.

Mary's teenage life was promising. She had a father who was wrapped around her little finger. She had a best friend in Penny, who shared her life at a boarding-school in Dublin. And when she came home, her older cousin Ivan was waiting with all his attractive friends lined up to hang out with the two glamorous girls who were at school in the capital. She was popular, attractive, quick-witted, curious and infectiously giddy. She loved photography, was a dab hand with a paintbrush and intelligent too, winning praise in most subjects. It was thought that she could be anything she wanted to be once her mind was made up. And at sixteen it was: she would move to New York City and become a photo-journalist. She would study photography and imaging at NYU, using the money her mother's family had left her to pay for her dream. In the meantime, she had given her heart to Robert Casey the first time he smiled at her.

They had got together six months later at a party in her cousin's house. He had guided her into the toilet under the stairs. They had kissed under a blue light on a white porcelain toilet while inhaling lavender. Meat Loaf was playing in the background and a queue formed outside, with teenagers banging on the door and pleading for the sake of their bladders. A little over a year later they lost their virginity to one another on a patch of grass under a summer moon where the forest met the water, which was lapping in the distance as they experimented with rubber. When she left for school their teenage hearts would break and promises were made. When she returned, they made up for lost time, desperately in love, the education system ensuring a burning fervour. Mary was passionate then. She was wild and free, believing the world to be some sort of giant playpen.

She had just turned seventeen when she discovered she was pregnant, doing the test in the toilets with shaking hands, an uncooperative bladder and three minutes of concentrated prayer.

"Oh, bollocks!"

Panic ensued. She knew the exact moment of conception. It had been the night she'd spent in the boathouse, having snuck past her friends, who were standing around the flames of a barbecue and chatting over her favourite band, Take That, singing "Pray".

"Damn you, Take That!"

They hadn't wasted time so the condom wasn't properly positioned. It came away easily but they didn't notice until it was too late. They had discussed the morning-after pill but agreed that the risk of exposure through visiting a local GP was greater than the threat of reproduction. This proved to have been a mistake.

It was two weeks before Easter. Penny was stuck at school, working on a project she had avoided for far too long, so Mary had returned home alone. Robert picked her up at Killarney station, proud of his newly acquired driving licence.

She broke the news on the mountain. He had stopped the car and pulled in dangerously close to the cliff edge. His face had changed colour and his relaxed demeanour had metamorphosed into something twisted. Their conversation quickly descended into screaming and shouting, and he had taken off his seatbelt so that he could face her. He also had plans: he was set to become an architect. They acknowledged that their perfect futures were in terrible jeopardy. After a while, their debate in deadlock, he decided to start the car. Without thinking, he rammed it into first gear, needing to get back onto the road and drive fast to clear his head. He put his foot on the accelerator and the car drove straight over the cliff.

If you'd asked Mary about the accident she wouldn't remember anything after the argument, but those looking down from the skies could tell you every horrifying moment. Mary had heard Robert roar and saw him turn the wheel in mid-air. She felt the terrible drop as the car plummeted. She watched the glass in front of her shatter and her boyfriend sail through it, leaving her alone to face the ground below. She braced herself to smash and die. *Oh, Dad, I'm so sorry!* And then for her there was nothing. A busload of German tourists had witnessed their fall and, in a world before the mobile telephone, the bus driver radioed the depot. The staff there informed the police and ambulance. One of the tourists, a doctor, had insisted on being winched down on a climbing rope to where the boy lay broken, the other tourists and bus driver holding the end, praying they wouldn't let him fall and wondering where in hell the rescue team were. The boy was dead, the girl far down in the gorge and the doctor's rope too short. His fellow holidaymakers wanted to pull him up and away from the body but he insisted on staying with the boy until the ambulance sirens could be heard in the distance.

Mary was cut out of the car. They said it was a miracle she had emerged at all. Both her legs were broken and her left arm had shattered against the windscreen but it had been Robert, grazing the side of her head at 200 m.p.h., who had induced the coma. The car should have crumpled and she should have been dead, but its frame had somehow managed to withstand the impact, and when the rescue team made it down the mountain, they found her unconscious but alive. Later in the hospital her father discovered that not only had his daughter survived against all odds but, unbelievably, so had his surprise grandchild. As Robert's mother roared and screamed in the background and his father pleaded with the doctor to turn back the clock, Mary's dad had held her hand and prayed she would survive childbirth, unlike her mother.

"I don't care. Do you hear me, love? It doesn't matter. You're not in trouble. Just survive. And when you wake up we'll take care of this baby together. Don't you leave me now." He patted her hand, glad she didn't have to witness his eyes leaking. "Don't you leave me now."

She didn't wake for three months. Some had given up hope that she would be anything other than an incubator for her baby, but her dad was sure his daughter would return to him, and Penny was sure too, knowing that Mary hadn't survived merely to sleep. She would come back, and her best friend spent as much time as possible sitting by her side, gossiping and playing her favourite music.

"Music will bring her back," she had told Mary's father, having filled the room with CDs. She gave him a schedule of songs for morning, afternoon and evening listening, divided into weekdays and weekends. It was important he adhere to it, she said, as Mary would not stand for a weekday song at the weekend or a morning song in the evening. Paul Simon's "Fifty Ways To Leave Your Lover" was a weekday song, preferably to be played in the morning – afternoon would be pushing it and it was most definitely not to be played in the evening. Leonard Cohen's "Everybody Knows" was another weekday song but this was deemed appropriate for evening, not morning or afternoon.

Prince's "Little Red Corvette" was a weekend evening song, late afternoon would be OK – she'd noted in the margin that it should not be played before four p.m. And so she went on until Mary's poor dad was fully apprised and entrusted with this weighty task when she was forced to return to school in Dublin to complete her Leaving Cert.

When she was gone Ivan picked up the slack. Every day after school he'd visit and talk or read to Mary so that her father could take a shower or drink a fortifying coffee. Every day her tummy grew under a hospital blanket and Robert's parents would call to visit the part of their son that wasn't buried in their family grave. They'd speak in whispers and Robert's mother would cry and his dad would insist on shaking Mary's dad's hand.

She came back one Tuesday on a warm June day. It was around half past five. Ivan was reading aloud from *The Lord of the Rings* while Van Morrison's "And It Stoned Me" was playing on CD. Her hand had jerked. He ignored it at first as spasms were not unusual. Then it moved again. Her fingers appeared to be searching rather than twitching randomly. Slowly he lowered the book and watched her. Her eyes flickered and blinked and at the same time her mouth opened and breath escaped. He froze and her eyelids peeled apart – slowly, as though they were coming unstuck.

"Mary?"

"Iv . . . zan," she responded hoarsely, her mouth and throat like sandpaper.

"Oh, Jesus on a jet-ski! You're back!" He jumped up and ran out of the room, leaving her to wonder what the hell was going on.

She could hear him screaming, hailing her return in the corridor, and it wasn't long before a team of doctors, accompanied by her tearful father, revealed how long she had been lost, that Robert had perished, she had missed her Leaving Cert exams, and she was just shy of six months pregnant, soon to be a mother. Lying there surrounded by strange, harried faces, looking down at her swollen self, with her boyfriend dead, her limbs uncooperative, and slurred speech braying in her addled brain . . . lying there disoriented yet painfully aware that the girl who had got into her boyfriend's car would never emerge . . . Through the haze of this new reality, her mind settled on Van Morrison's familiar beat. He spoke of water and prayed it wouldn't rain all day.

In contrast to his new neighbour, Sam's entrance to this world was joyful. He was born to a tired but grateful mother and a proud cigar-toting father, his older brother, then a toddler, inquisitive and keen to stroke his tiny face. His early memories were of train sets, a mother's perfume, a father's laughter, a brother's teasing, but it was his granny who took up most of his head space, she being the one who had raised both boys while their mother worked in her husband's Manhattan restaurant. Sam's days were spent accompanying her to the local grocery stores where she'd barter with old friends while catching up on gossip, making the men laugh with her flirtatious wit and the women smile at her kindness. Granny Baskin had moved in with her daughter and son-in-law a year before the birth of her favourite grandchild and just after her own husband had quietly died while sitting on a steel girder thirteen hundred feet from the ground. Granny had often talked of Sam's grandfather and the day the sky had taken him from her. She wasn't bitter: he had been in his late sixties, which some considered young, but to Granny Baskin it was long enough for a man such as her husband to be grounded. "He was never meant for this earth," she'd say. "His head and heart were always skyward." Then she'd look up towards the heavens and wink as though he was watching.

Most afternoons she'd collect Sam and his brother Jonah from school and take them to the park so that she could catch up with her old friends playing chess and telling stories, while the birds fed on the scraps they sprinkled about themselves. Jonah would run off with other boys and play football or basketball with any ball they could find, and if they didn't find one he would run as though he was chasing something invisible. Granny Baskin would laugh and wink at Sam, who preferred to sit by her side and listen to a group of old immigrants reminisce about their home-lands, comparing stories of the plight of the old world, each one bettering the last's tale of woe.

Sam had thought it odd that they could tell such sad stories yet laugh and joke so easily, until Granny had coun-selled that time was a great healer. He was six so he didn't have a clue what she was talking about, but when she said it she gave him the smile that came with twinkling eyes and pushed a sweet into his hand so he'd remember it. Mr Grabowski and Mr DiRisio would often fight for the old woman's attention and even a six-year-old could work out that his granny was as sassy as she was old, as wrinkled Mrs Gillespie always said.

It was his grandmother who encouraged his love of Irish music, sharing with him her taste for the Clancy Brothers, the Chieftains and the Dubliners. Luke Kelly made her cry, but her tears were always accompanied by a smile. She introduced him to all kinds of music – jazz, blues, bluegrass, rock, pop, and the only artist they ever disagreed about: Neil Diamond. She bought him his first guitar, telling him that once he'd learned to play he would never be lonely. She saw it in him first, the singularity that would polarize him for his peers. Normal kids didn't hang out so willingly with their grandmothers. He was an old soul content to remain friendless. His parents weren't worried that he wasn't a great mixer: all kids were different and he'd grow out of it. Teachers felt that he was merely shy and agreed it was most likely a phase. Granny Baskin knew better. Her grandson's eyes betrayed a certain melancholy which, as an Irish emigrant, she was more than equipped to recognize. He wouldn't fit in with the crowd and there was a chance he wouldn't fit in at all.

"Who were you before? A warrior or the wounded, my sweet boy?" She'd ruffle his hair and he would smile as though he knew the answer but dared not share it.

Sam had started out in the world as a gawky creature, too skinny for his large or piercing facial features. The kids at school made fun of his square jaw, often referring to him as "Desperate Sam the Pie-eating Man". It hadn't bothered him – at least, not at first. He was too busy locked in his thoughts and playing riffs in his head while others around him talked nonsense just to hear themselves speak. But as the years passed the noise grew louder and their contempt became harder to ignore. He often wondered why they couldn't just leave him be. But jealous souls demand to be heard, and his ambivalence taunted them as surely as their bullying haunted him. He was in his mid-teens when he began to fill out. His features no longer overtook the rest of him. His blond hair was shaped into a crew-cut by the local barber.

"As handsome as your grandfather in his day," his granny whispered. He might have had a rocky start but she'd always known he'd be a heartbreaker one day.

The girls in school noticed too and suddenly he was considered deep instead of weird. He instantly recognized the hypocrites for who they were and retreated further into himself, distrustful of his new-found popularity and cursing his appearance for drawing unwanted attention. Instead of hanging with the guys, getting drunk and exploring girls, he hid for hours in his room with his guitar, losing himself in melody, playing from his heart – a heart that was full of all kinds of music. His gran would bring him tea, shaking her hips; he'd grin when she'd twirl around without spilling a drop or letting a biscuit slip from the plate.

"You'll be a star some day," she'd say proudly.

He'd shake his head modestly, but deep down he prayed he'd reach the dizzying heights his loving granny dreamed of. Playing guitar was the only time he felt he was honest with the world.

It was just after his sixteenth birthday when his granny keeled over in the kitchen, taking a pot of mercifully cold tomato soup to the floor with her. She woke up a day later, the left side of her face sliding towards her shoulder, her speech impaired, an arm and a leg now useless. He sat with her and talked while she stared blankly at the ceiling, one eye blinking. It was only when he played his guitar and a tear escaped her that he knew she was still with him.

His parents flew into action. First they put a bed downstairs in the unused drawing room. Then they hired a nurse and a physiotherapist, who would call three times a week. But Granny wasn't improving at home – or not the way the professionals thought she should. After six months Granny Baskin was moved to a hospital that specialized in stroke-victim aftercare. It was Sam who helped his mother to wheel her to the car. She hung on to him loosely while his mother removed the chair from beneath her. His strong arms manoeuvred her into the front seat, where he smoothed her skirt when it rode up her leg. His mother was busy attempting to fit the chair into the trunk, cursing silently when she scratched the paintwork.

It was then that his granny leaned forward, almost flopping, with a sideways grin. "Don't let the bastards get you down!" she managed. It had been the first real sentence she'd spoken since the stroke. With her good arm she ruffled his hair and he could have sworn that, after all those months, the twinkle returned to her eye, if only for a moment and just for him.

His mother drove away, leaving him to sit and rock on the stairs that led to his bedroom and the world his old granny had helped him create. The pain of loss engulfed him, tearing his insides out. The fear of what lay ahead of her burned his chest as surely as a hotplate would a naked hand. Worse, he couldn't break her out and take her to a better place. He couldn't tend her. He couldn't save her. She had given him everything and he had let her down. He cursed himself and his inadequacy. He hurt himself punching his fist against the hard wood banister that didn't budge, further highlighting his failure. On the day his grandmother was taken into hospital, Sam sat with his head in bleeding hands, sobbing and wondering if he'd survive without her, and if she could without him.

A year later Sam's granny died and he mourned her a second time, but since she had left his home, life had moved on, and although he missed her he was used to her not being there now – he had really lost her two years before on the day of her stroke. He'd also found a girlfriend. Hilarie was a strange-looking punk with green hair, a pierced nose and cherub tits. Like him, she was an outsider. They had met when he auditioned for a garage band. She was the only girl. The other guys were noncommittal but she had wanted him from the moment he'd walked through the door. Luckily she had the deciding vote. She liked it that he was insular, speaking only when necessary. It made a nice change from the shit she had to listen to from the other guys.

She also liked it that he didn't come on to her every chance he got, and especially when it became clear that she would have to make the first move. She waited until the night of their first gig when even her solitary new band-mate had reached a level of exhilaration that opened him up a little. She spotted the chink and before he knew it he was leaning against a tiled toilet wall, with a bass player on her knees sucking so hard that his knees threatened to give way. Afterwards, when she kissed him, he could taste himself. He missed his granny, and sometimes still ached for her, but he had a window of opportunity to become a person deemed normal – until the bullying started again. This time it was more menacing. In the end it took just one night to destroy any chance he had of ever being OK.

*

Ivan was a funny fish – at least, that was what his mother always said. He loved the sea, learned to swim as soon as he was dropped into water and spent his childhood and early teens sitting at the end of a fishing-rod, pondering his existence while awaiting a tug at the pole. His older twin brothers, Séamus and Barry, and younger brother Fintan were more interested in GAA – Fintan and Séamus being the footballers and Barry an avid hurler, which ensured that he'd lost most of his teeth by the age of eighteen. His parents paid for caps, while cursing the cost of dentistry, so Barry had what his twin would describe as a movie-star mouth. Throughout their childhood, Ivan's brothers would win the medals but Ivan would bring home the tea. He was born relaxed and never changed. No terrible twos. No challenging teenage years. He just got on with it, and as long as he could fish for a few hours a day, he was as content as an old man sitting out on a warm day.

He was always popular with the girls, even as a kid when he was supposed to dislike the opposite sex. The fact that he was a year older than his cousin Mary never seemed to affect their relationship: from cradle to adulthood they were drawn to one another. He found he had more in common with her than he did with his older brothers. His mother had deliberately left a five-year gap between the twins and her second pregnancy, despite what the Church thought. Unfortunately for her the contraceptive method that had worked so beautifully for the five years preceding Ivan's birth failed miserably in the months after, and Fintan was conceived all too quickly.

Ivan was the archetypal middle child, happy to blend in with whatever was going on. He experienced his first love at twelve with a fair-haired, blue-eyed whippet of a thing called Noreen. They kissed behind the dressing rooms on the football field, holding their lips together until he had counted to sixty. After that she wouldn't talk to him, but the memory of her lips against his ensured he wouldn't be behind-the-door about discovering someone else. He lost his virginity at fifteen, which was young in the 1980s, to a seventeen-year-old at an Irish college. He hadn't learned much Irish but, as far as he was concerned, the three weeks he spent shagging on an island off Cork was money well spent.

When he wasn't breaking hearts, he was hanging out with Mary. She was the only girl he ever shared his thoughts with. She felt like part of him and he could never accept that he'd experienced something unless he'd shared it with her. Luckily for her, she wasn't one for embarrassment so when he described his first sexual experience it was without reservation and Mary, mesmerized, made mental notes for when she dared adventure as her cousin had.

When Ivan nearly lost his best friend and confidante he re-evaluated the world around him. He didn't bother with his Leaving Cert, which, despite the year he had on Mary, he was due to take at the same time. He didn't need it anyway, not for what he wanted to do with his life. His parents put up a battle but, with their niece in a coma and their son as stubborn as he was calm, they were forced to surrender. While the rest of his classmates studied, Ivan sat by his cousin's bed day and night, sharing sentry duty with his broken uncle. He philosophized and recited her favourite song lyrics into her ear. He also read to her the books he thought she'd like and that he'd researched during the few hours he was apart from her. Her pregnancy came as a horrible surprise and he blamed himself for it – perhaps his confidences had led her to follow in his footsteps. He wondered if the baby that had survived tumbling down a mountain would suck the life out of its mother. If so, he would despise that child for stealing his best friend.

The baby surviving had been the first miracle. Mary waking had been the second. That she'd survived without brain damage, the third and final. Her skull was weakened and headaches would haunt her, but medication would keep them mostly at bay and she would be back to herself soon enough. There would be a wheelchair and physiotherapy, a wig to hide the hair loss as a consequence of the operation she had undergone to insert a metal plate into her skull. The baby would grow inside her and Ivan would be at her side through it all, yet they would never speak of her boyfriend's death or her miracle child. That part of her was closed. But Ivan knew she'd come back to them and every time he made her laugh he knew he was a step closer.

It was during this time that he first fell in love with Norma. She was a quiet town girl, bookish and pretty. She would ask after his cousin and talk about treatments she'd read about. She planned to study medicine and he was falling in love with her. Mary had been out of the rehabilitation hospital a month when they announced their engagement and Norma's pregnancy. Their child was less than a year old when Ivan first left his home town for a faraway oil rig that would earn him enough money to support his family, leaving his new wife behind with a baby. She never did become a doctor and it would be too late by the time her husband realized that she felt desperately cheated.

*

And then there was Penny – poor Penny – daughter to two solicitors and an only child. Her conception was deemed a mistake as children had never been on her parents' agenda. They weren't bad people – at least, not as far as she knew. They weren't around much and their house was a base rather than a home. Both parents worked mostly in Cork, staying in their apartment there, only popping back at weekends. Their child was cared for by a series of live-in nannies until she was old enough to be sent to boarding-school.

"If it's good enough for royalty, it's good enough for you, darling!" her mother would say, smiling.

Mary had plonked herself beside Penny on that first train journey, taking them towards their new life in Dublin. They didn't really know each other as they had attended different primary schools but Penny's face was familiar – they had grown up in the same small town. Penny had been sad but Mary was excited at the prospect of a new school and a new world, and by the time they had reached Dublin she had managed to infuse that excitement into her new best friend. Penny and Mary were kindred spirits from the start. Mary might have been the child that the townspeople pitied – she was the one they whispered about as she passed, her dead mother never far behind – but Penny suffered from her parents' rejection and Mary understood that. She had no mother but she did have a father, which was more than Penny had. From the day she sat down beside Penny, Mary would do everything to guarantee that she wouldn't feel lonely again, including introducing her to one of Ivan's best friends, Adam. Mary swore he was perfect for her. She was right: Adam and Penny were inseparable from the start.

When Mary nearly died, Penny thought she might just

die with her. She returned to an empty house and spoke with Adam on the phone. He told her that her best friend might not live through the night. He was desperate to be with her but his parents wouldn't let him leave the house, not after his friend had plunged to his death leaving his half-dead girlfriend with child. That night, alone in her big empty house, she opened her parents' drinks cabinet and poured herself a whiskey. When she'd finished it, she poured herself a second and a third. After the fourth she passed out on the sofa, waking up the next afternoon, still alone.

The first time she'd seen Mary in hospital, she waited until they were alone before she stroked her bandaged head. "You'd better not leave me!"

She wasn't allowed stay away from school, it being her Leaving Cert year, so she went back to study for a college place she didn't want. Luckily for her she was clever, and even though she had spent four months without opening a book, she breezed through the exams, as her parents had before her. She wasn't there on the day that Mary woke, but Adam called to let her know and she cried down the phone. She wasn't allowed home until the weekend, four days after her best friend had come back to the living. When Penny entered the room Mary burst into tears and Penny's heart soared because she was so happy to be recognized. That night, to celebrate, she and Adam drank three bottles of her mother's Christmas wine stash. Penny knew emptiness, but no matter how hard she tried she could never fill it.

Adam was the kind of kid who would never set the intellectual world on fire, but if you put him in a field with a ball or a stick it was like watching genius. He loved his sports and would have been a much more suitable friend for Ivan's brothers than the sport-shunning Ivan. But there was something about Ivan that drew Adam to him from the first time they met. He liked his calmness and admired his simplicity. Ivan didn't care about appearances and Adam enjoyed his friend's lack of ego – his easy ways relaxed him. If Ivan was the easygoing one and Robert the adventurous one, Adam was the funny one. He could make anyone laugh, even the sternest of his teachers, so he often talked his way out of trouble. Of course, his abilities on the field got him a place on the Kerry youth team and with this came a hint of celebrity – his capacity to pick up a cup and make a joke to a local TV crew had further endeared him to the inhabitants of his small town. But his heart belonged only to Penny.

A long time before his friend had introduced them, he had watched a young girl with the prettiest blue shoes sit on the wall that separated the primary school from the road. The school was empty, the bell having rung long before, but there she sat, alone, staring at her pretty blue shoes. He hid behind a bush that separated his friend's father's land from the road that lay between him and the girl. He was eleven and had been making his way home across the fields when he'd caught sight of her. Her pretty blonde hair shone in the evening sun, and when she eventually raised her cherubic face, he was reminded of an angel in the prayer book his mother had often made him read. He scrambled to hide in the undergrowth in case she caught sight of him.

The teacher came out, looking at her watch. "Well, Penny, there's no answer at home," she said, failing to disguise her annoyance.

"I'll be OK," Penny said. "I'm sure someone will be here

soon." Her voice was full of the kind of sadness that only kids can convey. Adam heard it, but her teacher didn't.

"This is the second time this week, not to mention three times last week," the teacher said. "This is not a baby-sitting service."

"I'll be fine," Penny said.

"I can't leave you here," the teacher said. "I'll try your neighbour."

Adam watched the woman leave the girl called Penny on her own and he watched the fat tears roll from Penny's eyes. *Don't cry,* he thought. *Please don't cry.* Every minute she sat there alone and in tears seemed like an eternity and each moment a lifetime. He was too scared to move, although he wanted to place his arm around her shoulders, so he just sat in the grass pretending he was beside her and willing her to be all right. Penny dried her eyes before her teacher returned to tell her that the neighbour was on her way. Twenty minutes later a car pulled up beside Penny, who jumped from the wall and silently slid into it. The teacher spoke with the woman in hushed tones as Penny stared straight ahead. Adam wondered what she was thinking and if he'd see her again.

He, too, was an only child but, unlike Penny, was smothered with his parents' love. His every whim was catered for and it was a testament to all concerned that he didn't end up a spoilt brat. He saw the joy he brought to his parents and it inspired him to attempt to bring it into the lives of those around him. He'd score a goal or a point or throw a basket or make someone laugh. Pleasing people came easily. He was no pushover, though. He was a winner, and all winners have the ability to put themselves over others when it really matters.

That was where he and his friend Ivan differed but it was a trait he shared with Robert. The first time Adam dressed up for Hallowe'en he was Superman, the next year he was Spiderman, the year after that he was Batman. Batman lasted three years because his outfit was way cooler than that of the tights-wearing Superman/Spiderman. At twelve he had fancied himself as some kind of hero like Westley in *The Princess Bride*, which was his favourite film (although if his friends had asked he would have told them it was *Rambo – First Blood*). But consumed by football, hurling, basketball, movies, Nintendo, music, friends and family, he had yet, unlike Westley, to find his true love Buttercup until the day he saw Penny crying on her school wall.

*I'll save you.*

Summer came quickly and the girl he had watched sitting on the wall, sometimes for five minutes and sometimes for an hour, vanished. He didn't know that her mother's mother had a house in France to which she was sent every year. He prayed they would end up at the same secondary school, but that September he was bitterly disappointed.

Three months later, Adam was formally introduced to Penny by his friend Ivan's cousin Mary. The three boys, Ivan, Adam and Robert, had been sitting on a bench in the woods smoking cigarettes and drinking Coke when Mary appeared with Penny in tow. Ivan was preoccupied with the news that his favourite chocolate bar was being taken off the market. Robert had a thing for Mary, but he was still with Shauna Ryan – he was busy flirting with Mary anyway – and Adam was lost to the girl who reminded him of Buttercup in *The Princess Bride*. Ivan wanted to play video games at the chipper and Robert had to meet Shauna, but Adam was going nowhere. Mary tagged along with Ivan, leaving Adam to walk Penny home, talking about everything and anything along the way. He made her laugh easily and her eyes lit up. Later that night they sat on her wall and at last he got to put his arm around her. When he was leaving they kissed and for both it was a first. *My Buttercup.* The trouble was, Westley married Buttercup, not a Dutchman's daughter.

Sam had taken his book to bed, falling asleep some time after two. Around the same time Mary emerged from the woods, frozen inside and out. Mr Monkels had forgone his usual fourteen-hour sleep and was standing to attention by the door, ready to welcome her home as if to remind her that, despite all she had lost, she still had him. She straightened the picture of her son holding Mr Monkels on a better day. *Goodnight, baby boy, your mammy loves you.* She rubbed Mr Monkels's head and he followed her upstairs. She undressed quietly and fell into bed, exhaustion taking hold. At last sleep was inescapable.

Penny continued to slug from her tumbler of vodka while flicking through TV stations, propped up by pillows, feigning interest in reruns of bad sitcoms so that she could finish the bottle. Breaking up with Adam had been hard enough but losing him to Cork City was unbearable. The neat spirit flowed down her throat like water, and it was after three when the glass fell from her hand and her head lolled forward. When she vomited, it was messy but she was safe.

Ivan was restless. He wasn't used to being uneasy – it clashed with his nature. He was worried about his kids – a phone call earlier had left him perturbed as his son, ten and usually a smartarse, had been subdued and his daughter, seven and a chatterbox, quiet and hesitant. His ex-wife had attempted to allay his concerns, noting that they were kids and being moody was part of the deal, but she, too, had sounded off form. He wondered if she was stressed – but then again, for five days out of any month she suffered with severe PMT, during which time she could take a man's head off if she had a mind to. It was hard to forget that the slightest infraction would induce a tearful tantrum that had to be seen to be believed.

During their stilted conversation he had casually glanced at his wall calendar and surmised that, if the pattern remained unchanged, she should have another good week of sense in her. He knew she didn't really like talking with him. He could hear it in her voice. She was friendly and polite but it was obvious she was glad to have escaped. Although, after a nasty patch, their eventual parting had been amicable enough, she was always quick to get him off the phone. He missed his kids, even if they were moody, and in truth he missed his wife – even if she had run off with some English tourist, taking his life with her. He had never been one for television so he listened to the ticking of an old clock.

Adam returned to an empty house in time to take a call from his frosty wife. The phone rang and silence ensued because there was nothing left to say. His head hurt – it was so full of obligation and desire, love and hate, bitterness and regret. He, a winner, was in a no-win situation. His children or his lover? With no room for manoeuvre he had to do the right thing, which meant losing everything. He would miss his home, Kenmare, his parents and friends, but mostly he would miss the girl in the blue shoes, who had stolen his heart when he was eleven. When he fell asleep he dreamed of her.

# 6. Meeting the people

Sam woke early. He was hungry, having merely staved off starvation with his reticent neighbour's scraps. Yet he was slow to leave his new home to venture forth into the town he had travelled so far to explore. He picked up the book that had fallen to the floor when he had dropped off to sleep. He meant to read a few pages only but he lost himself in another man's imagination. It wasn't unusual that he found himself comfortable in make-believe, and some would have said that, as a seasoned heroin-user, fantasy was a state to which he was well accustomed.

Next door, considering the previous night's heartache, it was surprising that Mary's morning had started so full of promise. She had awoken from a blissful sleep. Her son's anniversary was behind her and the giant invisible weight had lifted from her mind. She felt bright, breezy and full of vigour. She'd even danced in the shower while Dolly Parton belted out "Nine To Five" and Mr Monkels head-butted the glass door. Dolly was one of his favourites although her bluegrass stuff made him whine.

Mary didn't have to be in the bar until midday so she pottered around the house. She cleaned the kitchen, drank coffee and spoke with Penny on the phone.

Penny told her about Adam's bombshell.

"She knows?" said Mary, aghast.

"I've no idea how she found out. Still, after five years, I suppose it was about time."

"It's a miracle you got away with it for so long. God help her."

"God help her?"

"He did marry her, Penny."

"Yes, he did."

"Finding out your husband has been having an affair must be a nightmare," Mary added.

"To be honest, I always thought she knew, at least on some level."

"Just be glad she's not on your doorstep causing murder," Mary said, relieved that Penny's adversary could comport herself with such dignity in the face of her husband's betrayal.

"Why would she? She's won. They're moving to Cork," Penny said angrily.

"What?" Mary immediately began to fret. She really did hate change.

"The hotel's going up for sale. She's already found a house she likes, the stupid bitch."

"He's leaving us? Unbelievable!" Mary said, screwing up her face, as she always did when she was puzzled, upset or embarrassed. In this case her wrinkled forehead indicated distress.

"At least we had one last dance."

Mary could almost hear a tear rolling down her cheek. "I'm so sorry, Penn."

"You'll miss him too," Penny said, and she was right.

Mary would miss him. They had all been friends for so long. "Why don't you come into the bar tonight?" she said.

Penny wasn't sure, saying she wasn't feeling so well. "I'll probably stay in and keep my head down."

"Well, the offer's there if you change your mind."

"Cheers, Mare."

Mary hung up, feeling sad for Penny and Adam and for herself. She would miss her friend. Adam was impulsive to Ivan's dependable. He was funny, sharp and often the centre of attention. "Born with charm" was how her dad had once described him, and indeed he was charming, but he was also terribly unhappy and she worried for him. Moving to Cork was possibly the worst plan ever. He wouldn't want to leave his home, his friends and, most of all, Penny, the girl he had fallen in love with while she was sitting on a wall. *Oh, my God, was Adam the boy in the hood?* Poor Penny and poor Adam. Of course they were in the wrong – Adam's wife was the victim in all of this – but Adam's wife wasn't Mary's friend.

Later she sent a text to Adam, asking to meet him during her break. He responded instantly, agreeing to rendezvous at seven.

Another hour passed and, even though he was surely about to discover who had killed Boy Staunton, the ferocity with which Sam's insides burned proved too great to ignore. He put the book onto his bedside table and went to the shower. He washed and shaved in minutes, got dressed, grabbed his neighbour's dish and left his new home.

Mary found her jacket and picked up her handbag, which signalled to Mr Monkels that it was time for a furry kiss. He walked in step. She opened the french windows into the back garden. "In or out, Mr M?" she asked.

He took a step outside and faced her.

She bent down. "Good choice." Then she kissed his face, rubbing her cheek against his before he turned towards the bird table to resume the battle he had begun earlier that morning.

Sam's intention was to leave the bowl outside Mary's front door, as directed the previous night. He certainly wasn't in the mood to be scowled at. The sky was a vibrant blue and the day was unexpectedly sunny, in contrast to the rain that had washed him into this small, curious place. The light danced on the water – now a clear colour approaching a pale blue or a deep green, depending on which angle you viewed it from. Sea air filled his lungs, clearing his tired mind. Overhead a seagull squawked a greeting – or told him to eff off. He grinned to himself. If it had flown in from New York harbour the sentiment was definitely the latter.

He opened the gate to his neighbour's house slowly, attempting to avoid the squeak it had made the previous night, afraid it might herald his presence. He put the bowl on the step and turned away, then back: a bowl on the middle of a step might be stood on, resulting in a visit to an emergency room. He bent down to move it next to the large flowerpot that contained a hardy-looking red-leafed plant and a deep-blue pottery hedgehog. It was the hedgehog that caught his eye, and delayed him in standing upright.

He didn't hear the door open and his neighbour didn't see the man stooped over her step so she walked straight into him – his face embedded itself in her crotch – unbalancing him. Her initial shock gave way to horror when he clutched at her arse. Beating him about the head with her handbag was her only option and she did so with gusto. A strange man's face in her crotch will provoke that kind of reaction in a woman.

In Sam's defence, he hadn't planned the assault and her handbag had buckles.

"Get off, you frigging perv!" she roared.

"Your bowl!" He pointed with one hand, while protecting his face with the other.

She gave him one last clout and the onslaught ended. Unfortunately that one drew blood.

"*Aaaah!*" he yelled.

Mary took a moment to survey the damage she'd inflicted. "Oh!" *Frigging buckle.*

"What?" Sam said urgently – as with most men, any minor injury was tantamount to the end of the world.

"Your eye is bleeding. It must have caught on the buckle."

Sam took his hand off his face. It was red, the blood pooling in his palm. He heard her sigh – a frustrated sigh. She really did have a nerve.

Mary was embarrassed at having gone one step too far, yet his reaction to a tiny cut was amusing, even endearing. "I have a first-aid kit," she said.

He would have told her to shove it but he had always been squeamish around blood, which had proved a handicap when he was a heroin addict. Of course, the promise of liquid Nirvana had enabled him to get over it, but now he was clean, his weak stomach and wobbling legs had made a surprising return.

Unsteadily he followed her inside and she indicated that he should sit at the kitchen table. He closed his eyes, his hand tight against the cut just over his eye. He could hear

78

her shoving pots and pans about and then she was standing over him. "You have to move your hand," she advised.

Eyes closed, he was almost sure he could hear a grin in her voice. He was slow to comply.

"It's a tiny cut. You're not going to lose an eye here."

*Easy for you to say, you bag-wielding lunatic!* He lowered his hand and his good eye opened in time to see her approach him with a cotton-wool bud.

She held his head, arching it back. "This will sting a little," she warned, and he braced himself.

It wasn't that bad. She was surprisingly gentle. Using another bud she applied antiseptic cream and then a small plaster covered the even smaller cut. "There, all done!" she said.

"I guess I should thank you," Sam said, still a little shocked at sustaining a head injury so soon into his trip. It wasn't hard to detect a hint of sarcasm in his voice.

"Don't bother," she said, brushing herself down.

He got up, sensing she wanted him gone – he was only too happy to oblige.

"Sorry," he heard himself mumble, as he walked quickly to the door.

She followed and once outside she attempted to reciprocate his apology, conceding that it had all been a misunderstanding and that, in all probability, he wasn't a pervert. Still, it was clear to him she was not entirely convinced.

(In fact, he was so desperate to prove his innocence she almost felt sorry for him but she wasn't about to let him know that. She'd had way too many foreign neighbours – the best of friends one day and the next gone for ever – and didn't need the hassle, so she allowed him to think she wasn't convinced of his virtue. *That should keep him at bay.*)

She was getting into her car when he realized she would know where he could get a decent lunch. She rolled down the window. "Everywhere is good," she said, and drove off.

"Everywhere is good," he repeated. "Thanks a lot, lady."

Sam decided to walk. He reckoned town was ten minutes on foot and, as he was still a little light-headed, he deemed it better not to risk driving – this in a man who, one night six months previously, had driven from Boston to New York having pushed five hundred bucks' worth of heroin into his system that day. He was halfway to town when it struck him that he cared about his welfare now, which reminded him that he had indeed come a long way. *I hope it lasts.*

He reached the top of the town and looked down at the sloping street that led to a church with a steeple. The sky above was a deeper navy than that over the water and yet it seemed as bright. Stratus clouds passed quickly above him towards the sea. Below, everywhere was busy with cars beeping and people waving as they popped into and out of the colourful shops.

While Sam sauntered through his new world, Mary parked half a street away in her father's yard and entered the kitchen to be met by Pierre, who was in foul form, having borne the brunt of Jessie's frustration.

"Oh, that woman!" was his greeting, and Jessie wasn't far behind.

"I heard that," she said, red with anger. "Arse-crack!" she bellowed, following him to the storeroom at full speed. It was a term Jessie used at least three times a day.

Mary went into the dining room where her dad was behind the bar. "Have they been like this long?" she asked, laughing.

"All morning – they're like feckin' caricatures," he said. "Are you OK?"

"Thanks for the flowers, Dad. He would have liked them."

"You're both welcome." He patted his daughter's back. They had been through hell over the years but as long as she was OK he would be.

The place was busy enough, and within seconds of her arrival Ivan was sitting up at the bar ordering his usual seafood salad. "Don't you ever want to eat something else?" Mary asked.

"No," he said. "What about you? I hear you're meeting Adam for a drink. Is there something I should know?" He was chuckling.

"Shut up." She grinned, then became serious. "I can't believe he's leaving."

"I'll believe it when I see it," he said, playing with the redundant menu.

"Penny says he's definitely going. He's got a job managing some restaurant in Cork and they're selling the hotel."

Sam was too hungry to survey the many restaurants and planned to eat in the first he found. He didn't have to walk too far. The menu was plastered on the front door and it looked good. Better still, the aroma coming from inside could only be described as mouth-watering. The place looked homely – pottery and luscious plants filling the window and ornate furniture bedecking the entrance. Once inside, he wasn't disappointed. Faces and events from another era lined the walls, mingled with a few paintings. The dark wooden tables and red velvet sofas suggested warmth and, even on a bright day, the burning candles didn't seem out of place. He melted into his chair, having already decided to start with the crab salad and to follow with the house omelette. Someone had left a newspaper on the seat. He began to read what he thought would be local Irish news but which turned out to be international, with much criticism of the Iraq war. He put it down just in time to see his basher neighbour behind the little bar. "You're kidding me," he mumbled.

"Crap!" Mary disappeared.

Ivan bent over the bar and looked at her crouching on the floor. "What are you doing?" he asked, intrigued.

"Frigging American," she mumbled. "Of all the frigging places. I have to go." She stood up again and disappeared into the kitchen.

Ivan glanced around and spotted the blond boy. *Interesting*. He refilled his coffee cup, then went over to Sam's booth. "Excuse me?" Ivan said. "You're on your own?"

"Yeah," Sam agreed.

"Not from around here?" Ivan noted.

"New York."

"Ah," Ivan nodded, "you're the new fella by the pier who Jerry Sullivan nicknamed 'Uncle'?"

"Yeah?" Sam shook his head, amazed.

Ivan laughed. "I bumped into Mossy first thing."

"I don't know Mossy."

Ivan grinned. "You will."

"Man, this is one small town."

"You've no idea," Ivan said.

A fat woman in her fifties took their orders. To say she wasn't in a good humour was an understatement. When Ivan made a joke she smacked him over the head with her order book. Ivan had laughed but Sam was unwilling to risk further injury at the hands of a crazy Kerrywoman.

Over lunch they conversed easily. Sam liked Ivan mostly because he was easygoing and not intrusive. The guy was more interested in talking about fish than asking probing questions. He found himself relaxing, although it was obvious that Mary had seen him and was steering clear. The crab salad was to die for and Ivan had gone to great lengths to explain why. "I'm talking about fish too much," he ended sheepishly.

"You really are, man," Sam agreed, but he was enjoying himself.

Ivan liked the American too. He wouldn't have stayed on for a pint with him if he hadn't.

Mary made herself busy chopping onions in the kitchen so that she could avoid her neighbour. If he hadn't asked her to recommend a place to eat and if she hadn't been so dismissive, she wouldn't have felt the need to hide. Having said that, he had asked and she hadn't volunteered her own establishment. Seeing as she'd drawn blood, the offer of a free lunch was possibly the least she could do in recompense. *Of all the frigging places.*

Jessie wondered why she was staying in the kitchen. "I chop. You lord it over everyone. What's changed?" she asked insultingly.

"I'm hiding," Mary admitted, and Jessie was suddenly interested.

"From who?" she asked, on her way to the door.

"Jessie!" Mary called.

Jessie didn't even have to open the kitchen door before she copped it. "It's the American," she noted triumphantly.

Mary was impressed. "How did you know?" she asked, despite herself.

"Why wouldn't you hide? He looks like an arse-crack."

"He's not," Mary answered, without thinking.

Jessie's eyebrows rose. "Really?"

She looked at Pierre, who grinned. "Ah, *chérie*, you like him, no?"

"What?" Mary was alarmed. "Don't be ridiculous."

The enemies had converged, nodding at one another, enjoying her moment of torment.

"Arse-crack is a disgusting expression, that's all I'm saying," she said, chopping into her eighth red onion.

It was over the third pint that Ivan offered to take Sam out in the boat with him. Sam was enthralled by the idea of fishing so Ivan promised they'd go the next day, adding that as it was Sunday he had to eat with his family so it would have to be late afternoon. Sam could see no problem with that and it would give him time to finish his book. He insisted that his new friend allow him to pay for his meal.

He made his way home, feeling a little dizzy but full and happy. He also felt a little guilty. Drinking three pints was as close as he'd got to oblivion since rehab. He wasn't an alcoholic so drinking wasn't entirely against the rules. *But does it make me want to get high? No. Definitely not. OK, this is cool. I'm just a little happy. I'm fine. Everything's fine.* This was a relief, but he'd have to keep an eye on himself. He wasn't strong enough yet: he was still on a precipice and the slightest ill wind could knock him off.

# 7. Past and Present

It was the third time in six months that Penny had been awakened by the smell of her own vomit but, hung-over, she remained unaware of it until she looked into the bathroom mirror and discovered the extent of the previous night's debauchery. *Oh, sweet God!* Disgusted with herself, she stripped off and got into the shower. The water was pounding against her skull, which felt as fragile as her mother's ugly fine-bone china. Her legs were shaking under the weight of her surprisingly heavy head. She leaned against the wall and slid down towards the shower tray. She didn't attempt to stop herself, and sat with her knees under her chin and her hands cupping her head to protect it against the water.

Later she took painkillers with a pint of chilled water and made coffee while two DJs bantered about Madonna and her latest religion. She had three espressos before she opened her emails. She answered some of her editor's queries and typed a redraft of her lottery story, and by mid-morning her limbs had stopped quivering.

When Mary called, she cried, which she had promised herself she wouldn't do. She had declined Mary's offer to come over, telling herself that, like any wounded animal, she needed to be alone. That wasn't the truth. She hated being alone but she knew she wouldn't get through the next few days exchanging pleasantries and girl talk. Instead, as soon as she had finished a telephone interview at three, she would open a bottle of vodka. When it was gone she might break out another – and she didn't need any witnesses. After that, she promised herself, she'd emerge from the haze tomorrow or the next day and everything would be fine.

Ivan always woke in time for sunrise. In spring and summer he would enjoy it from his veranda, drinking coffee while the birds sang from the branches of the many trees that lined the boundaries of his home. In autumn and winter he would be on his boat when the sun came up. Whatever the season, he would enjoy five hours of good fishing before he headed into town for lunch. Ivan was a creature of habit, so much so that many people had commented they could set their watch by him.

His afternoons he spent at home locked in his study, reading magazines on stocks and commodities or trading shares online. He was never going to be the cause of Donald Trump losing a night's sleep but he was smart enough to know when to buy and sell. He enjoyed risk but was never seduced by it. Sometimes his judgement let him down but those occasions were rare. Ivan was no mathematician but he was a pretty good economist.

It was curious that he had deviated from his routine, and it was perhaps curiosity that had driven him to do so but, whatever, he had thoroughly enjoyed drinking a few pints with the American. It had been a nice break from the mundane and it was even nicer to be away from his home in the afternoon even if only for a few hours.

Ivan's large house was a symbol of success to the onlooker but its many empty rooms reminded him of his failure. When he had uttered the words "I will" and "for ever", he had meant them and, foolishly, he had believed his wife when she had repeated them. Years later when she had come home one night, battling tears to make an announcement, he had been shocked to the core. In the weeks following her desertion he was numb, but at least she and his children, whom she had left with the very night she'd dictated their split, were still in Kenmare.

Originally she had planned a new life for them somewhere in England, which had ignited in Ivan a fierce anger. It was then he considered fighting her for custody. He consulted a solicitor and was told that his rights were secondary to his wife's. He had argued that she was the adulterer, the home-wrecker, the assassin, that it was she who had killed their family – and there were plenty around him who weren't shy to point that out. If necessary, they would have stood in a court to swear to it. He argued that he had been a good provider, a good husband, and that he'd never strayed. He had loved his wife and he adored his children. He would never have risked them. He asked why he should lose everything. His solicitor had no answers but, despite this, Ivan was determined to fight for his kids.

Then one day, having witnessed his daughter's confusion and tears, it dawned on him that this was about his kids, their life and his love of them, not about the woman who had abandoned him. His kids needed her and, despite her failings as a wife, she was a good mother and the prevailing force in their children's lives. He couldn't rob them of her as she had robbed him of them. When he had finally admitted to himself that he would lose them, he had quietly fallen apart.

Earlier that morning, alone on his boat, he had found himself reflecting on the day that he had driven his children to the airport and out of his life. He remembered that, following their mother and her lover in the car ahead, they had cried all the way. Neither had wanted to move away from their dad and their friends but he had told them to be brave and to enjoy the adventure and that their home would always be waiting. Everything inside him had threatened to snap but he held on tight to reason and reminded his children that he loved them. He told them to think of England as boarding-school because they would spend all their holidays with him at home. When they walked through the departure gates he had struggled so hard not to cry because a father's tears could scar a child. Instead he wept all the way home, having to stop the car a number of times because he couldn't see the road.

For two weeks he hibernated in his soulless home, dressed in an ill-fitting tracksuit, holed up watching daytime TV with the phone in his hand. Then Mary had sorted him out. She had let herself in with his spare key and, ignoring his protests, she had cleaned the pigsty his home had become, then cooked a spicy lamb stew, his favourite of her dishes. He showered and shaved, but only after she'd threatened him with a kitchen knife. He joined her at the freshly laid table, silent and distant, and attempted to eat while she talked to him about all the things he could do with his kids when he saw them.

"Remember when Chris was a baby?" she asked.

"It seems like a lifetime ago."

"Nah, not so long. You were abroad working for a lot of that."

"Don't remind me," he said, his hands over his ears.

"Did he forget you then?"

"No."

"No," she agreed. "He used to sit on the doorstep waiting for you to come home." She smiled at the memory. "You're their dad. You're the one they love. So miss them while they're out of sight but remember it's not for ever. You'll see them again."

Suddenly he was embarrassed. "I'm sorry. I know it's not the same as losing Ben."

"This isn't about me," she said. "Not everything that happens has to be measured against losing Ben. You have a right to your pain. I just want to make sure it doesn't swallow you up."

He reached across the table and took her hand in his. "What would I do without you, cousin?" he asked.

"What would I do without *you*, cousin?" she responded. "Life goes on."

"And the only choice we have is how we want to live it," she replied.

At first Ivan's kids had groused and griped about their new life. They bashed their friends, school, teachers and their mother. They turned grumbling into an art form. Ivan would spend hours on the phone attending to their complaints. Their problems were not so different from the ones they'd left behind, and with time they made new friends and became accustomed to their environment. Intermittently he'd receive some positive information about an outing or something that had happened at school. They had settled in, and Kent was not as far away as he'd first thought. Kerry airport was only half an hour down the road and there were cheap flights to three London airports every day of the week. The journey took less than an hour. When he worked out that it would actually take them longer to travel home to Kerry from Dublin than it would from Kent, he felt a lot better.

And just when he'd relaxed his kids stopped talking to him. No more whingeing and whining, no more bitching and moaning. No more stories of friends or outings or anything. Their conversations became stilted, and again he worried that he was losing them, but something in the back of his mind told him it might be worse than that . . .

After his few pints with the American he didn't feel like going home so he returned to his boat. The evening sky contained a hint of purple and the weather was mild so he located a beer in the fridge and sat on deck sipping it and watching the dark waters as the Waterboys sang "Fisherman's Blues" from an old CD player he'd fitted in the cabin. Ivan liked to think he'd inspired the song as he'd met the lads a few times when they'd played in Kenmare.

So, while the rest of the world busied itself, he sat in contemplation. He was glad to see that the previous morning's cloud had passed and that his cousin was in a lighter humour. He had realized the date and its significance, which was why he'd checked in on her the previous morning, but he would never have mentioned it. Being there for her was enough – and she always made a lovely breakfast. Her reaction to Sam had struck him as odd. Mary was not inclined to fluster. Then again she often behaved peculiarly around the time of Ben's anniversary. To be fair, the American seemed like a really nice fella and he looked forward to introducing the city boy to the sea.

*

It was just after seven when Mary made her way into the Horseshoe bar. Adam was sitting at a table picking at a bowl of mussels and sipping a pint. The bar waitress saluted her and made some joke about her being the competition. Adam stood and they hugged.

"You've had some week." Mary wasn't one for beating around the bush.

"I've had better." Adam was a bush-beater.

"So, you're really leaving?"

"Yeah – you know I wouldn't put Penn through it if I wasn't."

Mary raised her eyebrows. "You've put her through everything else."

Adam conceded that she had made a good point. He loved Penny too much to cause her pain intentionally but pain caused, whether intentional or not, is still pain. It was such a pity he didn't love his wife.

"You're in a pretty terrible fix," she added.

"I am," he agreed, "but it's no different from the fix I've been in for years."

"It is. You won't have Penny," Mary said, and instantly regretted it. "I'm sorry. I shouldn't have said that."

"Why not? It's true."

"Cork is only sixty miles away," Mary said, trying to compensate for her previous comment.

"Cork is a lifetime away," he said.

Mary ordered a gin and tonic and he ordered another pint. Then he explained how his wife had worked out that he was having an affair and how she had threatened to take his kids to the Netherlands and how he had to make it work. He had no choice: he'd witnessed what losing his kids had done to Ivan. Mary squeezed his hand: given the choice, she would have traded anything or anyone for her own child. People wasted so much time seeking out the love of their lives in the shape of a partner, when the truth was that for most the real loves of their lives were their children – and everyone else was dispensable. Once, when Ben was still a toddler, she had used this theory to explain her lethargy in seeking companionship and now, years later, Adam and Penny were proving it had legs.

Adam's wife had gone to Cork to set up home but her spies were everywhere. When Peggy Dawson passed she leaned in to say hello to Adam but the manner in which she looked Mary up and down, accompanied by a deep line-furrowing frown, suggested that what she really meant was "Your card is marked." Mary wanted to point out that she wasn't Penny, but as she was Penny's closest friend, Adam was deemed to be fraternizing with the enemy. He was as nice as pie to Peggy and even managed to make his wife's friend laugh. Mary also made an effort to smile at the local gossip and harridan, who had often described her as the Angel of Death. Peggy continued to eyeball them until they finished their drinks and left.

Adam wanted her to go with him to McCarthy's for another but she needed to get back behind the bar. He asked her if she wanted company and, as Penny had decided to stay at home, she agreed. He sat up at the bar and she poured him a drink while he riffled through the available CDs as she'd promised him the music would be his choice. Her father was tired and she had assured him she would be OK on her own, with Adam to step into the breach if necessary. He didn't need to be told twice.

Adam picked Damien Rice's *O* and handed it to her.

"Again?" she asked, hand on hip.

"What do you mean 'again'?" Adam asked, with mock-horror.

"I swear to God you're turning into Ivan," she said.

"Ivan has eaten the same salad for fifteen years. I've requested this record three times."

"Yeah, well, it's a slippery slope." She grinned.

Once the CD was playing, Adam settled on his bar stool while Mary wiped the counter. "Is she drinking?" he asked, out of nowhere.

"A few bottles of wine last week but she's OK."

"You sure?"

"No, but she's favouring staying at home rather than going to the pub so that's good," she said. "Last week was the first time I've seen Penny drunk in an age and, let's face it, she'd just been dumped."

Adam nodded guiltily. "OK."

"She will be as soon as you leave," Mary couldn't stop herself saying.

"You're a cold-hearted bitch," he said.

"And you're a cheating bastard," Mary said.

"I'm really going to miss you." He smiled.

"I'm really going to miss you too."

Interrupted conversation followed as they talked about this and that while she served drinks and swapped pleasantries with other locals. Adam told her about the restaurant at which he'd secured a management position, the legal wrangling involved in selling the hotel, and the place his wife had found for them to live. It wasn't all that bad: the restaurant was an award-winner and there were some excellent schools. Mary had told him about her new neighbour and was pleased when Adam enjoyed her report of the tourist-bashing incident.

It was after ten when Tin Fitz and Roy Rice plonked themselves on the bar stools at either side of Adam.

"Adam," Tin said.

"Tin," Adam responded.

Tin sniffed. "Caught rotten."

"I suppose so," Adam agreed.

"You'll have a drink," Roy said, and Adam nodded.

Roy ordered three pints from Mary and within moments the three men were immersed in a conversation about Kerry's chances of winning the All Ireland hurling final.

A few hours later, when last orders were finally served, Mary joined the three lads at the counter.

"Mary, have you decided to marry me yet?" Tin asked, grinning.

"I hadn't heard you'd divorced," she said.

"I haven't but I've a big bed. I'm sure Nora would make room."

"That's some image," Roy said, and laughed to himself.

"I've always believed two wives were better than one," Tin said, and nudged Adam. "It'd sort out a lot of hassles."

Adam refused to be drawn.

"What's that called?" Tin said to Roy.

"Polygamy," Roy said, and drained his glass.

"How you fixed for a bit of polygamy?" Tin winked at Mary.

"I'd rather gnaw through my own foot, thanks, Tin," Mary said.

Adam and Roy laughed while Tin shook his head. "All right – if you feel that strongly I'll get rid of Nora."

Later, when the bar was cleared out, Adam and Mary sat drinking coffee and reminiscing.

"Remember the night on the boat?" he asked.

They had been on the boat hundreds of times but she knew which night he was referring to. Of course she remembered. "The water was like glass. I still can't believe Uncle Pete didn't catch us or that we didn't crash," she said, grinning.

"Crash? Ivan could drive that thing in his sleep even at sixteen!" Adam was laughing. "Penny and I were hot and heavy that night."

"I threw a bottle of water on you to cool you down."

"And night swimming!" he lamented.

She smiled widely at the memory of her first skinny-dip. Ivan had been embarrassed to take off his trunks in front of his cousin but he'd been with a girl called Bridget and she was definitely one to see in the nip so he'd agreed, based on a borderline system. Then, under cover of darkness, the six of them had spread out with only the moonlight to guide them to their partner.

"Robert was the first to jump in." Adam sighed, remembering his long-dead friend.

"Robert was always the first," Mary said, remembering her first love with all the warmth a fond memory could bring.

"He wanted to be an engineer."

Mary nodded. "Yeah, and to play guitar for Bon Jovi." They laughed, remembering their friend's youthful passions.

"Do you miss him?" he asked.

Mary was taken aback. "Not really," she answered honestly. "Mostly he's a stranger, a kid I knew a long time ago, but on nights like this one, when we talk and reminisce, I do – but it's fleeting and not real. We were just teenagers finding our way . . . It's likely we wouldn't be together now if he was alive."

"Like me and Penny," he said sadly.

"No, not at all like you and Penny."

"How long will it take her to forget me?" he asked, looking into the dregs of his mug.

"A long time."

"It's killing me," he said.

"I know." There was nothing else to say.

Mary got home just after one. Mr Monkels was extremely put out that he had been outside for the entire evening, even though he had been well fed and there was a shed with a deluxe quilted dog bed at the end of the garden. He articulated his feelings with various forms of sustained groaning. He was not impressed with his owner's timekeeping and was determined that she should be aware of it. Mary gave him a bar of chocolate to shut him up. This was the act of a bad mother, dogs being intolerant of chocolate, but he loved it and she only gave it to him on a very special occasion or as a response to guilt.

The light was on next door and when she went into the back garden to retrieve Mr Monkels's bowl, she could hear Billie Holiday singing in her neighbour's kitchen. She stopped to enjoy "April In Paris".

Next door Sam was sitting, book in hand, having resumed his journey to Deptford and beyond. He didn't worry about the cut above his eye or ponder on his new life in a small south Kerry town. He didn't worry about those he'd left behind. He didn't think about anything. By one a.m. he had long ago left Kenmare.

# 8. Sunday, bloody Sunday

It was Sunday and Ivan was having lunch with his parents, his twin brothers Séamus and Barry, Séamus's wife Vicky, their four-year-old twins Beth and Bonnie, Barry's boyfriend Steven and their puppy, Pluto. He was accustomed now to attending his mother's lunches alone. He still found it hard. The friendly noise made it harder to go home to silence. He missed the familiar sounds of a full house and envied his older brother but, having said that, it was obvious that Séamus was at the end of his tether.

"Beth! Bonnie! Leave the dog alone!" Séamus shouted. Neither child heard him, so busy were they in trying to capture Pluto, who had managed to squeeze himself behind the TV.

Steven was beside himself: "Pluto! Daddy's here!"

The girls were reaching in as far as their little arms allowed them and Pluto was squealing, waiting for Steven to save him. Steven, in haste to get to his pup, tripped over one of the girls' Disney Princesses nearly knocking himself out on the edge of the coffee-table. Barry, seeing his partner crumpled on the floor, dropped his cup of coffee and slipped on it in his haste to get to his boyfriend. Séamus helped his brother up, still roaring at the girls who were still determined to catch the dog. Ivan attended to Steven while his mother attended to Barry. Séamus stormed out of the room with a little girl under each arm, calling to his wife, who yelled that she was in the bathroom. Well used to blocking out sound, Ivan's father snoozed in his chair.

At the table Steven insisted on eating lunch with Pluto attached to his chest in a dog knapsack. Bonnie and Beth were strapped into their chairs, both a little too old for high-chairs but a little too hyperactive not to be tied down. Séamus and Barry talked about the Cork v. Kerry game. Steven, Ivan's mother and Vicky complained to one another about the price of cashmere, then discussed Greece as an all-round holiday destination. Bonnie and Beth threw food at each other while Ivan and his dad silently enjoyed their meal.

Ivan's mother had always known Barry was a little differ-ent from her other sons, and even his love of the GAA hadn't encouraged her to look forward to grandchildren. The first indication that he might not marry had come when he was four. She would often find him asleep in her ward-robe with a face full of lipstick and wrapped in one of her dresses. At six he broke his leg while walking in a pair of her heels. His dad had taken him to the emergency room and told the doctor he had fallen from a tree but Barry had cheerfully corrected him. During his teenage years he had thrown himself into sport and his mother worried that he was doing so to escape himself. His other brothers, Séamus, Ivan and even the youngest, Fintan, were all sluts, each week a different girl, but not Barry. His father pretended that this was because he was studious and a consummate sportsman. She wasn't sure how to tackle her son's ambig-uous sexuality but after long consideration she thought it best to allow him to discover himself. She sat back and waited, but made sure he knew that he lived in a house of tolerance and acceptance.

Barry came out at a Sunday lunch during his last year in college. His mother was relieved and kissed her son, ruffled his hair and told him his boyfriends would always be welcome in her house. His father was a little pale but resigned – after all, his wife had been preparing him for this over many years. He put his arm around his son, patted him on the back and said, "Never mind." Ivan and Fintan didn't seem to care either way. Ivan was preoccupied about how he should tell his parents he'd got his girlfriend pregnant, and Fintan was working out how to dump his latest, who was a great kisser but had a flatulence problem.

Séamus had been the most put out by his twin's revelation. Barry had joked that his brother's storming out of the kitchen suggested he thought that maybe Barry had tried to have his way with him in the womb. His mother had attempted a laugh before asking him to follow his brother and to have a quiet word. It turned out that Séamus was upset because what had been so obvious to his mother had not been obvious to him. He had always thought they had a special bond and that he knew all there was to know about his twin and suddenly Barry was a stranger. After that, their relationship had changed a little. They had always referred to each other as twins, but now they were merely brothers.

Over the years, most revelations had taken place at Sunday lunch – Barry's coming out; Ivan's impending fatherhood a mere two Sundays later. Ivan had not been met with the same understanding as his brother – in fact, his mother had threatened to have him shot and his father had had to hold her back while shouting at his son to run for it. A few months later it was Ivan and Norma's engagement, a much more sedate affair, with congratulations and champagne – initially his mother had worried that he was moving too fast but by dessert Norma had won her over. A few years later Séamus's engagement to Vicky became yet another announcement over the Sunday lunch table. Ivan's wife's infidelity was imparted over a salmon starter, the separation a few Sundays later. Fintan's decision to move to New Zealand to start a bungee-jumping business had been the most recent.

But on this Sunday, aside from Barry and Steven nearly knocking themselves out, the twins being terrors and Pluto's nervous disposition, all was going well. Until Ivan's mother advised them that she had an announcement to make. Everyone fell silent and braced themselves.

"I'm pregnant," she said.

Barry nearly choked, Ivan went red and Séamus stood up. Vicky looked confused and Steven seemed impressed.

Ivan's mother laughed and his dad joined in.

"Only joking."

Séamus sat down. "Very funny, Mother. You nearly gave me a heart-attack."

Her face changed a little. "It's funny you should say that." She wasn't joking any more. She squeezed her husband's arm. "Your father had a mild heart-attack last Monday." Everyone stared blankly at her.

"Everything's fine. They only kept him for two nights in Cork. He'll have to go back for tests and maybe a little oper-ation. It's nothing serious but of course he'll have to change his diet." She looked at her husband. "His cholesterol is off the chart but I won't go into that." She smiled at him and he grinned sheepishly at her, then at his kids, who remained blank. Steven was shifting in his seat, appearing embarrassed.

Barry spoke: "Dad had a heart-attack."

"Yes," his mother confirmed.

"And you didn't think to call one of us?"

"No."

"I cannot believe –"

Barry's father put up a hand, silencing him. "I told your mother not to say anything. I didn't want a fuss. It wasn't serious – I was never at death's door. The only reason we're telling you is that I may have a genetic heart condition." He stopped, as though he'd said enough.

His kids and their partners stared at him, waiting for the punchline. He picked up his fork and continued to eat.

Their mother took control. "It involves thickening of the valves. A good diet can be preventive but you should all get checked out. You're young men so it shouldn't be a problem, but it's better to know." She sat back in her chair.

Vicky looked at her husband with concern. Steven looked at Barry with the same concern. Even the twins were silenced. Ivan stared at his plate. His mother leaned over and squeezed his hand. "It'll be fine," she said to the table.

Afterwards the others made their way into the sitting room. Ivan insisted on helping his mother in the kitchen. She allowed him to, knowing that he hated being in the crowded sitting room alone to be reminded of the family that had left him. Halfway through drying up, he sat up on the counter. "Wow, a separation and a possible heart condition all in the space of a year. I must be on a roll."

She laughed. "Don't be ridiculous!" She scrubbed hardened potato from a sudsy plate.

"What do you mean?"

"You're not going to have a heart problem," she told

him. "You and Fintan take after me. It's Barry and Séamus who won't be able to eat a fry for the next forty years."

Ivan laughed – he couldn't help it. His mother wasn't a doctor, yet he knew that if she said he had nothing to worry about, it was the truth.

"Thanks, Mam," he said, leaping off the counter like a teenager. He gave her a kiss on the cheek.

"You'll get checked, though?" she asked, and he nodded. He walked to the door.

"Tell me this," she said, "who's your new lunch mate?"

He was confused.

"The American," she said.

"Oh, Sam!"

"Tell my niece her auntie Sheila likes the cut of her new neighbour." She winked.

Ivan grinned. "Will do."

"Tell her to come and visit, and sure if she likes she can bring him along."

Ivan left the room laughing.

By five he was on the water and in the company of the American the whole town seemed to be talking about. Sam wasn't much of a fisherman but he was a quick study and Ivan enjoyed guiding him. The sea was crystal clear and the mackerel were biting so it was shaping up to be a pleasant evening. They had been fishing for more than an hour when Sam broached the topic of his standoffish neighbour and commented on her unfavourably. Ivan let him speak, then mentioned that the woman he was dismissing was his own cousin and best friend.

"You're kidding me?" Sam said.

"I'm not," Ivan replied, and laughed heartily, thoroughly enjoying his new friend's discomfort. It was then he had offered him two pieces of valuable information. One: a warning never to speak ill of a local unless he was absolutely sure there was no connection between the person to be spoken of and the person being spoken to. And two: the reason why his cousin was as she was.

Ivan spoke of how he'd watched Mary beat the unbeatable, surviving a devastating crash to go on to give birth to her dead boyfriend's son, and then he had told him where his neighbour's little boy had died. The tale was devastating. A beautiful child broken and a mother's screams. She had held him in her arms knowing that death was instant and that no doctor could bring him back. Others had stood around, silently bearing witness to her agony while clinging to their own children, covering their small faces from the horror before them. As a storyteller Ivan could transport his listener to another time and place. Sam felt a lump in his throat and sat quietly, feeling pretty guilty for judging the unfortunate woman.

Ivan was silent for a while and Sam didn't know what to say so he concentrated on the water. After a few minutes, the pole bobbed and then he felt strain. Ivan returned to the present to help him hook the smallest fish he'd seen in a long while. They laughed and threw it back. Then they shared a flask of coffee and shot the breeze about nothing in particular.

But Sam wanted to hear more about Mary and about what had happened in the aftermath of such tragedy. Ivan didn't seem to mind returning to it.

"Well, we thought we'd lost her," he said, scratching out

the sea salt lodged in his hair. "We thought there was no coming back." He nodded, affirming it. "Her mother she could get over – sure she'd never known anything different. Robert, well, he was just a boy – 'twas hard on us all but we knew she'd recover. But after Ben 'twas different and no one was sure if she'd ever be right again."

"But she was," Sam found himself interjecting.

His new friend smiled. "After a long time, she came back to us," he said.

"But not the same?"

"No," Ivan said, a little sadly, "not the same." He put down his pole to pour some more coffee into his cup.

"How long has it been?" Sam asked.

"Six years this week."

"Holy shit!" Sam breathed.

"Yeah. It's always a bad time for her but it's over now and summer's around the corner."

Sam's pole bobbed, the line tightened and so did his grip. This would not be a small fish.

Later that evening when Ivan had docked the boat outside Sam's, Sam had wandered past it and made his way to the wood. He walked until he came across the plaque that bore his neighbour's child's name; a sodden teddy bear and wilting flowers lay beneath it. He had no idea why he felt he had to sit by a stranger's memorial but recently he hadn't had much reason for anything.

That night Ivan went home and phoned his kids. Chris was out playing soccer with some new pals but Justine was there and she seemed to be in a lighter humour than when they had last spoken.

"How's school?" he began, predictably.

"Jenny Thompson's dog got run over!" She seemed quite excited.

"Oh, I'm sorry to hear that," he said.

"I'm not!"

"You're not?"

"No."

"Why not?"

"The first time I went to her house he bit me and, anyway, he only broke a leg." She spoke as though she'd been waiting for him to get his comeuppance.

"Fair enough so," Ivan conceded.

"He has a cast and everything."

"Yeah."

"It's funny."

He could hear the smile in her voice and grinned. "How's Chris?"

"He's a pain."

Ivan laughed.

"Mam wants to talk to you," she said, with a sigh.

"I love you, Justy," he said quietly.

"Love you too, Dad."

He waited for her to pass the phone to her mother.

"Dad?" she said.

"Yes, love."

"I can't wait to see you."

Before he could answer she had passed the phone.

"Ivan."

"Norma."

"Look, I was thinking that maybe you could take the kids for the Easter holiday." She was rustling papers.

"I'd love to have them," he said.

"Good."

"Doing anything nice?" he asked.

His question came as a surprise – normally they restricted their conversation to the children – and caught her off guard. "No, Des and I just need some time alone," she admitted.

"Oh." He regretted asking. "Well, I can't wait," he added, with delight.

"OK, then."

"Right." He put down the phone.

His kids were coming for an unexpected visit in less than a month. He thought about painting their rooms but decided against it. Justine feared change almost as much as her auntie Mary and, indeed, he did.

Sam made his way out of the wood in time to bump into Mary, who was coming home from the pub. Sunday nights were always quiet and her father was happy enough to close on his own. He was trying to open his wooden gate as she got out of her car. The damn thing seemed wedged shut and refused to budge. He shook it and shook it, cursing under his breath.

"You have to kick it," she said.

"Kick it?" he echoed.

"It probably swelled in the rain."

"Swelled," he repeated.

She put her handbag on her car and gave the gate a good boot. It swung open. She picked up her bag and walked into her own garden.

"Thanks," he said.

She responded by putting her key into the door.

"I said thanks." He wasn't used to being ignored and didn't like it.

"I heard you," she replied.

"So say, 'You're welcome,'" he ordered, and the pity he had felt for her earlier all but disappeared. Nothing excused bad manners.

"You're welcome," she said, and closed her door.

"Did that kill you?" he mumbled, putting his key into the lock.

# 9. All is forgiven, Brinkerhoffs

A red sun lit the dusky evening sky. Sam walked along the path, eyes north, watching the colour seep. The various shades of this small town had fascinated him during his two weeks in residence. This evening he was wandering again through the wood, a little conservation area that nestled between the golf course and the river. This place, with a Gaelic name he couldn't even begin to pronounce, was filled with trees, swamp and water, all overlooked by low hills. There were wooden benches, a bat sanctuary, leafy trails and scampering teenage would-be lovers, and it was the place his granny had talked of most. Before the days of conservation, wooden benches and a bat sanctuary, this was where she had been a girl full of romantic dreams for a bright future anywhere but in a small, depressed town in south Kerry. This was the place where she would lie on her back, count the stars and pray that some day she would cross them to reach her destiny. Even as a child, his granny had known she would not stay in the beautiful little town yet in some small way she would mourn it all her days.

"Caught between two lovers!" She'd laugh. "Ireland versus America." Her smile would fade just a little. "Heart versus head." There was nothing in Kenmare for his granny in the early 1930s. The war had scarred the whole country and there was little opportunity, especially for a woman who didn't believe in marrying for the sake of it. Her mother had despaired of her but she was the apple of her father's eye. Her five brothers treated her like the princess they felt she was destined to become. Her mother had found a man to take her but she'd stood firm, not willing to compromise in a time when compromise was the way of life.

Maybe her feisty nature had turned her mother against her, but it had ensured her doting father's support and her brothers' admiration. When her mother had tried to force her daughter's hand, the men in her life had contrived her escape. Her father could have put his foot down, but he knew that, married or not, his daughter wanted more from life. She was desperate to taste the New World and he was desperate to give her all she wanted. Instinct told him his beloved girl belonged to another place, so he drove her to the boat and sobbed as he handed over the money he and his sons had worked for to secure her emancipation. He had held her close while the whistle blew insistently, willing them to part, then pushed the money into her hand. "It's up to you now, girleen," he'd said, his voice choked and eyes brimming. "We can't help you when you're gone. America is so far away."

She wiped the tears from his eyes. "I'll always be in here, Daddy." She laid a hand on his chest so that he could hold it there. "You tell the boys that I won't let you down." She was crying because she knew she might not see him again.

They used to call the party that was held before a family member moved to the States the "American Wake". Emigration was tantamount to death. Sam's grandmother didn't have an American wake and her mother never got to say goodbye to her. In hindsight her father might have admitted this was a mistake, as his wife was not the same after her only daughter had deserted her. The boys hadn't made a fuss either: each one had packed a small token in her bag and kissed her goodbye on a day she thought she was accompanying her dad on a job. She'd only realized she was leaving when they were on the docks and he'd handed her a bag filled with her clothes and her brothers' farewell gifts.

"I love you, Daddy."

"I love you, *mo chuisle*." And with that he turned and walked away, not looking back at the daughter he would never see again.

Sam's granny had often talked to him about the boat journey to America with enough money to last her a week or two. She would speak of her fright that first night at sea, feeling desperately sick in the bowels of the ship, without a soul to comfort her. But then she'd tell him she need not have feared facing the New World alone because on the third day of the voyage she met the man she would marry. Together they would get off the boat and together they would forge a new life better than the one they had left behind.

When Sam was dragged to the première of *Titanic*, he had smiled at the story, which seemed somewhat familiar – aside from the treacherous lover, the large jewel and the sinking ship. His granny had loved to talk about how she had fallen for his grandfather over a game of cards and one too many whiskeys. She'd spoken of home too, lamenting its beauty and the love of those she'd left behind. Even as an old woman, the small town had been part of her identity, although it had become as foreign to her on the day she died as America had been on the day she stepped off the boat as a teenager in love.

Sam looked around at the old trees, all witness to his grandmother's youth. The grass, the sky, the water that lapped against the rocks renewed themselves but the trees held time and one a message from the grave. Now her grandson, a New Yorker through and through, was tramping through her old sanctuary, looking for the one tree in a million that bore her carving. She had only mentioned it once. "I left my mark," she had said, smiling. At the time Sam hadn't understood what she meant but now, an adult in Kenmare and with time on his hands, he was determined to find the tree. Unfortunately this entailed a lot more work than he had anticipated – for a small wood, there were a hell of a lot of trees – but he was as determined to find her there as she had been to leave.

While he was surveying trees he had time to contemplate his short time in Kenmare. Since the incident with the swollen gate, he had tried to keep out of his rude neighbour's way but Fate had acted against him. It seemed that every time he'd opened his front door she was in her garden, coming in or going out, on the pier with her dog or sitting into her car. When he ventured into his back garden to hang clothes, she'd come outside with the same intention, just a wall away. They'd attempt to ignore one another, which was uncomfortable due to their proximity. He didn't enjoy awkwardness and with each encounter he'd curse coincidence, yet he would have been lying if he'd said he didn't miss her on the rare day he didn't catch a glimpse. Mary wasn't over-toned or plastic. Her skin glowed, her body was soft and it occurred to him that she could have been the embodiment of an earth-mother if she hadn't been such a bitch.

When he thought of her past he felt sorry for her, but

whenever he saw her she didn't seem like a victim and it was difficult to empathize with someone who so obviously didn't like him. Sam wasn't used to this. Of course, a hell of a lot of people in the business disliked, even hated, him but they had good reason. This woman had disliked him on sight but that was OK: he didn't need some stranger's approval. He had his recovery to focus on, so if she ignored him, he'd ignore her. If she sighed at the sight of him, he sighed louder. If she made a face, he made a worse one. Their annoyance had become a game and it was getting old.

Besides, now he had his project to keep his mind active. He tied a small red band around a branch of the last tree he had surveyed. This would signal where his search would next begin. It was getting late and he had promised Ivan he'd help him move furniture.

Adam's wife and children had driven away from Kenmare, leaving him to finish off packing their belongings before he followed them on the long road away from his home. Ivan had attempted to keep things light and Adam endeavoured to maintain a brave face. Sam had kept his head down, conscious that he was assisting a new friend in saying goodbye to an old one. It was on their last trip, while they were carrying a heavy ornate mahogany desk, that he and Ivan had emerged into the evening light to be confronted with Adam and Penny wrapped round one another, kissing deeply and tears flowing. Sam was acutely embarrassed – and a little confused, having waved off the man's wife less than an hour before. He and Ivan put the desk on the ground and went back inside, unseen by the parting lovers. Ivan made tea and Sam sat looking around Adam's empty home. Although he felt sorry for him and his predicament, he was also a little jealous that he had never felt as strongly about anyone as the man outside clearly did.

Mary had turned up just in time to say goodbye to her old friend and to put an arm around a distraught Penny. Adam put his car into gear and, with one last look back at the love of his life, flanked by his two best friends, he drove away. Sam stood back, watching them all from the doorway, but it was Mary who captivated him – her tenderness and strength, and the way she held her grieving friend. He found himself thinking she would have been a beautiful mother. *Damn shame she's such a bitch.* Ivan had suggested they all go and get something to eat and, despite himself, Sam hoped that Mary would agree. But Penny was too distressed so Mary took her home. He watched her drive away, one hand on the steering-wheel and the other stroking her friend's hair. She hadn't once looked him in the eye.

Penny stood under the shower while Mary surveyed the contents of her fridge. The ingredients were sparse but when Penny emerged in a towelling robe a Spanish omelette awaited her.

"I can always rely on you to cook in a crisis."

"Just eat," Mary scolded. "When's the last time you ate a decent meal anyway?"

"Now," Penny said, before shoving some into her mouth.

Mary worried about the amount of vodka in the fridge but said nothing. Penny always liked to have a stash in case of a party and she often gave one, mostly after the pub. Mary guessed she wouldn't for a while, so with that in mind she made a mental note to pour some of the vodka down the sink as soon as Penny's back was turned. *Just in case. She probably won't even notice.*

Penny was silent.

"What can I do?" Mary asked.

"Nothing."

"What are you thinking?"

Penny sighed.

"Honestly?" Mary urged.

"I thought he'd pick me," she admitted. "I know he has kids, but when it came down to it, I really thought he'd pick me." Tears rolled down her face and her nose ran. She sniffed.

"I'm so sorry, Penn."

"I know I'm selfish," Penny said, wiping her nose with her hand.

"You're human."

"I wanted Adam to abandon his children."

"Penn, I don't give a frig about any of that. I think you're it."

Penny looked at Mary. "You think I'm it?" she said, with an emerging smile.

Mary nodded. "I do."

"What? Are you sixteen?"

"No. I just look it." Mary grinned.

After that Penny said she felt better. Mary insisted on washing up and mopping the floor, having decided that Penny was too traumatized to engage in such menial tasks. Penny argued but Mary had taken on her in-charge mode so she sat with her coffee while Mary cleaned.

"So, what's the story on the American?" Penny asked, stirring her coffee.

"He's everywhere," Mary said. "Every time I turn around there he is with a stupid face on him. The other week he actually pulled me up on my manners."

"He did not!" said Penny, amused.

"He did. And I wouldn't mind, but I'd helped him with his stupid gate. I never thought I'd say this but I miss the Brinkerhoffs. At least they knew how to keep to themselves."

"The Brinkerhoffs were wanted by Interpol," Penny said, with a slight smile and, annoyingly now, still stirring her coffee.

"And he's Ivan's new best friend. Three lunches last week, two nights in the pub, and clay-pigeon shooting last Sunday." She shook her head. "It's unbelievable."

"Ivan's lonely," Penny commented.

"So he should get himself a girlfriend," Mary said.

Penny scoffed. "Yeah, right, because that's so easy. And what's your big problem with the American anyway? He seems nice enough. He helped out today."

"That's exactly what I'm talking about, Penn. Four life-time friends saying an emotional goodbye to one another and there he is, Mr In-Town-On-A-Wet-Day-Tourist, stuck in the middle of it."

"This isn't you. What's going on?"

"I don't know," Mary answered honestly. "There's just something about him. I can't put my finger on it but I don't like it."

"Oh, are you being the all-seeing psychic again?" Penny had never really bought into her friend's abilities. "He's not featuring in any angry eggs, is he?"

"No." Mary smiled. "I don't know what it is but some-times when I look into his eyes I want to cry."

"Weird," Penny said.

"What do we know about him anyway? He could be a psycho killer."

"Psycho killers don't usually look like movie stars," Penny said, and returned to stirring her coffee.

"I don't know – Ted Bundy wasn't bad."

"He was the one with the gold VW Beetle?"

Mary nodded.

"Yeah, OK, he was all right. Not worth dying for, though."

"My point exactly," Mary said. She took Penny's spoon away from her and threw it into the sink. "It's stirred."

Penny was glad her friend had stayed, and their idle chat had lightened her mood, but eventually she was happy to see her go. She waved her off and closed the door. Then she went to the fridge and pulled out a bottle of vodka. She thought about it for a moment and put it back. She had promised herself she would take it easy, so instead she reached for a bottle of white wine. She spent a minute or two looking for the corkscrew, which stubbornly refused to be found. *Fuck it,* she thought. She opened the fridge and grabbed the vodka. *Fate has spoken.*

Once seated, she poured a tall glass, took her first sip and switched on the TV. *I could have sworn this bottle was more than half full.*

Mary parked outside her house, content that she had left Penny in lighter spirits than she had found her. The blue sky was fading to light purple and the water was still, reflecting the two upturned half-moons of the imposing bridge under which the river Roughty joined with the Sheen. Inside, she made her way to the back yard to alert Mr Monkels to her homecoming. Usually he would sense her from halfway down the road or he'd hear the car engine – either way he'd be sitting at the glass patio door panting hello. He wasn't at the door. Instead he was lying flat out on the ground in front of the shed, half concealed by an untamed bush.

"Mr Monkels!" she called. "Mr Monkels?"

She picked up her pace and her heart started to beat in time with her feet. She bent down to him and it was clear that he was breathing but he wouldn't budge. She stroked him and he whined a little. "OK, buddy," she said calmly, "everything's going to be OK." She tried to lift him but he groaned and she knew he was too heavy for her to carry without fear of dropping him. She could hear that the American was in because the sound of gospel queen Mavis Staples was leaking from his kitchen. *What is it with that man and gospel?* She wasn't going to ask him for help so instead she ran to number three, hoping against hope that Mossy would be there. He opened the door with his hands caked in clay and a joint hanging from his lips.

"Mary of the Sorrows, always a sight for sore eyes," he said, wiping his hands with a tea-towel. He seemed unaware that he had referred to her by her nickname.

"I need your help," she said, although from the size of his pupils she was in no doubt that he was pretty stoned.

He stood over a table on which lay a piece he was working on. "What do you think?" he asked.

*It looks like a brown banana – that or a piece of* . . . "Lovely," she said. "There's something wrong with Mr Monkels. Can you help me get him into the car?"

"Oh, sorry, Mare, I can't," he said.

"What?" she replied, not sure she'd heard him correctly.

"I'm out of my gicker." He giggled. "Seriously, I've got this new stuff and it's off the wall but really getting the inspiration juices flowing."

She took a second look at the piece of crap on the table. "Yeah," she nodded, "thanks anyway."

"Ask the American," Mossy advised her. "He seems like a very accommodating fella."

She was stuck. Mrs Foley in number five had difficulty carrying a cup of tea, never mind a large dog, and she couldn't waste any more time. She knocked on her new neighbour's door.

Moments later he opened it. "Can I help you?" he asked, appearing nonchalant.

"I'd really appreciate it if you could," she responded, careful to mind her manners. *I don't have time for a hissy fit.*

"What is it?" he asked, delighting in this unexpected power.

"My dog. He's not well. I need help lifting him to the car."

"Oh," he said, without a hint of his previous smugness, "sure."

He followed her to her back garden and where her dog lay panting. He seemed bigger when lying out flat – in fact he seemed a lot bigger and heavier. Sam's back already ached from carrying heavy furniture but he could see the anxiety on his neighbour's face. "OK, how do you want to do this?" he asked.

"Mr Monkels, we're going to lift you now," she said to the dog. "You take the back end," she instructed Sam.

Sam squatted. Mary placed her hands under the dog's

upper body and Sam did likewise under the dog's hind-quarters.

"OK, on three," she said. "One – two – *three*!" They proceeded to lift.

It was then that something in Sam's back clicked out of place. He froze. "Holy shit!" he exclaimed.

"What?"

"My back!"

"What's wrong with it?" she cried. They were holding the dog between them. "Oh, my God!" she said. "Put Mr Monkels down," she ordered, as calmly as she could.

"I can't."

"What?"

"I can't move. I think it's locked!"

"Knickers!" she said. "OK, I know what to do. Don't move. Just stay calm. I'm going to lower the dog to the ground head first. Do not move."

"You don't have to keep saying 'don't move'. I *can't* move."

"Don't get snippy."

"Snippy?" he inquired, as she lowered Mr Monkels's head to the ground while his hindquarters remained raised in Sam's custody. "Holy shit – the pain."

Mary stood beside Sam and placed her hands beside his under the dog. "Let go!" she ordered.

He did, and she lowered the dog until he was once again lying on the ground. She stood up while Sam remained bent forward.

"I'm going to die," he mumbled, at which, like Lazarus, Mr Monkels rose to his feet and shook himself, then pottered into the sitting room, jumped onto the window-seat and made himself comfortable as though he had not a care in the world. All the while Mavis Staples was singing "Oh Happy Day".

"Am I fucking dreaming?" Sam asked earnestly, facing the ground.

# 10. Back to back

Mary managed to negotiate her injured neighbour into her house, then called her doctor. Sam was unable to do anything other than lean over her kitchen table. "I'll make you some tea," she said, wondering how long it would take the doctor to get there.

"No, I'm good," he said, with a hint of sarcasm.

She couldn't hold that against him – he'd just sustained his second injury at her hands. "OK. Can I get you anything at all?" She knew she sounded stupid.

"No. I'll just wait for the doctor," he said, through gritted teeth.

"OK," she nodded, "good idea." She wasn't sure what to do next. "Would you like to be alone?"

"That would be great," he suggested, again with that hint of sarcasm.

*I thought Americans didn't do sarcasm.* "OK." She left the kitchen, closing the door behind her.

Half an hour later Dr Macken arrived. "Hello, my dear," he said, happy-go-lucky as ever. "You look well," he added, fixing his comb-over.

"He's in here," she said, in no mood for pleasantries.

He followed her into the kitchen, where Sam remained in the position in which she'd left him.

"Oh dear," Dr Macken said, and chuckled. "That does not look good."

Sam did not respond but Mary could see he wasn't happy.

Dr Macken put his bag on the table beside Sam. "A cup of tea would be lovely, Mary," he said, rubbing his hands.

Sam's face fell and Mary heard him mumble, "You're kidding me."

Suddenly she wanted to laugh but suppressed the urge. She turned her back on the disgruntled patient and her GP.

"Now this may hurt but bear with me," Dr Macken said.

Mary gulped and filled the kettle.

Sam braced himself. "Holy shit!" he cried out.

"Hmm," Dr Macken observed.

*"Ho-ho-ho-lee shit!"*

Mary switched on the kettle and bit her knuckle.

"Ever slipped a disc before?" Dr Macken asked.

"No," Sam said, clearly perturbed.

"Well, son, it looks like you could have slipped one now." He went to his bag. "Now, if you're lucky it might just be a serious muscle spasm."

The kettle whistled.

"Milk, no sugar, Mary," said Dr Macken. "Now, I'm going to give you something to relax the muscles and then I'm going to prescribe painkillers."

He walked into the sitting room and Mary followed him with his tea.

"We're going to need a fairly hard mattress. You'll have to move the sofa but he'll be fine here for a few days," he said, taking the mug from her.

"Excuse me?" she asked, alarmed.

"What?" Sam shouted, from the kitchen.

"Well, you'll hardly send him in next door."

"Why not? That's where he lives," she whispered.

"I'm not staying here!" Sam shouted.

"He can't be left on his own, Mary girl, and, besides, you have a downstairs bathroom."

Silently Mary cursed her extension.

"I am not staying here!" Sam shouted, despite the pain it caused in his lower back.

"Do you have a suitable mattress?" Dr Macken asked, ignoring all objections.

Mary rolled her eyes, much as she did each time he tapped her head and made some annoying comment about her metal plate.

Dr Macken was assisting Sam into the sitting room while Mary wrestled the mattress from the spare room down the stairs.

"Oh, that'll do nicely!" the doctor remarked.

Sam was a whiter shade of pale. Dr Macken resumed a conversation with his patient to which Mary had not been a party. "You either take the muscle relaxant or you end up in this particularly amusing stance for the rest of your days."

"Not until you tell me what's in it."

"Is there something in your medical history you'd like to share with me?" Dr Macken asked.

"No," Sam replied.

"And you're not allergic to anything?"

"No," Sam confirmed.

"Then take the pill."

The doctor held the glass of water in front of him and he swallowed the tablet and drank until the glass was empty.

"Good," Dr Macken said.

He helped Mary to move the sofa, and when the mattress

was dressed, he reintroduced Sam to the art of lying down, ably assisted by his unwilling aide, Mary, who was charged with providing cushions to prop up the patient's knees. "As he loosens up, take away the cushions," he ordered.

She responded with a heavy sigh. Sam covered his face with his hands and inhaled deeply.

"Well, I can see this little sleepover is going to go beautifully." Dr Macken laughed. "Hah, Robocop, I'd say it's a match made in heaven!" Dr Macken turned to Sam. "It's a wonder she can't pick up a few more channels on that thing," he said, pointing to her head while she pursed her lips to stop herself telling him to make himself scarce. Sam snickered a little. Dr Macken softened. "Still, it's a wonder she's with us at all!" He smiled at his toughest patient, then became serious. "Any headaches since I last saw you?"

"No," Mary said, embarrassed by the question in front of a stranger.

"You're due a scan," he said.

"I know."

"I'll make the appointment," he said, picking up his bag.

"OK." She walked towards the door. Thankfully, he followed her.

"I'm giving you a prescription for painkillers."

Sam called from the floor. "What's in them?"

Dr Macken laughed. "Don't worry, just a little opioid – they won't kill you."

*He probably thinks I'm one of those health freaks he reads about,* thought Sam, *the kind of guy who dates in oxygen bars and whose idea for a great weekend involves colonic irrigation.* Sam knew he couldn't touch an opioid unless he wanted to end up an addict again and right back where he'd started. This meant that he'd be in pain without relief. *I'm on the fucking precipice.*

On the morning following Adam's departure from Kenmare something clicked in Penny and she emerged from her booze-laced cocoon. She had been drinking for three weeks straight and, like a reluctant genie, it took courage to emerge from the bottle. She had hidden away and licked her wounds, and her friends had given her the space to do so, knowing that Penny liked to do things her way. But they were unaware as to what exactly her way entailed.

She had spent the greater part of her day cleaning herself and then her house until she felt there was no visible trace of her transgression. Her clean start was tiring work but it kept her mind off the fact that Adam was gone. She'd avoided Mary's five calls. Later she packed her car boot with empty bottles and drove to the recycling centre. It was late evening so she hadn't anticipated meeting anyone. Unfortunately she was halfway through unloading when she spotted one of Adam's wife's more vocal friends, Bridget Browne.

"That must have been some party," Bridget said, with a sneer.

"You've no idea," Penny said, her cheeks threatening to shatter under the strain of her fake smile.

"You have a thick neck!" Bridget said, passing so close they almost touched.

Penny faced her but Bridget walked on. "Excuse me?" She didn't need to take this crap from a woman who had once been one of the town's biggest sluts.

Bridget turned back to look her up and down with contempt. "You heard, you callous bitch!"

"Hey, Bridget, guess what?"

"What?"

"Your husband recently fathered a child in Sneem." She watched Bridget's face fall. "Is that callous enough for you?" she asked.

Bridget was momentarily stunned, and immediately Penny realized the depths to which she had sunk. She might have apologized but the moment passed, and so did Bridget's shock.

"*What did you say?*" she screamed.

A little panicked, Penny shut her boot, still half full of bottles, and walked around to the driver's seat.

"*What did you say, you bitch?*" Bridget said, thundering towards her.

Penny opened the car door quickly, knowing that the other was on her way to launch a well-deserved punch at her face.

She locked the doors just in time and backed out of the recycling centre with a screaming and red-faced Bridget pounding on the roof of her car.

Once she'd made her getaway, she broke into laughter born of mild hysteria and tears quickly followed. *Oh, God, what did I just do?* Revealing a husband's secret love-child was brutal, petty and maybe even despicable. An internal debate followed in which she reasoned that, although she had done something terrible, Bridget was a horrible human being who had often revelled in the misery of others. She silently accused Bridget of being the kind of person who liked to lord it over others and was only too happy to judge all and sundry. She still felt a little sick until she remembered that Bridget and her husband had been known as the town bikes for years. It had been bound to come out sooner or later. By the time she'd driven halfway home, she'd decided that Bridget deserved it.

The truth was she didn't deserve it, and if Penny hadn't been bitter, broken-hearted and hung-over she would never have torn apart anyone, even someone of Bridget Browne's bad temperament. She dried her eyes and decided to forget her verbal assault by buying a bottle of her favourite red wine – she was off the hard stuff but wine never hurt anybody.

Penny had decided to throw herself back into work and, by coincidence, the next morning the Cork correspondent was forced to take a sudden leave of absence. Penny had a fluff piece about an obese cow in north Kerry and was covering the opening of a restaurant in Dingle but, despite time constraints and impending deadlines, she readily agreed to cover his story. She worried briefly that her decision to help out a colleague was based on Cork being Adam's new home, but concluded that it most certainly was not. She reminded herself that Adam had made his choice. Furthermore he hadn't even told her where he would be working or whispered his address – not that she wanted to know either. That ship had sailed and she was moving on, except of course that she wasn't. Instead she was drowning. The emptiness made her insides ache but she wasn't about to ask Mary or Ivan for information on Adam's exact co-ordinates because then they would know that she was desperate to see him, even though she had almost convinced herself that she wasn't. In any case, if he'd wanted to see her he would have called and he hadn't, not that she was waiting for him to call. In fact, she probably wouldn't have taken his call, so determined was she to start afresh.

However, upon arriving into Cork City she found she wanted to explore it more than she had in previous years. She might even have walked around the city centre for a few hours paying particular attention to the restaurants, peering at the menus stuck to the windows and accidentally catching glimpses of front-of-house staff, none of whom was Adam. Then again, she'd always been a fan of restaurants and Cork was full of them.

Late afternoon, and after a long walk, she arrived at her destination. The piece she had been asked to cover was a story about a young Corkwoman, Lacey Doyle, who'd travelled to an exotic location only to become a bomb victim, returning home minus her legs. Despite this she'd been deemed lucky: her best friend, who had been standing less than ten feet away from her, could only be identified by DNA. The crux of Penny's story lay in the revolutionary new limbs Lacey's supporters had paid for. It was all very complicated and Penny wasn't sure how they were different from any others. They were state-of-the-art in a weird futuristic way. The manufacturers had made no attempt to create the illusion of real legs. The girl's skin met metal and at the end there was a shoe but she didn't seem to care. She spoke a lot about their flexibility and was happy to demonstrate. Every time she exposed her stumps, though, Penny felt a little sick.

"It's horrible, isn't it?" Lacey asked chirpily.

"No," Penny lied, "it's fine."

"My legs were ripped off – it's OK to feel a little repulsed."

Lacey laughed at Penny, who had gone very pale.

"OK," Penny conceded, "I do feel a little sick."

"I couldn't look down for six months," Lacey admitted.

"What changed?"

"I got bored looking up." Lacey giggled and Penny joined in.

"I don't know how you get over something like that," said Penny. She was a lot more interested in the woman who'd lost her legs than the revolutionary replacements.

"You don't," Lacey said. "You just get on with things. You either do that or you rot." She grinned. "And there was George."

"George?" Penny asked, intrigued.

"My boyfriend – well, actually he's my fiancé now. We got engaged last month."

Penny's mouth almost fell open.

"You're surprised anyone would marry me," Lacey said.

"No." Penny was horrified that she was so transparent.

"I was surprised too," Lacey confirmed. "It was a year before I could let him touch me, never mind anything else."

Penny wasn't sure she wanted to hear any more.

"Sex was a nightmare at first," Lacey said, "but it got better," she nodded, "and now it's good."

Penny was glad she was sitting down as her own legs were feeling a little shaky.

"You're sickened again, aren't you?" Lacey asked.

Penny smiled. "Yes, but it's not what you think."

"What, then?" Lacey asked.

"I'm jealous."

"*Jealous?*"

"Pathetic, isn't it?"

"A little bit. Can I ask why?"

"At least you're not alone," she said, and a tear escaped.

She had burst into tears in front of an interviewee – was she having a breakdown? Penny couldn't face driving home so she booked into a hotel and headed for the bar where she ordered vodka on the rocks.

"Tough day?" the barman asked.

"I met a bomb victim without legs who's happier than I am," she said quietly, raised her glass and drank.

"Jaysus, your life must really suck," he said, and grinned.

"What part of Dublin are you from?" she asked automatically.

"What part do you want me to be from?" He winked.

"A part where they answer direct questions with direct answers," she said, draining her glass.

He laughed. "Crumlin. You want another?"

She nodded.

"What about you? Where are you from?" He handed her the refilled glass.

"Nowhere," she said.

"You're homeless, then?"

"Home is where the heart is," she said, with a bitter laugh.

"And where's your heart?"

"Lost." She raised her hands in the air, then drank the vodka in one.

"Women! Does the drama ever end?" he said.

"You tell me," she said, with a hint of a grin.

The bar was quiet and he had little to do but flirt with her so she stayed there, drinking vodka after vodka, talking with the barman from Dublin. When he got off his shift she led him up to her room.

"I'm married," he said.

"So was my boyfriend." She closed the door behind them.

The next morning she awoke alone with bruises on her arms and thighs. The room was in a state, too, as a result of Penny and the stranger taking out their frustration on one another. She had a bruise on her hip from where he'd slammed her against the dresser and her leg was scraped, she couldn't remember why. He would have been marked, too, and she wondered how he'd explain it to his poor wife or even if he'd bother. Her neck was sore from when he'd held her against the wardrobe until she couldn't breathe, but she'd kicked him onto the ground and, when she had been on top, she'd bitten him hard. Her nipples were raw, and when she went to the loo she bled a little.

After a cleansing shower she decided not to drink alone any more, only with friends. Then she wouldn't over-indulge until she was sick or prostituting herself. *Jesus, what was last night about?* She had made a mistake but she was OK and wouldn't put herself in that position again. *Easy. No problem.*

# 11. Knowing me, knowing you

Ivan was late but only by half an hour. Sam hadn't noticed – he had disappeared into his thoughts, accompanied by Roberta Flack's melodic melancholy. Ivan's knock broke the spell, returning him to earth and Mary's floor.

Ivan looked down at his new friend. "Well?" he asked.

"Agony."

Ivan shook his head. "Four days later. I'm telling you, the Bone Man will sort it in five minutes."

Sam sighed. "So you keep saying."

"Well, if a thing's worth repeating it's worth repeating," Ivan said, chuckling to himself while he got comfortable on the sofa.

"What do you think, Mary?" Sam asked, having established a kind of rapport with her over the previous ninety-six hours.

"I don't know," she said. Ivan gave her a dirty look. "I don't know," she repeated to her cousin, flinging her hands into the air.

"What about Tommy the Coat?" he asked.

"What about him?" she replied.

"He was on his back for four months. One trip to the Bone Man and he was dancing a jig three days later."

She shrugged her shoulders. "I don't know. The doctor said it could be a disc and a disc isn't bone."

Ivan was exasperated. "Bone Man is just his name. He deals in back problems – all back problems."

133

"I'll think about it," said Sam.

Mary went back into the kitchen to finish making dinner while Ivan nipped to the loo, leaving Sam alone.

The front door must have been on the latch because it opened at Penny's push. She closed the door behind her and she walked past Sam apparently without noticing him. "Mare, there's an American on your floor!"

"Where have you been?" Mary asked, ignoring the matter of her lodger.

"Cork," Penny said.

"Cork?" Mary's tone suggested she was alarmed.

"Not with Adam. I was working."

Ivan emerged from the toilet. "Hey, Penn, where've you been?"

"Cork."

"Cork." His tone was similar to Mary's.

"I was working!"

"OK. Good."

"Are you hungry?" Mary asked.

"Starving," Penny said. It had been a while since she'd eaten an actual meal.

Once more Mary returned to the kitchen, and Ivan and Penny sat on the sofa with Sam at their feet. Ivan apprised Penny of the details of Sam's accident. Penny suggested he see the Bone Man.

"Hah! I told you!" Ivan was vindicated.

"Who's singing?" Penny asked.

"Roberta Flack."

"Nice." Ivan nodded.

"You had your music brought in from next door?" said Penny.

"Sure. I'm going through a phase."

"Wow!" Penny laughed. "Mary won't like that."

"What do you mean?" he asked.

"Well, she's funny about music," Penny said, and Ivan concurred.

"I don't understand," said Sam.

"She has a band or a sound or a song for every mood, emotion or event in her life. You could say she lives her life to a soundtrack and now you're here and messing it up." She was laughing.

"You're kidding me?"

Penny and Ivan shook their heads.

"Unusual," he murmured.

They had dinner in the sitting room so as not to leave the patient alone. Mary cut up his food, helped him onto his side and positioned cushions to support him as he ate. She put a straw into his drink and pushed it towards him. Then she sat down in the armchair opposite her friends. Both Ivan and Penny had noted the significant shift in Sam and Mary's relationship with some interest. Of necessity he relied on her, but more importantly he appeared comfortable with her and she attended to him deftly, knowing exactly what to do.

"What?" she asked her friends, whose mouths were slightly agape.

"Nothing," they said together.

"Do you want to change the music?" Sam asked, out of nowhere.

"No, it's fine," Mary said, unsure why he was asking – he'd taken over her CD player and been listening to nothing but American black women since he'd arrived.

"Are you sure?" he asked.

135

"I like it," she replied.

"OK."

Penny and Ivan laughed.

"We mentioned your analality regarding music," Penny confessed.

"Analality isn't a word," said Mary.

"Well, it should be," said Ivan.

"I'm not anal."

"Hah!" Ivan said, snorting.

"When Mary listens to Radiohead . . ." Penny began.

". . . she's sad," Ivan finished.

"When Mary listens to Dolly . . ."

"Happy."

"And when Mary listens to Nirvana?"

"Frustrated," Ivan said firmly, and Penny stuck out her tongue at her mortified friend.

"Wow!" Sam said. "The wall between us is pretty thin and she listens to Nirvana a lot."

Mary bit her lip.

Penny and Ivan left together. As Ivan put on his coat, Mary asked after his ex-wife. He told her she seemed fine. Mary seemed unsatisfied by his answer. "Is there something wrong?" he asked.

"No."

He crossed his arms and waited for the truth.

"I mean I don't know," she admitted, screwing up her face.

"What did you see?" he asked, a little alarmed.

"Oh, for God's sake!" Penny exclaimed.

"It's nothing," Mary said, embarrassed by Penny's indifference to and Sam's ignorance on the subject of her dubious psychic abilities.

"Mary!" Ivan had always believed in them and now he was worried that something wasn't right with his ex-wife.

"OK." She sighed. "I saw her calling for you."

"Calling for me?"

"That's it. She was calling out for you."

"How?"

"What?" Mary wished the conversation would end.

"For God's sake!" Penny said again. "Was she calling out in a Heathcliff-it's-me-Cathy kind of way or in a kids-come-in-for-your-dinner way?"

"Oh. Neither. I don't know."

"Was it real?" Ivan asked.

"I don't know."

Penny harrumphed. "I wish you'd stop wrecking your head with all of this stuff," she said to Mary.

Sam was wondering what the hell was going on.

Penny pushed Ivan out of the door. "I'll give her a call tomorrow," he said, then added, with a grin, "Tonight I'm on a date."

Penny and Mary stopped in their tracks.

"A *date*?" Mary quizzed.

"Ah, yeah," Sam remembered aloud, "good luck with that, man."

Mary looked from Ivan to her uninvited guest.

Ivan laughed. "Sam'll fill you in." He winked and closed the door behind himself and Penny.

Mary was wondering what in the name of knickers was going on.

Sam, a practical stranger, filled Mary in on her cousin's exploits in McCarthy's bar the previous week. They had been having a few pints and a girl whose name he couldn't remember had sidled up to them. She had sat beside Sam and asked him to a party. He explained to Mary that he had declined the invitation.

At this point Mary interrupted to clarify that the woman Ivan was dating had originally asked Sam out. He considered this for a moment, then conceded this was so. Mary screwed up her face at her cousin's having opted for sloppy seconds. Sam laughed at her distaste, and explained that when it was his turn to go to the bar, Ivan and the girl had struck up a conversation and had got along so well that by the time he'd returned with the drinks they'd forgotten he was in the room. Mary gazed at him sceptically and he assured her it was true. She wondered how it was possible that a week had passed without her cousin confiding in her, and acknowledged inwardly that his omission was made all the more grievous by her uninvited guest's delight in knowing something about him that she didn't.

But of course Sam was delighted – the horror on her face was comical.

After that Mary cleaned the kitchen while he flicked channels, bored with TV but too tired to read.

During Sam's short sojourn with Mary he had noticed she followed a series of routines. For instance, in the evening she cooked, she ate, she washed, she dried, she brushed the floor, she emptied the bin, and while the kettle boiled for tea she covered the leftover food with clingfilm and put it into the fridge. It was always in that order, and it was a pretty innocuous thing to notice, but noticing the innocuous was one of the things that had made Sam great at his job. She wasn't a clean freak but she liked everything in its place, possibly to a pathological degree. If he put his book down for more than five minutes, it mysteriously appeared in the magazine rack, which, considerately, she'd left close enough for him to reach. The second he dropped the remote, it found its way to the left-hand side of the coffee-table on the TV guide, which was placed so that its edge met the rim of the table. *Weird.* Her CD collection, which was vast and too far away in the corner for him to see, appeared to be in alphabetical order, and a disc was only out of its case when it was playing.

Her friends were right: behind her calm exterior she was anal, but it wasn't overt. She was also painfully honest in both word and deed. When he smelt she told him so. When she promised she'd close her eyes while she helped him to wash, she didn't open them once, even when she somehow swallowed some suds. He had guessed that she'd given up any attempt at lying years before as her expressive face would have given her away. In that respect she was nothing like him.

Every night before she went to bed she adjusted a photo on the wall – the one closest to the door of her son and the damn dog. She never straightened any of the others, and it was always the last thing she did before turning out the light and leaving him with the glow of the television, as per his request.

She had noticed a lot about him too. He didn't like questions but then again neither did she, so that was OK. Still, he could sidestep an uncomfortable or uninvited query as well as or better than a seasoned politician, while she was forced to resort to rudeness. This irked her. He liked American soul, R&B and gospel singers, but she'd known that already. When he laughed she'd noticed that his nose crinkled, his jaw stuck out – he unconsciously covered it with his fist as though he was suppressing a cough – and in that moment the darkness lifted from his eyes, if only briefly.

He could play the guitar too. During his first day on her floor Jerry Letter had arrived with a package that turned out to contain a very valuable instrument, which he'd had shipped from the US. She had helped him to sit up, if only for a few minutes, so that he could examine it for damage. When he told her it had been Scotty Moore's she was impressed, and he was impressed that she knew who Scotty Moore was. This pissed her off until he apologized for presuming her ignorant. He had proved himself stubborn as he only asked for help when he was desperate for the loo and unable to travel the distance unaided. He laid the guitar on his chest and strummed and, although he messed up a lot and cursed under his breath, she enjoyed listening to him; as he was loosening up now, he improved each time he picked it up.

She noticed he was what her father called eagle-eyed. It was annoying when he pointed out her foibles, which she had no idea were so many, but it was also interesting, if not a little disturbing, to have a mirror held up to her face. She liked that he seemed relaxed in her care and that he didn't pander to her past. If he thought badly of her he said so, while most people tiptoed around her, afraid of breaking the shell she'd constructed around herself.

"Why do you work in a bar?" he'd asked, out of the blue, that very morning.

"Because I do," she answered, yawning and clutching her morning mug of coffee.

"You're better than that," he said, as though he was inter-viewing her for a job rather than taking up half her floor.

"Excuse me?" she'd said, annoyed at his arrogance.

"It probably made sense once, but not any more." He looked at the wall where the pictures of her son hung, then met her widened eyes. "Those photos you took are truly beautiful. Trust me – I have an eye."

"You'll have a black one if you don't shut up," she said, getting up and striding to the kitchen.

"I was only saying!" he called.

"Yeah, well, nobody asked you," she said, and slammed the kitchen door behind her.

Of course, seated at the kitchen table, she started to think about what he had said. She'd tried not to, even singing "Ring Of Fire" in her head to escape it, but she couldn't because he was right. Why, after six years, was she tending bar when she had once been so full of ambition? Ben had stopped her becoming the photographer she had always dreamed of being, but what was stopping her now?

Despite Sam's unwelcome observation, Mary had to admit it was nice having someone to take care of.

And it was nice for Sam, the guy who had painted himself as invulnerable to the world for so long while he had been silently destroying himself, to be taken care of. Like Danziger, his nurse in rehab, Mary was stronger than he was, and it felt weird being there but also good – even if he did think about the pain pills he hoarded under his mattress a little too often and even if the stupid dog, the cause of his predicament, attempted to sit on him at least twice a day.

That night Ivan shared his first official date with Sienna. They had agreed to meet for dinner in Packie's because that was Ivan's favourite restaurant and, a creature of habit, when he ate out his order never deviated: a herb potato pancake followed by a medium to rare steak with the softest, sweetest carrots in the world, creamy cabbage colcannon and caramelized onions on the side. He wasn't a dessert man so that was never a factor in his choice of venue. The other places, as good as they were, didn't offer the same menu, or not exactly, so when he'd asked her to Packie's he hoped to God she'd like it.

When Sienna said she was happy to allow him select the wine, he panicked a little as he was not a connoisseur and to order the house wine might seem cheap. So he deferred to his helpful seventeen-year-old waitress.

They sat together in warm, low lighting, surrounded by well-dressed people. They ate slowly, concentrating on the conversation – of which neither was short.

Sienna had been living in Kenmare for six months. She was working on reception in the Sheen Falls Hotel, having worked in a number of five-star establishments. She was used to the trappings of wealth but it was apparent that she had little time for luxury. Sienna had flaming red hair, much like Mary's, soulful brown eyes and a heart-shaped face. When they stood he had to look down. She was five six to his six four, and a hippie at heart. Beads were threaded into her hair and she sat comfortably in a dress that flowed from rather than clung to her body. On her right hand she wore two rings, on the left three, one a tiny Claddagh ring. They were all silver – she preferred it to gold.

She was two years younger than Ivan and had never been married. Her one serious relationship had lasted four years. He had left her on 6 August 1999 – her birthday – and she had not heard from or seen him since. She liked animals but didn't own one. She had come to Kenmare because her flatmate in Adare was annoying. She knew of Ivan's past and, although she sympathized, she didn't fuss or make him feel like the arsehole whose wife had left him. She liked it when he talked with passion about fish. Her father was a fisherman in Galway Bay and she'd spent many a summer gutting fish on his boat. If this didn't seem too good to be true, she loved the Waterboys. When she laughed it came from her belly, and by the end of their evening together he was desperate to shag her. They were the last to leave. Ivan thanked the seventeen-year-old for picking a feckin' nice wine and she thanked him for a large tip.

He walked Sienna home through the busy town. Spring had arrived and with it the bars, restaurants and streets were repopulating. The stars rested over the mountain, and when he put his arm around her she rested her hand in his pocket. When they reached her apartment they kissed at her doorway. She was soft and he could taste the wine. She asked him inside and internally he leaped for joy. *Please, God, let me have sex!*

Penny made her way to Mickey Ned's. The bar was busy and she waved at Tin and his wife before passing them in favour of Josie and Jamie, the beautiful black-haired Casey twins, Kerry roses who had gone on to become bored wives of very wealthy men in Kilkenny and Tipperary respectively. They waved madly, delighted that someone slightly less tedious than their present company had entered. Penny approached while signalling her drink order to Ger, the barman. He knew exactly what she wanted – the same as always: vodka on the rocks. Josie and Jamie both hugged her at once and told her how great she looked. Jamie managed to squeeze the bruise on her arm and Josie rubbed against the really sore one on her hip. She grinned through the discomfort and welcomed the girls home while nodding at their husbands who were deep in conversation about VAT. The three girls found seats near the corner of the bar. The twins were grinning insanely.

"So you've heard I'm an adulterer?" Penny said, matching the grins to disguise her humiliation.

"Technically he's the adulterer," Josie said.

"You're the coveter," said Jamie.

"And, yes –" Josie said excitedly.

"– we can't believe it!" finished Jamie.

"Maire McGowen said it'd been going on in secret for years," said Josie.

"I don't know how you did it," Jamie said in awe. "I mean, nobody can keep a secret in this town."

"Yeah, well, I'm the Inspector Clouseau of sluts," Penny said, chortling at her own joke. The sisters didn't get it. "I wore disguises," she qualified.

They laughed, but she could tell they still didn't understand.

"You're filthy," Josie observed ruefully.

"You've no idea," Penny said, and swigged her drink.

"You and Adam," Jamie said, "even if we didn't know you were actually doing it, there was always something between you."

Suddenly Penny felt like crying. Clearly Jamie spotted this because she ordered her another drink, and Ger was quick to bring it.

"Is he gone for good?" Jamie asked.

Penny sighed and nodded. "I believe he is."

"You're better off without him," Josie said.

"I'm really sorry," said Jamie.

"Thanks," Penny replied. "Me too."

After that the twins spoke of their kids, and how their husbands played golf too much, and when they weren't playing golf they were working, and when they weren't working they were watching sport, and when they weren't watching sport they were flicking channels as though they were brain-dead. The kids didn't get a look in, as far as their fathers were concerned, and yet when the men did the smallest thing the kids considered them bloody heroes. Jamie was remodelling her house and the builders were her new nightmare. Josie was taking yoga lessons and her periods had become heavier since she'd started. Still, she was sticking to it because it was nice to get out on a Tuesday morning and her thighs felt firmer. Penny made jokes and they told her she'd always been a scream. All the while they drank and neither sister noticed that their friend was imbibing three drinks to their one, so delighted were they to offload their crap and so happy that she could make jokes to lift them from their perceived misery.

"Josie?" Penny leaned in, drink in hand.

"Yes?"

"I know your husband's a dick but look at it from my point of view," she drawled.

"And what's that?" Josie played along.

"Men are like car spaces – the best ones are always taken and the rest are handicapped."

The twins laughed, and Penny silently gave thanks for joke email.

Eventually they asked for her news but, aside from the

scandal, she didn't have any, which, for a journalist, was pretty sad. She could have talked about work but why bother? They could read that and, anyway, it wasn't hers, it was someone else's. Instead she stuck to making them laugh and drinking.

"So, is there anyone here you're interested in?" Josie asked, as she surveyed the bar.

"Are you looking for me or for you?" Penny queried.

"Ah, stop it!" Josie said. "For you, of course . . . Still, the one in red with the black and grey speckled hair, the sharp jaw and the dick the size of a large foot towards your left looks interesting."

Penny and Jamie's heads spun towards the man in question. "I believe that's his hand rather than his foot in his pants." Penny squinted to negate the double vision.

"Oh, my God!" Jamie spluttered, and Bacardi Breezer dribbled from her delicate nose.

"As I said before, the best ones are taken and the rest are handicapped." Penny smirked.

The two girls were crying with laughter when she called for more drinks.

# 12. A diamond day

The next morning Mary woke up around seven. She was meeting her dad at the bar at eight. She showered quickly and fed Mr Monkels, who seemed sleepier than usual. He ate his breakfast and flopped back into snoring. Sam hadn't woken so she closed the door to the kitchen and quietly ironed a shirt while she had a slice of toast. She drank her coffee in the car.

Her dad was standing outside the bar. He waved and got in. They hugged.

"Morning, Dad."

"Morning, love."

They drove to the graveyard in silence. Mary parked the car and lifted the large bouquet of her mother's favourite flowers from the back seat.

Her dad smiled. "It seems to get bigger every year," he remarked.

Mary inhaled the lilies as they walked together through the little iron gate that brought them to the grassy hill, covered with graves. Like the living inhabitants of Kenmare, the dead also overlooked the water. Mary and her father strolled along the narrow paths, making their way to the family plot. The sky was white and the water glistened, as though fresh from a diamond downpour. Mary held on to her dad so they didn't trip over the rocks that poked inter-mittently through the hardened mud surface.

When they arrived at the grave they began their yearly ritual. Mary would lay the flowers on it and her father would bless himself. They would stand in silence for approximately five minutes, although on a rainy day this was cut to between two and three because Mary's dad was susceptible to bronchitis. Then he would signal that it was time to say goodbye. Mary would lean down and place a black marble pebble on the white marble gravestone to signify the passage of another year, and her father would blow his wife a kiss.

"She turned out all right, love," he'd say. "You'd be proud of her." He'd take his daughter's hand and they'd walk back to the car.

Years before, when Mary was a child, her father had decided that to avoid his daughter enduring the pain of her mother's anniversary on her birthday he had to separate them. Of course, it was impossible to change the date of his child's birthday or the date of his wife's death. The only answer was to change the day on which he remembered her. Every year on his wife's birthday he and his daughter would lay flowers and remember her so that Mary's birthday was for Mary alone. That way the dead could rest and the living could get on with it. And he had decided that because his daughter had been robbed of her mother he would ensure that on his wife's birthday they would spend the day together, and each year he would tell Mary something she didn't know about her mother.

It had been a great idea and had worked very well, especially when she was a teenager. If she was going through an awkward phase he could pick a memory of his wife that would speak to her even if *he* couldn't. Of course, as the years passed it was harder to find a memory he hadn't already shared. Sometimes he might think of one during the year and write it down in preparation but then he'd lose it – he'd never been known for his organizational skills.

They drove to the Silver Strand and took a walk on the beach. A man was throwing a stick for his dog – she was pretending she hadn't noticed, preferring instead to rub her face in the sand. They didn't talk on the beach, just listened to the wind, the waves hitting rock and the birds screeching, taking turns to dive into the water. The dog barked, and the man yelled, "Fetch!" Mary smiled at her dad as they walked arm in arm. He smiled back, but he was far away – not with his daughter but his wife and they were courting.

When he was a boy and she was a girl, they'd walk the strand and she'd talk to him about her latest craze. One week she'd be into knitting and she'd arrive with a woolly jumper full of holes and ten different stories about the making of it. The next week she'd be an avid swimmer, regaling him with the benefits of the breast-stroke. Then she'd find swimming lonely so she'd move on to Irish dancing, which was very social and she was quite good at it.

She made him laugh and he liked her flightiness: she was always moving on – but he noticed that she didn't move on from him. Their walks on the beach were his favourite memory of her. It was when she was outdoors with the wind in her face and hair that she entertained him with her whole self, expressing her every thought about dreams and reality, habits and doubts, plans and obstacles. It was on the beach that she was most alive. And while he walked with his daughter, his wife's voice was calling to him inside his head.

"Jack, put it on!" she said, and he could see her holding the oversized jumper and beaming at him.

"I don't even know if I can," he replied, trying to work out the neck from the sleeve.

She laughed. "Sure the way you're built it won't make a difference."

He put on the jumper, which gaped at the neck and met his knees, with a hole in the side. He stuck his hand into the hole.

She took it and placed his arm at his side, covering it. "There now! You can't see a thing wrong with it."

"You want me to keep my hand by my side for all time?"

"I do."

"And what if I need to use this arm?" he queried.

"Now, Jack, you're a man of industry and I have no doubt that, whatever needs doing, you'll find a way." She laughed and he pledged that, for her love, he would.

Later, behind the dunes, she had stripped him of his new jumper and they had fooled around until they were interrupted by an old man and his wife tutting and warning them of the wrath of the local parish priest.

Now Jack laughed to himself and Mary squeezed his arm, bringing him back to the present. "What are you thinking about?" she asked.

"Your mother," he admitted. "You look so like her."

"I know I do, Dad."

"And you're as bold as she was."

"Maybe once," she said.

They walked on in silence.

Later they had lunch in a small restaurant in the middle of nowhere. Each year they found a new place to eat – they liked to keep the day fresh. The food was good, and as Mary was driving, her dad allowed himself a Guinness, which was rich and creamy. He held it up. "Now that's a good pint." He admired it as an antiques dealer would admire a rare teapot.

After they had consumed their steaming beef stew, he placed a small wrapped box on the table. "That's for you," he said.

"Dad!"

"It's not from me, it's from your mother," he told her, bowing his head.

Mary opened the gift. It was a solitary diamond on a short gold chain. "Dad, this is beautiful!" She was shocked and delighted.

"It was your mother's engagement ring – I had it melted down," he said, sad and happy at the same time.

"Why now?"

"Well, initially I thought that if a young man ever asked for your hand in marriage and he was a little stuck, I could slip him the ring."

"Father!" Her outrage was pretence.

"Anyway, no one ever did because they weren't given a chance to, and time's pushing on so I thought 'twould be nice to see that diamond worn again and sooner rather than later."

"So you've given up on me?" she asked, giggling.

"No. I wouldn't say that – but I wouldn't say I was holding my breath either!"

She looked at her diamond necklace. "Thanks, Dad," she said, hugging him.

Mary and Jack arrived home around six. Pierre and Jessie had been handling the bar alone all day and it was a surprise to find them laughing together in the kitchen. Jack, the greatest victim of their ongoing dispute, had to ensure this was not a momentary ceasefire. "You're friends?" he asked tentatively.

Jessie looked at Pierre and nodded to indicate that he could speak for them both.

"We are." Pierre bowed.

"Oh, well, isn't this just the greatest day?" Jack grinned widely. "And thank the Lord above for it."

Pierre and Jessie shared a smile and Pierre mumbled something about God having nothing to do with it. Mary's eyes narrowed.

"Yes, Mary?" Pierre asked.

"Am I ever to know how this amnesty occurred?" she asked, knowing the answer.

"Of course, dear," Jessie told her, "when your father sells this place to me for fourpence."

Pierre laughed.

Mary's dad entered the kitchen with a bottle of his favourite wine and poured four glasses. "Here's to the team back together again! And may whatever it was that was driving us apart be no more! Here's to a bicker-free future!" He raised his glass as did Pierre, Jessie and Mary. Of course, at that moment Mary's dad was the only person who wasn't aware of how the argument between Pierre and Jessie had started but that didn't matter: some sort of peace had been reached. It would seem that all they had needed was time alone to work it out. Mary did wonder what had been said to bring about peace and how she could find out.

After they had drunk a second toast to Mary's long-departed mother, Pierre and Jessie went home, leaving Mary and her dad to tend the bar.

After a glass of wine and wearing her mother's diamond, Mary was in high spirits when Penny arrived, bearing news of Ivan's second date with Sienna. She had accidentally encountered them lunching in the Horseshoe. She described the woman and Mary knew instantly who she was talking about. "We use the same hair dye," she said.

"What?"

"We had words in the chemist over the last box of dye about three months ago."

"Words," Penny said.

"And a slight tug of war."

"Who won?" Penny wondered.

"She did," Mary said, rolling her eyes. "I called her a pushy cow!"

After that Penny stayed for a drink and promised to check in on Sam. Mary was worried about him – she'd left him alone for the entire day. Ivan was supposed to have looked in but in light of his new romance she was afraid he might have forgotten.

Penny made her way up the street ostensibly on her way to Mary's house, but before she reached the top of the town another bar lured her in. She intended to stay for only one, but then Jerry Letter bought her a drink to demonstrate that, despite his own clean record, he was not one to sit in judgement on others and Pierre, still celebrating the end of his row with Jessie, was only too happy to include the partying Penny in his round. Five drinks later she remembered the American on the floor. *Oh, Christ.* She slipped away unnoticed.

She was halfway down the hill and towards the pier when the oxygen kicked in and she felt kind of dizzy. She sat on a wall for a minute or two and concentrated on sobering up. She got up and pushed herself down the road, zigzagging all the way. By the time she reached the house she'd convinced herself that she'd recovered enough to pull off the appearance of sobriety. She opened the door with the spare key Mary had left under the hedgehog in the pot beside the door. Sam was playing his guitar but stopped when he saw her.

"Still alive, then?" she slurred.

"I'm fine," he replied. "Where's Mary?"

"Working," Penny said, and burped. "She asked me to check on you."

"As I said . . ." He seemed uncomfortable with her there.

"You eaten?" she asked, realizing she herself hadn't had anything since lunch.

"Ivan brought me something."

"Oh, good old Ivan! Even in the afterglow of a long-awaited shag he remembers those less fortunate!" She grinned while feeling for the sofa so that she could plonk herself onto it. "Always thinking of others!" She perched precariously on the edge of the sofa, and laughed. "You look so helpless." Her grin turned into a yawn. "Maybe I should come down there."

"I don't think that's a good idea." He sounded nervous.

"I promise I won't hurt you." She leered at him. "You're so beautiful." She sighed. "I bet you get that all the time," she nodded, "but she won't notice . . . she'll never notice, no matter how pretty you are." She laughed to herself.

Sam remained silent, not wishing to engage with her despite his outrage. *She won't notice me. Who? Mary? Why should I care?*

*I don't want her to notice me. I'm on the fucking floor, for Christ's sake.*

Suddenly Penny was on her knees leaning over him, and her hand was reaching to stroke his face. Painfully aware of his vulnerability, he pushed her away so that she fell back. She giggled and attempted to get back to her feet. "I think you need to stop drinking," he said. "It doesn't suit you."

She appeared to sober up briefly and hurt was evident but suddenly her face changed colour and her hand flew to her mouth.

*Oh, my God,* thought Sam, *I'm going to be vomited on.*

She got up quickly and staggered to the downstairs loo. He heard her evacuate the contents of her stomach, then the flush. Minutes later she was back, wiping her face as though nothing unusual had occurred.

"You seem fine," she said, "so I'll leave you to it." She let herself out of the front door before he could answer.

Mary came in after midnight and was careful to be quiet – she didn't want to wake Sam if he'd managed to fall asleep. She had come to notice that his sleeping patterns were as erratic as her own. He spent much of any night awake, staring blankly at the TV, while upstairs she tossed and turned until she pulled a book from under her bed and lost herself in it for a while.

She had also noticed that he was not taking his prescribed pain medication. It was never going to make the difference between him recuperating or not but she wondered why he chose to hide it under his mattress rather than take it or, indeed, simply refuse it. She had found the stash, having taken the opportunity to change his bedding while he was in the loo, but hadn't asked about it. She didn't need to open any can of worms – life was hard enough.

It had been a long day and tonight she fell asleep instantly.

Mary was standing on an empty street. A red light glowed above her head, reflected in the rainwater pooling by the grating at the side of the road. She was wondering what she was doing there until the teenage boy with the hood concealing his face came around the corner. He was running as before and she sensed his heart beating hard. He turned in time to see the boys following. She called to him but he couldn't hear her.

She ran out into the road with her hands up to stop the boys but they ran through her. She turned as one grabbed the hooded boy and pushed him to the ground. She watched helplessly as the blows rained down. The gang divided. Three kicked and punched him while he attempted to protect his head. A large boy, built like a bear, loomed in the middle distance. He was holding an empty vodka bottle like a tennis racket and screaming that it was his turn. Another boy was leaning against a car watching the beating and it was obvious that he was the rabble's leader. He was surrounded by darkness. He turned to watch the large boy dance with the bottle. His slash-like mouth bled into a grin and he called to the three who were kicking. She heard him laugh as he pointed at the bear with the bottle.

"Look, Topher's excited!" he sneered.

She looked around wildly for help but the street was otherwise empty. *Somebody please come. Somebody save him.* She ran until she saw a man and woman and willed them to turn to where the boy was being attacked but they got into a car and drove away. *Oh, God!* She ran back in time to hear the gang's leader say, "Give Topher a go."

The boy-bear moved in and the others made way for him, leaving the hooded boy on the ground, too injured to run. She felt his broken knuckles clutching at his face and his body curled into the foetal position to protect his balls from the oncoming onslaught – and woke with a start.

She was shaking, and her heart was racing, her pulse too. Her hair was damp and a migraine was coming on. She could hear the TV murmuring faintly through the floor. She needed to take a pill but she kept the bottle in one of the kitchen cupboards. She put on her long cardigan, the one that made her feel like Miss Marple, and made her way downstairs.

Sam looked up from the floor. "Are you OK?" he asked, concerned.

"Just a headache, that's all," she said, passing into the kitchen.

"You look like you've seen a ghost," he remarked.

She returned with a glass of water and a pill that she popped into her mouth and swallowed.

"Stay!" he called.

She stopped.

"After all, we're both awake," he added.

She nodded, knowing that sleep would not come easy. She sat on the sofa and he lowered the TV volume.

"Are you getting a migraine?" he asked, as though he'd seen her medical file.

"I think I've caught it in time."

"You're shaking," he pointed out. "What's wrong?" Clearly it was more than a headache.

"Just a nightmare." Without warning her eyes filled with

fat tears that threatened to tumble. *Oh, my God, I'm mortified. Do not cry!* she warned herself but a rogue tear rolled towards her chin. *Knickers!*

"It must have been a bad one," he commented, evidently surprised by the tear.

"It was."

"You want to share it?"

"No," she said, wiping her eye.

"I have nightmares too," he said, with unexpected honesty, "a lot. I guess that's why I have trouble sleeping. It's hard to sleep when you're scared to."

Mary was as taken aback by his candour as he had been by her tear. "It seemed so real," she said.

"Like one of your visions?" he asked, and she eyed him, suspicious. "Ivan told me."

"No – usually they're pretty surreal."

"Like the cat on the flying mat?" he said, with a smile.

"Yeah." She laughed, then became serious. "This was like a movie and somehow I found myself in the frame." She rubbed her forehead.

"But it's just a nightmare, right?"

"I don't know. I've had it before. It was exactly the same except this time I got to see a little more. It's never happened like that before. Maybe it was a dream but something's not right." He was silent and she watched him from the corner of her eye. "You don't believe it could be anything more than a dream, do you?"

"It's nothing personal but I don't believe in much," he admitted.

"That's OK. Penny thinks I'm a basket case – maybe she's right."

She warmed some milk for them both and they chatted freely. Sam admired her diamond necklace and she told him about her day spent remembering her mother. She shared some of the tales her father had told her and he talked about his grandmother. In the telling, he inadvertently revealed his nerdy origins.

"I can't see it." She laughed.

"Well, trust me. My teenage years were a nightmare."

"You're not alone."

"Oh, shit, sorry."

"Don't be." She smiled. "It was pretty good up to the coma, dead boyfriend and freak pregnancy."

He laughed and she stood up. "I should get back to bed. I'm in the bar first thing and you have a full day on the floor ahead of you."

"Actually, I'm booked in with the Bone Man. Ivan set it up earlier."

"Good for you."

"You think it's the right thing?" he asked, betraying a little panic.

"You've got nothing to lose."

"Well, except for the ability to walk."

"You'll be fine," she soothed.

"Thanks for taking care of me."

"You're welcome," she said, with new warmth. She stopped to straighten the picture of Ben and Mr Monkels, then made her way up the stairs and back to her bed.

# 13. Rear window, hard ground

Although Sam was capable of straightening and, with great difficulty, assuming the seated position, the pain that followed was so excruciating that it brought tears to his eyes. Mary wanted to insist he take his medication but thought better of it.

Ivan tried to take his friend's mind off his discomfort with what his own mother often described as idle chatter. His description of Sienna's performance in bed got them to the other side of Killarney. "Jesus, she's a wonder!"

Sam laughed despite the pain.

"I tell you, my balls could have been on fire and my wife wouldn't have licked them," Ivan continued happily.

Sam wondered what woman in her right mind would lick balls that were alight.

Ivan was rubbing his nose on his sleeve. "Jesus, she's a wonder!" he repeated. "And as for positions!" He slapped the steering-wheel. "Jesus, she must come from circus folk!"

"I'm happy for you," Sam said. "She sounds like she could be the one."

"I tell you, it's a wonder I don't have to visit the Bone Man myself!" Ivan turned onto a long and winding road that seemed too narrow for the car, not to mind the oncoming one, but he was used to it and carried on unconcerned.

Later Sam asked if he had called his wife.

"This morning."

"And?" Sam asked, curious as to whether Mary's vague premonition had any merit.

"And," Ivan said, "she told me I had some ego for an eejit. Apparently I'd be the last person in hell she'd call out for." He sniffed, wrangling with the glove-box in the quest for tissues. "Feckin' hay fever."

"So Mary was wrong?"

"She is not," Ivan said, blowing his nose.

"You still think your wife wants you?"

"Oh, she doesn't want me but she might need me because there's something wrong. I know that much."

"So what are you going to do?"

"Well, I'll wait until the kids come for Easter and I'm going to ask them," he said matter-of-factly, and turned into a farmyard. "We're here."

Sam couldn't conceal his concerns when it emerged the Bone Man was in fact a farmer and his surgery was a table in the back of a barn. But Ivan swore by him and Sam was only hours away from submitting to the painkillers prescribed by the GP – or, at the very least, smoking the cannabis Mossy had so generously offered when he had called in to apologize to Mary for being too off his head to help with the dog. Sam knew he couldn't risk taking any drug, prescribed or not. He couldn't be any worse off, he'd thought – until he met the Bone Man. He had hands the size of shovels, wild curly hair and a big beard. He reminded Sam of one of the crazy homeless guys in New York. He did as he was told, though, because the guy was six eight and almost as wide. In the end it took only a moment. He heard a loud click, felt an excruciating pain that lasted one second and then relief. The effect was much like heroin.

Sam wasn't dancing a jig like Tommy the Coat but he was home and back in his own bed that night. Although he was happy to return to isolation he found himself missing Mary. In the absence of the TV he had grown accustomed to, he turned his full attention to the guitar he had previously only tinkered with. It had been odd that he had been so comfortable playing in front of Mary. His ex-girlfriend had begged him to play many times, but he had refused. Then again Mia was a world-renowned recording star and Mary tended a bar so he guessed it was most likely something to do with that. He didn't have anything to prove to Mary, and even if he'd felt he did, she wouldn't have given a shit. He'd felt good when she'd stopped to listen to his version of Bonnie Raitt's "I Can't Make You Love Me". To him, it had sounded shoddy but she hadn't noticed or maybe she just hadn't cared. It was nice.

When Jerry Letter had knocked on the door with Sam's prize possession carefully boxed – her emancipation reliant upon a signature – it had been a good day, despite his unfortunate circumstances. Once the front door was closed he had set about freeing her with a ferocity that matched a zealous child's on Christmas morning. However, he was forced to leave the unveiling to Mary. And, once she was revealed, he had paused to gaze at her as though he was seeing her with new eyes and new appreciation.

"Hello, Glory!" He'd sighed.

"It has a name?" Mary inquired.

He didn't care if she thought him stupid – a hero of his

had named that guitar and that was good enough for him. And now, alone in his own home and fabulously free from pain, he took Glory out and held her on his lap, his right hand sliding up and down her neck, his left cupping her body. Until his time on Mary's floor he hadn't played guitar in years – in fact, he'd only ever played this instrument once before on the night it was presented to him by Leland when Sam's first signing for Seminy Records had gone platinum. He had taken her home and tinkered with her, but he was drunk and she was the original Scotty Moore Gibson ES-295, so he'd thought better of it. When he was sober, the guitar embarrassed him. As much as he loved her and the idea of her, he had a deep-rooted fear that he wasn't worthy of her. She was used to being played by one of the all-time greats and Sam had long ago proved that he was mediocre at best. So Glory's new owner retired her and Scotty Moore's Gibson was designated to become a museum piece, an expensive element of a businessman's décor.

Alone and lost in a distant memory, he held her for five minutes before he strummed. She needed tuning. He didn't have a tuner so he set about doing it by ear. This took a little while but when he'd finished she was perfect. He placed his fingers on the first chord and then she sang "Hotel California", one of his granny's favourite tracks. He followed up with "Life In The Fast Lane" forgetting the mid-eight but returning to it after the second verse. He played it again three or four times until it flowed and his hand was less stiff. The Kinks were next – working out "Louie Louie" took him until tea-time. He stopped to fry up some French toast, then resumed, playing Steely Dan, the Grateful Dead, a little Floyd and, of course, he couldn't resist Led Zeppelin. It was after ten when he put her down and, exhausted, took to his bed, his mind buzzing with something he had long ago forgotten about. Sam's gospel phase was over.

Music had mattered to him once, before he'd been disappointed too many times. His first band Diesel, featuring Hilarie, the dick-licking bass player, had lasted a mere six months. They'd broken up when the drummer fractured his leg in a car crash and Hilarie decided she wanted to be a nurse.

Sam had also been hospitalized but for different reasons. He hadn't broken any bones, but his injury would take the rest of his life to heal. He had also moved schools that year and spent his last year of high school as a recluse. He didn't bother with college but, desperate to leave home, he found himself a job in a music shop and rented a boxroom in a tiny apartment he shared with a lesbian couple, Ronnie and Sue. It was Ronnie who had introduced him to the bass player in the band Limbs, an all-guy unit made up of three art-school dropouts, Fred, Paulie and Dave. They used to joke about it, saying they were missing a limb, as if it was funny, but he guessed that when you were twenty-two and high, it pretty much was.

The music was serious, though. Fred was the bass player and lead vocalist – he had a set of pipes on him. Paulie was the drummer, and what he lacked in talent he made up for in raw energy and enthusiasm. Dave, on guitar, was the quiet one and the main songwriter. They wanted a second guitar player and Sam fitted the bill. He would have been designated "the pretty one" but the epithet was used only once: Dave and Fred had to pull Sam off their terrified drummer, who sustained a black eye and a fat lip. Although Sam apologized for the seemingly unprovoked attack, he didn't explain to his new band mates why he had torn into Paulie.

Sam was desperate to be in a successful band and he knew that, with the right songs, these guys could go all the way. Dave's were shit so he hoped that after an apprenticeship he could introduce a few of his own, and maybe then they'd rocket and he'd no longer be window-dressing. It didn't work out like that. Dave was precious and, although Sam's songs were infinitely better, Dave was boss. It was his band and Sam could fuck off if he thought he was coming in to take over. So he did fuck off. Instead of trying to hook up with another band he auditioned for his own. That was how he met Sophia Sheffer, the rocker chick with the big hair, hips and voice. He knew instantly that she was the one. He also knew that she was into him, and he slept with her that first night, sealing their newly formed partnership. He wrote the melodies and she wrote the lyrics – she insisted they had to mean something to her. He didn't mind because she wasn't bad and it felt right that she should sing about chick stuff – he definitely couldn't write that.

He plugged them as the Carpenters of the late eighties. Of course they sounded nothing like the Carpenters, and their songs were hardcore rock anthems, which they considered an antidote to Karen and Richard's squeaky-clean soft pop-rock. Also, they weren't related, which was good because they had sex at any given opportunity. It wasn't love, and Sophia understood the concept of opportunistic fucking – she was a rocker, after all.

They worked well together; he secured them paid gigs early on and free recording time, finding that he could schmooze with the best of them. She was serious about improving vocally, became stronger with each passing day and was dedicated to working on her image. Neither batted an eyelid when the other slept with someone else. He acted as manager and found that for some reason doors were quick to open. Maybe it was because he flirted with the PA to every record-company executive in New York and maybe not, but their demos were always heard. Sam was always working. When they weren't gigging, they were writing. When they weren't writing, they were practising. When they weren't practising, he was networking.

They'd been together for nearly two years when the buzz started. Vocally, Sophia had found her niche – one critic describing her voice as husky, dark, warm, sexy and pitch-perfect. The music was strong too, reminiscent of Janis Joplin's raw iron but hinting at what would later become grunge. But music is all about timing: what's hot today isn't tomorrow, and it turned out that Sam's burning, pain-soaked anthems were a little ahead of their time. The world was still into metal-inspired rock 'n' roll and the charts were dominated by bands like Guns N' Roses teasing the girls and instructing the guys with tracks like "Patience", and on the other side, U2's *The Joshua Tree* had delivered America a new-found church: the Church of Bono. Record companies with little imagination were looking for the next U2 and the next GN'R. Sam and Sophia didn't fit the bill but Sophia alone – well, she had a voice that could raise the roof, just like Axl and Bono and all those guys, but she was different because she was a girl. Better than that, she was a girl with balls and Max Eastler, the hottest A&R guy on the east coast, had wondered the first time he'd seen them play how much better she would be with a shit-kicking band around her.

He'd sat back and watched her on the stage, analysing her dirty against her guitar player's pretty. He had liked the songs but the songs were the guy's and he was a complication. Besides, Eastler *had* songs – great writers, great producers, great players were all available to him – so all he had to do was get rid of the blond kid.

It wasn't hard to persuade Sophia to abandon Sam – after all, they had no allegiance to one another, not sexually and certainly not emotionally, and, hey, business is business, after all. Just when they had a chance to get somewhere, she walked and his faith walked with her.

"Please don't do this," he'd begged.

"It's done," she said, unable to look him in the face.

"Please." He was on his knees.

She shook her head. "You're a good player, Sam, but we both know that you're never going to be great." She still couldn't meet his eyes.

"I'll work harder," he pleaded.

"Max is right – talent like yours is . . . Well, you're expendable. I'm sorry." She paused and added, "This is my shot and I can't blow it on some guy I probably won't even remember in ten years."

Sam was crying when she left, and he hated himself for it but he hated her more. Her desertion and her reasoning had hit him hard, knocking his confidence so much that he retired his guitar and swore he'd never trust anyone again or ever again show weakness. He meant it and was blessed – or cursed – with great resolve.

During his time with Sophia he had realized something

167

interesting about himself: he was an intuitive businessman and, better than that, he had the gift for spotting talent. He could walk into any club in New York and put money on the bands who would make it versus those who wouldn't. And if he had been Max Eastler, he would have done the same thing, because Sophia was better off without him. Still, he despised her for doing to him what he knew, given the chance, he would have done to her, and he was determined she would pay.

Within weeks he'd picked himself up and made a decision. He was never going to be the next Santana but, sure as shit, he was going to be the next Clive Davis, the next great music executive in America. He'd never again be expendable. He'd be the best in his chosen profession – and if being the best meant being a complete fucking asshole like that guy Eastler, then so be it.

Fate must have taken him in hand because a week later he bumped into a blue-eyed blonde called Frankie. Mesmerized by her unaffected beauty, he offered to replace the coffee she'd just spilled over him. Half an hour later she had made the decision to dump her boyfriend of three months. On their second official date Frankie mentioned she was the daughter of Joe Merrigan, head of New Moon Records. Sam couldn't believe his luck. Six weeks passed before he met Joe for dinner in his mansion. Joe conducted the meal as if it was an interview and Sam, ever prepared, came through with flying colours. Afterwards, when Frankie and her mother were making drinks, Joe told Sam dirty jokes, which he described as his weakness and not tolerated by his wife and their squeaky-clean daughter. Sam indulged the old man by responding appropriately and telling a few of his own. Joe smacked him on the back, laughing hard, and Sam knew he wouldn't have to wait long.

When he wasn't brown-nosing Joe or having polite sex with the man's sensitive daughter, he was trawling clubs looking for that next big act. Early on he narrowed it down to six bands, following them night after night and gig after gig, then narrowing them down again until, four months into his relationship with Frankie, he'd found the Deadbeats, his first great act.

He'd phoned her dad in his office at around noon. He told him he'd discovered a great band and respectfully asked if he would attend their gig later that night. Joe had laughed, saying he had young guys who did that, but Sam was insistent. Joe broke, and met Sam after eight in a small club in Hoboken. The band played and Joe's initial bemusement turned slowly to interest. After their fourth song he was hooked. Over the months Sam had cultivated a relationship with the band and introduced Joe to them. As instructed they sucked ass. Joe was really impressed with their knowledge of his medium-sized company and of its many quality acts. He was especially impressed with their lack of ego and commitment to the process of making music – in which Sam had spent most of the day indoctrinating them.

Later at an all-night diner and over pancakes, Joe offered Sam his first job in A&R. He started the next day and at first he worked under a gay guy called George Le Forge, a coiffeur turned A&R in the late sixties after a chance encounter with Misty Day, a buxom blues singer he had introduced to Arista Records. She went on to sell eight million copies before she died of a coke overdose in the early eighties. Then he'd found a metal outfit who were doing nicely for Blue Moon. Sam guessed that George had been lucky – he'd only discovered two acts in ten years while he himself was planning on discovering one a year. Within six months Sam controlled the Deadbeats and George was back doing hair.

After he had successfully signed another two million-dollar acts, he migrated to RCA America, leaving Frankie and Joe devastated. Frankie had lost the man she thought would marry her and Joe a natural son-in-law and heir. Sam felt a clean break was best. As much as he liked Frankie, she was a little too fragile for his taste and, besides, he had enough of his own shit to deal with. He didn't love her so he reasoned that he was doing the right thing. He didn't look back, not even when Frankie ended up in hospital having starved herself for six weeks.

A year later, with two more massive acts tearing apart the charts, he was said to have the Midas touch, and described as a hardcore asshole. After he had taken over Max Eastler's job and axed Sophia's band Demonic – having explained to them that, in the current climate, they were expendable – he left RCA America to head up A&R at Seminy Records. The owner Leland Vander had made him an offer he couldn't refuse. Seminy was a hot new label nipping at the heels of the establishment.

At twenty-six Sam was one of the biggest players on the American music scene. He was sitting on top of the world and, deep inside, he knew that, for him, the only way was down.

Sam had navigated his way through eight weeks of rehab without really examining who he was, yet while he was alone and playing his guitar it was all he could do. He had been such an asshole for so long. He hadn't wanted to be – he'd just wanted to succeed so that the pain would go away. He'd believed that if he was the best nothing could touch him. He was wrong, of course. The gold records, the penthouse, the limos, the sexy girlfriend, the money, the suits, the great restaurants, the cool clubs, the awards – none of it had made any difference and, in the moment he'd realized he couldn't escape himself, he'd lost himself.

Sam played his guitar for two days straight until his hand was so stiff it was difficult to hold a fork. He hadn't seen Mary in those two days but she had made sure that he left her home with enough food to last him a week. Now he was looking forward to seeing her again. She had been such a surprise to him. The nights he'd spent on her floor had been illuminating. His once-frosty neighbour was warm and natural, not like most of the women he'd known, who were mostly too busy holding in their stomachs to be able to engage with him. She engaged, looking straight through his eyes and into his soul. He knew it would be difficult to hide anything from her.

# 14. Every day is like Sunday

Ivan woke with his seven-year-old daughter sitting on his chest. He opened one eye playfully, closed it and opened the other. She giggled. He raised his arms and she held on to them, lifted his legs and her feet met his. Suddenly she was suspended in the air, screaming and laughing. He dropped her onto the bed and she curled up beside him. "Happy Easter, Dad!"

"Happy Easter, Justy! Where's your brother?"

"Down by the water."

Chris, a ten-year-old who could have passed for thirteen, loved the water just like his dad. Ivan knew his son missed it in his new home and felt sorry for him.

"Eggs?" he queried.

"An omelette, with mushrooms, ham and cheese, and Granny Sheila's brown bread," Justine demanded.

"You don't ask for much!" Ivan ruffled her hair, happy that he'd stocked up.

Sitting in the kitchen she chatted about Granny Sheila and her twin cousins, and Auntie Mary, who'd promised to take her to Killarney to buy something pretty. Ivan attempted to question her about her new world but she remained closed off.

"Is everything OK with your mother?" he asked eventually.

She shrugged her shoulders and pretended to smile.

"Justine. Answer me. Is everything OK?"

She looked a little nervous, playing with the sugar bowl, and he could have sworn a tear sprang into her eye.

Chris opened the back door and came in rubbing his hands. "I could smell that omelette from halfway up the yard!" he said gleefully.

Justine laughed and Ivan winked at his son, happy his children were with him and temporarily forgetting his concern. After all, it was Easter Sunday and, for the first time ever, his mother had excused her children from their obligatory Sunday meal in favour of Ivan hosting a family barbecue to welcome his children home.

Ivan had missed out on most of his kids' lives. It wasn't just his wife's defection. A house and lifestyle like Ivan's didn't come from a fisherman's pay packet. As a teenager, when he had discovered Norma's pregnancy, he had had two choices: the first was to be poor and a full-time father, and the second was to train as a commercial diver, work in Saudi and make a mint. He'd already completed advanced diving courses during several summers while his brothers played football and hurley. The reality had meant leaving his young family for an oil rig off the Red Sea coast and working in hazardous conditions – but the pay reflected the danger, and if they were to have any kind of life, it was a risk worth taking. He had left his new wife and his baby boy to live on an oil rig.

He worked on it for four years straight, only returning when his nephew had died on a swing. Ivan had missed most of Ben's life and was shocked into deciding that he wouldn't miss the lives of his own children. He came home, bought a large house, a small boat, a number of properties in Cork and a few stocks and shares. He'd made it, and initially his wife seemed happy. After years of sustaining family life alone, her husband had returned. It should have been good. It wasn't. They were strangers, having grown up apart. Their break-up was assured but he hung on to the love they had once shared, desperate not to lose the kids he'd only just regained.

Sam had been surprised that his relaxed friend had once been a risk-taking daredevil, but to Ivan commercial diving had only ever been a job. Of course he'd have been lying if he didn't admit it was an adrenalin-charged and exciting way to earn a living – life-threatening activity usually is – but he didn't miss it. Diving had been a means to an end. He liked to fish, and diving for a few years, then making the right investments, would ensure that he could do just that for the rest of his days.

It was just a shame he'd lost his family in the process.

Penny sat in her living room, music blaring. If she had been more like Mary it would have been in tune with her mood but she wasn't – so, despite her desperation, Britney belted out "Hit Me Baby One More Time" while she slugged back a bottle of white wine. Red would have left tell-tale marks but white, if not her favourite tipple, didn't betray her.

She had attempted to get out of attending Ivan's barbecue to no avail. He wouldn't take no for an answer. He was in the mood for celebration and he felt it was as good a day as any for his friends to get to know his new girlfriend. Penny felt a little unwell, and the cause of her illness was jealousy, an unattractive quality she often battled.

However, her main reason for trying to escape Ivan's

party had less to do with his new girlfriend and more to do with Mary bringing Sam. She had avoided the American since her drunken attempted pass – she was monumentally embarrassed by it, and felt cheap and dirty and exposed whenever she thought about it. He had rejected her and had looked at her with the kind of horror reserved for circus freaks. In his eyes she had transmogrified into something grotesque.

The next morning she had awoken hating herself, but within hours and in the company of a stiff drink she had mentally dumped her self-loathing on Sam. After all, who the hell did he think he was? If Adam hadn't abandoned her, she wouldn't have looked at him twice. He fancied himself. It was then she decided he was an arsehole and a jumped-up arsehole at that. She didn't want to see him – she'd have to make polite conversation with him. She couldn't believe he and Mary had become friends over the past number of weeks. It was as though they'd done it to spite her. Just when she needed her best friend most, some stranger rolled into town and stole her away.

She finished the dregs of the bottle. It was the least she deserved.

Mary and Sam were up early so that they could fit in a few hours' tree-tagging before they headed to Ivan's. It had been the third afternoon in a row that Mary had joined Sam in his quest to find his grandmother's message.

At first he had been reluctant to share his pastime with his neighbour, but when he discovered that half the town was surmising he had some form of autism that related to trees, he explained himself to Mary.

Mary had grinned.

"What?" he'd asked, expecting sarcasm.

"Nothing."

He was freaked by her inane grin.

"It's nice, that's all. I hope you find her."

"She's dead. I'm not looking for her."

"Whatever." She was laughing now. Eventually she asked if she and Mr Monkels could join him on his quest.

It worked very well. They talked and Mr Monkels groaned and halfway through that first day, when Sam pointed to light streaming through a parting in a cloud, Mary got out her camera and took her first photograph in six years.

It was Sam's turn to be smug.

"What?" she asked.

"You took what I said to heart," he said.

"No, I didn't," she lied.

"Yeah, you did." He chuckled, so she pushed him.

After that she took a lot of photos – of Mr Monkels resting at the base of a tree, one of Sam running his hand over the bark and another of him hiding his face from her incessant clicking. A bird swooping low over still water was her favourite, or that was what she would tell people: actually it was one of Sam giving her the fingers. When they'd got back he'd helped her change her spare bedroom into a darkroom.

"Haven't you heard of digital?" he asked, while he gaffer-taped blackened cardboard to the window.

"One step at a time." She was grappling with the old black-velvet curtains her auntie Sheila had made for her, long ago.

Now the weather was getting warmer. Today Mr Monkels

had refused to budge when Mary had attempted to attach him to his lead. Instead he lay inside the french windows soaking up the heat against the glass.

Mary wished Sam a happy Easter, to which he grunted a response, and teased him about attending a service. He reiterated that he didn't do Mass.

"Me neither."

"But you believe in God," he said, his tone suggesting he thought she was crazy.

"Yeah."

"I don't get it." He took her hand to help her up a grassy verge.

"What's to get?" she asked, amused.

"With the way things have gone for you, it must have crossed your mind that He may have it in for you."

He was right – there had been a time when she'd believed that the Almighty was an arsehole, but one day that had changed. "A very wise woman told me once that the world doesn't revolve around me."

He arched an eyebrow questioningly.

"She said that those who had gone before had merely followed their own path rather than being a casualty on mine." She shrugged her shoulders. "We're all just visiting this world. Some stay longer than others."

"I hope for your sake you're not going to be disappointed."

"About what?"

"What if I told you that I'd died?"

"You *died*?"

"It was only minutes but long enough for me to know there's nothing." He was puzzled when she smiled.

"Ask me about what I remember during my coma," she said.

"What do you remember?" he asked, playing along.

"Nothing," she said. "Absolutely nothing."

"So?"

"So it doesn't mean there wasn't anything going on."

"It's totally different." He sighed.

"No, it's not."

"I just don't get why you would believe," he mumbled.

"Because if I didn't I'd lose my mind."

He nodded – that answer made sense to him.

Later, while they were making their way home, Mary returned to the subject of Sam's death. "Are you ever going to tell me about what happened to you?"

"Maybe some day."

She smiled. "It would be easier to get a straight answer from James Bond."

"I'm sorry. I don't like talking about the past."

"I understand. Some join the Foreign Legion and others come to Kenmare."

It occurred to Sam then that one of the things he liked most about Mary was that, although she knew little about where he'd come from, what he did for a living or the terrible mistakes he'd made, she did know him. In fact, she knew him better than anyone else.

It was after three when they arrived at Ivan's. Auntie Sheila and Mary's dad were vying for control of the grill. Mary kissed them both, her dad shook Sam's hand and her aunt told him that if her niece didn't have such a good left hook she'd steal him away for herself.

"We're just friends," Mary told her, for the fifth time.

"That's what they always say, and then someone gets pregnant," her aunt riposted, and nudged her brother.

"We're just friends," Sam clarified, before Ivan called him over to join in a game of football he was having with his son and his brother Séamus, who was running around the garden having the time of his life without his wife and twins. As luck would have it, one of the girls had been struck down with chicken-pox earlier in the week. Séamus had never had it, and while they waited to see if the spots would appear on her sister, the doctor had advised him to stay out of harm's way. To this end, he had moved in with his parents and was determined to make the most of his limited freedom.

Mary found Penny sitting at one of the garden tables toasting with Steven and Barry.

Steven jumped up to greet her. "Mary, you look like a diva."

"Isn't that your way of calling me a bitch?" She smirked.

"It's his way of telling you to take it easy on the hair dye," Barry informed her. "Or are you trying out for the Pussy-cat Dolls?"

Mary gave him a dig as Penny threw her head back, laughing.

"And you've competition," Steven said, throwing his eyes in the direction of Sienna and a blonde friend, who was helping her carry sauce bottles and condiments.

"Two redheads, but who is the reddest of them all?" Steven said, in his movie-trailer voice.

Mary looked at Penny. "You told them about the hair-dye incident."

"We heard it was more like a pushing-and-slapping affair," Barry put in.

Mary moaned. "Who's the blonde?" she asked, gesturing at Sienna's friend.

"Her name is Flory," Steven grinned, "as in Floor E."

"You're messing," Mary reproved him, but Barry and his boyfriend Steven shook their heads.

"And here's the best bit," Barry added. "The lovely Sienna has brought her along as a potential date for your new neighbour."

Penny started to laugh, which struck Mary as unkind although she wasn't sure why.

"Well, I wish her the best of luck," Mary said, as Steven stood up and took her arm so that they could walk to the makeshift bar together.

"Don't worry, she hasn't a patch on you," he whispered.

"We're just friends," she said, for the umpteenth time, and sighed.

Their friendship had been agreed upon over a meal in a local restaurant, which the hovering waitress, Minnie Morrow, had made uncomfortable by offering the new couple a free bottle of wine. Mary had tried to explain that her neighbour was merely thanking her for taking care of him during his convalescence to which Minnie had commented, "I bet you did," then leaned in to Sam and whispered that if it didn't work with Mary of the Sorrows he'd know where to find her.

When Minnie had gone, Mary had said, "Don't worry, I'm not looking for a relationship."

"Right back at ya," Sam had replied.

"I knew that. I just didn't want you to think I was sitting here with any expectations. I'm happy as I am."

"Me too," he had said, and raised his glass. "Here's to friendship!"

"Friendship," she'd echoed happily.

Mary made peace with Sienna over a hot dog, and told her how happy she was making Ivan. It was true – Ivan was like a playful puppy. When his wife had walked out, he'd lost his confidence as well as his family and Sienna had restored it so Mary was grateful to her. Ivan had put his arm around his favourite cousin and toasted his friends and family, while Justine sat on her grandmother's knee and Chris sneaked a sip of his uncle's beer.

Mary cornered Penny when she was pouring vodka for herself at the bar. "Hey, stranger! You've been keeping to yourself."

"I know," Penny said. "I've just been really busy."

"Maybe I could call over in the morning – I'll bring breakfast," Mary volunteered.

Penny glanced over her shoulder at Sam, who was talking with the blonde. "Great."

Mary had watched Penny from a distance and noticed she was never without a drink. But it was a party. She vowed to keep a closer eye on her. "You're OK, aren't you?" she asked.

"I'm fine," Penny said. "You want a drink?"

Mary nodded so her friend poured her one and they sat together.

Penny looked back towards Sam and Flory. "I don't trust him," she said, out of nowhere.

"Who?"

"Sam."

"Why?"

"I don't know. Why did you dislike him at first sight?"

"I didn't know him."

"Aren't you a great believer in gut feelings?"

"And don't you think my gut feelings are a load of crap?" Mary retaliated, attempting to defuse a potentially uncomfortable conversation.

Penny let it go – she'd made her point. She wasn't sure what it was. All she knew was that she didn't want to be around Sam, not after what had happened. He was an arsehole. She hoped he liked the blonde with the stupid name so that she'd get her best friend back. "Do you think he likes her?" she asked, her eyes on Sam and Flory again.

"I don't know. Maybe."

Later, when night had fallen and Ivan's garden was lit up from the porch to the sea, when Justine was asleep on her grandfather's knee and Chris was in the den watching a DVD with a friend who was sleeping over, the party continued.

Denis and his band, a Dubliners tribute called the Pale Pretenders, arrived a little after nine. The first time Mary had slept with Denis she'd mentioned that their name was pretty bloody stupid. He insisted on explaining its origins, hoping to change her mind. "You see, they're the Dubliners, meaning they're from Dublin. Dublin is also known as the Pale. We're not the Dubliners but we do play the music of the Dubliners so we're the Pale Pretenders."

"I get the reference and it's still rubbish."

"Fair enough," he'd acquiesced. "Any chance of a shag?"

He was the most relaxed man she'd ever met. Then again, he, like her neighbour Mossy, smoked hash like others smoked cigarettes, which pretty much explained his permanently numb state. Initially, although she was attracted to him, she had thought him to be one of life's losers, which hadn't bothered her at all. His grubby appearance suggested as much and his lackadaisical approach to life almost confirmed it – but that was before she had become aware of his past. He intrigued her, with his sharp green eyes, his matted hair and the clothes that were ten years old even though he owned half of Kildare. Later she would discover that he had bought his first property at sixteen, his second at seventeen, and while she was night-swimming and getting herself pregnant he had been building an empire. At twenty-six he'd got bored and learned how to play the guitar. He had always been a fan of traditional music, especially the Dubliners, so by the age of thirty-two he was a *bona fide* Traveling Wilbury, touring wherever the music took him. She had liked him instantly, especially as he was only in town for one night every few months.

Now he smiled, bringing her back to the present, and made his way over to the area that would become his stage. The fiddle player, Dillon, and the kid who sang with the voice of an old man followed him.

"Howya, Mary."

"Good, Dillon. You?"

"Just like jam."

She had no idea what that meant but guessed that it was good – he looked pretty happy.

As the band were setting up Mary brought Denis a drink. "It's nice of you to do this," she said. "I didn't know Ivan had asked."

"We were in Tralee last night. It was no problem."

It had been four months since she and Denis had seen one another.

"So, are we on tonight?" he asked.

"You don't waste time," she responded, swirling the contents of her glass.

"I think Jesus would be sad if I did."

She laughed. "I'm sorry – it's not a good night."

"No harm in asking." He grinned, glanced at Dillon and the boy, and suddenly there was live music and dancing.

Sam had viewed the guy talking with Mary from a distance. He looked like a hippie with dreads and was wearing a jumper two sizes too big. There was a hole in the sleeve that hung over his hand: his thumb, which bore a thick silver ring, stuck through it. He was tall, well built and his face was chiselled like rock. When he introduced their first song his voice was like gravel, briefly reminding Sam of Danziger. The guy beside him with the fiddle was smaller and rounder and the hair on his head had absconded. He made up for that with a long, grey-speckled beard. The third guy looked like a kid in a suit – short hair and rosy cheeks with freckles. He was engaging – close your eyes and it was Luke Kelly back from the dead – but Sam kept returning to the hippie, who spent his time staring at Mary.

Penny sneaked off to skinny-dip with Steven and Barry. She listened to the live band lying on her back in the water while the men, drunker than they'd been in a long time, frolicked, each pushing the other under water and taking turns to give chase.

Sam danced with Flory, who was possibly the most insistent woman he'd ever met. He had been polite all night as she clearly had issues with men. She had cried three times and every time he'd attempted to escape she'd grabbed his hand and wouldn't let go. When he'd caught Mary's eye she'd merely smiled and looked away. Everyone was having a good time but he was at a parallel party, listening to the problems of a disturbed woman.

Mary was sitting with her uncle, who was caressing the hair of his sleeping grandchild while he complained that his wife wouldn't feed him properly. "Who in the name of God in heaven eats whole grains?" he asked.

Séamus was dancing on his own with his shoes off and his trousers turned up. "God help him," his father said.

Mary looked at her cousin, then at her uncle.

"Twins will do that to a man," he said, nodding.

She looked past him towards the band, met Denis's eye and went past him to where Sam was kissing Flory. She got up, deciding she needed a drink. She met her dad at the bar. "A good night," he said, pouring her a drink.

"Yeah."

"You're OK?"

"I'm great."

"Right so." He left her to it.

Mary put her drink down. She had decided to go home.

# 15. A kiss is just a kiss

The pounding rain woke Sam some time after five the next morning. He needed the loo. After he'd emptied an alarmingly distended bladder he made his way downstairs, opened the fridge and took out a bottle. He was pouring water into a glass when he noticed that Mary's french windows were open. He looked over the wall and saw the rain pooling on her kitchen floor and drenching the curtains. It was a marvel to him how, in just a few hours, the weather had changed from a glorious spring night to a winter deluge.

The lights were out and he was sure she wasn't awake. He had seen her leave Ivan's party just after he had prised the insane blonde off him. He hadn't had a chance to say goodbye — she had been gone before he could speak to her. He wondered if she had seen the kiss. They were just friends, of course, but he didn't want her to know that he had kissed another woman. It would have been fine if that was what he had done, but it wasn't. Suddenly he realized it was very unlike Mary to leave her doors wide open and, considering the hour and that her wooden floor would suffer if he did nothing, he made his way towards her garden.

"Mary?" he said, but there was no answer. "Mary!" he said again, a little louder. Still nothing. He was getting soaked. The moss-ridden rock wall separating the two houses was slippery, not to mention sharp. Concerned for his back, he decided against trying to leap over. Instead he brought a chair out of the kitchen and stood on it, then manoeuvred himself carefully over the wall and dropped down on the other side. For some reason he felt like a criminal – his heart was beating way too fast to be good for him.

He took a deep breath and went into the kitchen gingerly. A heavy vase had fallen onto the floor and cracked. As he ventured further in he noticed that the place was a mess – in fact, the closer he looked the more apparent it became that he might be interrupting a burglary. A book of menus that had obviously been laid out on the table was now spilled across the floor along with CDs out of their cases. *She never leaves CDs out of their cases.* He listened carefully. He picked up a heavy wrought-iron poker from beside the fire and heard a thud upstairs. He grasped his weapon tightly and ran to the stairs.

It was after five when Mary emerged from the bathroom and made her way into her bedroom. Just as she was closing the door she heard a noise downstairs. She listened intently, interrupted only by Mr Monkels's thud when he fell off the end of the bed. He didn't even wake up – instead he rolled onto his belly and wheezed. She had worried that he might have had an epileptic seizure on the night Sam had hurt his back, but the vet had disagreed and the dog had displayed no symptoms since. She surveyed him intently for a moment or two – then heard another sound. She grabbed the hardback book she'd been reading and tiptoed to the stairs. They met halfway, their weapons held high.

"Sam?" Mary whispered.

"Mary! Are you all right?"

"I'm fine. What's wrong?" She lowered the book and beckoned him downstairs.

Inside the kitchen, he answered her: "This is what's wrong!" He swept the room with his hand.

"So I left a mess."

"Exactly. You don't leave messes."

"Well, I did last night."

"And what about the door?"

"I forgot about it," she admitted, picking up the vase before moving to close the french windows and standing in the pool of water. "Knickers!" she said, under her breath, and reached for the mop.

Absentmindedly, Sam sat down.

Mary raised her eyebrows. *He has a neck. One minute kissing the blonde and the next sitting in my kitchen.* She had convinced herself on her journey home that she didn't care about that kiss.

"Do you often leave your back door open?" he queried.

She pushed her hair off her face. "You know I don't." She felt the damp curtains. "Frig it! I just had those dry-cleaned." She moved across the room past Sam. Despite the damp, he smelt expensive. She was suddenly aware that she was wearing a pair of little black pyjama shorts and a vest top, especially now that her nipples were sticking out like bloody spare parts. She turned to the kettle, wondering whether he wanted tea and how long he was planning to stay. His closeness made her heart skip. He stood up, slipped his hand into hers and bent towards her. The impending kiss hung in the air.

She was paralysed rather like her dog had been two weeks before. Moments passed but they seemed like years. His face remained fixed at an intimate distance. *Oh, holy crap! Pull away, Mary! Pull away before he does something you'll both regret!*

It was at that moment that Denis came in. His piercing eyes took in Mary while seeming to ignore Sam. He walked right up to them and placed his hand on her shoulder. "Are you coming back to bed?" he asked.

Sam dropped her hand. She battled against the urge to throw up.

Denis left his hand on her shoulder while he registered Sam. He put out the other to shake Sam's.

Sam reciprocated while waging an inner battle of his own.

"You're the neighbour?"

"Yes."

"I'm the casual shag," Denis said, and Mary closed her eyes so that she didn't have to look at Sam's expression.

"I should go." Sam turned to leave.

She walked him to the door and opened it to let him out. "I'm really sorry," she muttered.

"Don't be," he said cheerily, as though nothing had happened – but, then, of course, nothing had happened.

He'd pretend he hadn't been about to kiss her and she'd pretend she hadn't believed he was about to kiss her. His momentary lapse would be ignored by both parties. He would pretend to be grateful for the reprieve Denis had provided – after all, he wasn't ready for a relationship or, indeed, anything other than friendship. She would pretend that she hadn't wanted him to kiss her and that it was a good thing Denis had been there to save the moment and their friendship. Both would determine that their friendship was not worth jeopardizing.

She watched him walk out of her little front garden. Denis's two band mates were waking from an uncomfortable sleep in the car parked out front. She motioned at them to come in for breakfast while her neighbour entered his house, closing the door behind him without glancing back. She guessed he'd seen enough for one morning.

*Oh, my God, he thinks I'm a whore.*

It was after nine and Penny was dreaming of a frog dancing a hornpipe on a blue carpet surrounded by GAA football players clicking their fingers.

Mary plonked herself down on her friend's bed and she sat up, still half asleep. "What? What? What is it?" she called, to the weird little frog clicking his heels.

Mary opened a bag of fruit scones under her nose. "I've got raspberry jam and fresh cream in the kitchen."

Penny's eyes opened slowly. "My favourite."

Mary went to the window to open the curtains.

"You wouldn't believe the weird dream I just had." Penny yawned.

"I wouldn't believe it if it wasn't weird," Mary said, going out of the door.

"What the hell are you so chipper about?" Penny grabbed her dressing-gown and followed.

"I had sex last night."

"Oh, my God, either pigs have taken flight or one-dimensional Denis had his way." Penny peered out of the window and into the bright blue sky. "No pigs. It must be Denis."

Mary was dumping beer bottles. "Did people come back here?" she asked.

"Yeah," Penny lied, not knowing why. Maybe because she didn't need questions about bottles so early in the morning.

"What the hell happened to your tooth?" Mary asked.

Penny remembered that when she'd got home from the party she'd needed a drink. After a few weeks of too much wine she'd decided to buy only beer. She hadn't been able to find the bottle-opener. After a few minutes of searching, she had become annoyed and annoyance had turned quickly to frustration. Eventually she did what anyone else would have done: she used her teeth to get the top off the bottle. Her endeavour was successful – at the cost of a cap on her left molar, bought by her parents many years previously. Now Mary scrutinized her as she felt the gap in her mouth with her finger.

"I said, what happened your tooth?"

"It's been loose for weeks. I must have lost it when I was asleep."

"OK," Mary said, as though she didn't believe her.

"Anyway, enough of that. How's one-dimensional Denis?" Penny said, in an attempt at distraction but also because she had a genuine interest in her friend's nocturnal activities.

"He's not one-dimensional."

Penny scoffed. "And?"

"He followed me home from the party." She started to make coffee.

"And the mood just came over you," Penny noted, shaking her head. "Well, after how many months? I suppose that kind of thing can happen."

"Ha-ha," Mary said, giving Penny the fingers. She knew how Penny felt about Sam, but she was desperate to talk about his possible kiss with Flory and to seek counsel on the handling of such a delicate matter – or, at the very least, confirmation that ignoring it would be beneficial to their friendship. She thought she'd test the waters.

"And do you know what else?" she asked.

"I can't wait," Penny responded.

"I had a late-night caller."

"A late-night caller?"

Mary nodded.

"Go on."

"Sam."

"What did he want?" The warmth left Penny's voice so Mary decided against confiding in her.

"He thought I was being burgled."

"What a hero!"

Mary changed the subject. "You really need to see a dentist."

"What am I like, Mary?" Penny made a face, exposing the gap.

Mary smiled but didn't respond – the question had been rhetorical, she knew.

After breakfast they sat out on Penny's patio, each clasping her coffee mug for warmth.

"I forgot Ben's anniversary," Penny admitted, gazing up at the light blue sky.

"It doesn't matter. You had a lot to deal with." The anniversary had been weeks before and it hadn't occurred to Mary to be annoyed that her best friend had forgotten it. Penny had enough problems of her own.

"It does matter. I'm really sorry."

Mary nodded. "Sam left flowers." She hadn't intended to mention him again that morning – it had just slipped out.

"You're joking," Penny exclaimed, in wonderment. "How do you know? Did he leave a card?"

"No. Cassie Boxer saw him. She told Rita Sullivan

Flowers who mentioned it to Jessie after Mass a week after he came here."

"That's weird."

"I know you don't like him, but I reckon I was wrong about him."

"It doesn't matter what any of us think," Penny said, eyeing her friend. "He's just passing through. This time next year he'll be a memory, like the Burkenheffs."

"The Brinkerhoffs," Mary corrected her.

"My point exactly," Penny said, smiling, "and in the meantime I hope he and Flory are very happy together."

By this time Mary had half forgotten his little indiscretion. *What the . . .?* She returned Penny's smile, then changed the subject again, in her get-ready-for-gossip voice: "You'll never guess what I heard last night."

"What?" Penny asked, gripped by the prospect of scandal.

"Bridget the Bike and her husband have split up." This was met with silence. "Someone told her he'd fathered that child in Sneem."

Penny inhaled sharply.

"I know," said Mary.

"Bridget Browne. Oh, dear God!"

"Apparently she discovered the truth weeks ago. They've been trying to work it out but . . ." Mary was shaking her head. "After all this time I wonder how she found out?"

"Well, the whole town's talking about it," Penny said.

"Yeah – but I wonder if it's really true?" Mary pondered.

"Of course it is," Penny said, betraying a little panic. "You think it's not?"

"It wouldn't be the first time a rumour was unfounded."

"Well, she's left him, so it must be true."

"Maybe. Still, I feel sorry for her. She sent me a lovely card when Ben died."

Penny wasn't ready to admit her part in the dissolution of the Brownes' marriage so, despite the emergence of guilt, she managed a smile and inquired whether or not her friend wanted more coffee.

Later Penny was sitting in her dentist's with a gap and a serious hangover. While she flicked through ancient magazines, she promised herself that she wouldn't mix her drinks any more. It just wasn't worth it. When she looked up, the woman opposite smiled. She smiled back, conscious of the gaping hole in her mouth.

"Cap?" the woman asked.

"Yeah."

"Hmm. I have false teeth." She loosened them in her mouth to demonstrate.

"Oh!"

"Eating steak's a pain in the face."

"Right."

"I miss them all the same."

"Right," Penny said again, not sure whether the woman was referring to steak or her teeth.

The nurse called the steak-deprived woman in for consultation, leaving Penny alone. This time she picked up a celebrity gossip magazine that was normally not to her taste. She stared at the singer Mia Johnson crying on the front page. She read the article with shaking hands – and not just because she was hung-over: in that picture, the ever-elusive Sam Sullivan was standing behind Mia. She thought about bolting but the gap in her gob forbade anything so radical.

Once her tooth was fixed, she drove straight home and went online. *Who is this man?* At last she had found a story worth reporting.

Saying goodbye to his kids was always hard but this time Ivan didn't experience the usual trauma. This time he had someone standing by him as he waved to them. Sienna had come to mean something to him. It had been just a matter of weeks, she was a bit younger and those around him, except Mary, felt he was too vulnerable to be serious but they were wrong: he had never felt stronger. He put his arm around Sienna as he watched his children disappear and she snuggled in tight.

"They're nice kids," she said.

"They are, even if they were little bastards to you," he said. Chris had practically ignored her and Justine had followed his lead, and when they weren't ignoring her they were either staring at her suspiciously or replying to her attempts at communication sulkily or sarcastically.

"They'll get used to me," she said, laughing.

"They have plenty of time," he ventured.

"Yeah."

Ivan sniffed a happy sniff and they made their way to the car park.

# 16. Digging for digging's sake

It had been two weeks since the kiss that had never happened. In that time Mary and Sam had bumped into one another and behaved politely, embarrassed and yet maintaining the façade of normality. This polite distance was annoying to both parties who, although they were unwilling to admit to feelings beyond friendship, missed each other. Sam was particularly freaked and for many reasons, the first being his near-inability to control the impulse to kiss Mary. *What the hell was that all about?* Not to mention his suffocating jealousy of Denis. *So she slept with the guy – big deal.* Her sex life, now revealed, had been a shock. Ivan had painted her as some sort of recluse and all the while she'd been boffing some travelling musician. *People never cease to amaze.* He worried that he was attaching feelings to her in a bid to escape from himself. A new relationship was not advisable within the first year of rehab. *I've got enough to deal with.*

But there was something else – something he wouldn't admit to. It was ego-related. Mary didn't pay attention to him in the way other women did. Sam often observed them looking at him. It was difficult not to, they made it so obvious. Some just stared and giggled or raised their voices in an attempt to gain his attention. Others grabbed at him, patting his ass while making suggestions into his ear, usually when they were drunk and at their least attractive. Other guys envied the effect he had on women, but Sam was bored with it. As with many men, for him the best part of an initial attraction was the hunt, but he'd had no need to exert himself since his late teens. It was rare that he wasn't the most beautiful man in the room and women were not ashamed to let him know of their interest.

He wasn't stupid enough to believe they were interested in him as a person. He had long ago come to terms with the fact that most women were far more interested in his looks than in anything he had to say. Sam was one of the few men on earth who could identify with a *Playboy* model. Of course, Mia hadn't been like most of the women who had crossed his path. She had seen past his face and loved him, but she didn't know him, not like Mary. *But how the hell could Mary know me?* And he knew her. *I just don't know why.*

After they had spent two weeks pussyfooting around one another, he was relieved when she asked him to meet her for dinner. He agreed straight away.

Mary arrived at the restaurant early. She was a stickler for punctuality, always overestimating how long it would take her to get from one place to another. After years of arriving between ten and twenty minutes early, she had learned to ensure that she always carried reading material. She ordered a glass of house red from Roni Shea, who was desperate to talk about the Browne break-up.

"So you've heard nothing?" she said, eyeing Mary while tapping her pencil against her order book in a slightly menacing fashion.

"No more than you."

"It's amazing – I mean, the child is six months old. You'd think she would have found out sooner," she pointed out astutely.

"Well, maybe it was the girl – what's her name?"

"Tracy Whelan – and, no, it definitely wasn't Tracy. Bridget attacked her after Mass on Sunday and gave her a black eye, and Lisa Harmon says she knocked out a front tooth." She was nodding animatedly, but speaking in a hushed tone.

"Ah, well," said Mary, afraid that Sam would catch her gossiping and wanting to end the conversation.

"It all happened in Sneem. The parish priest had to pull them apart. Apparently Tracy Whelan gave as good as she got. Of course, it's sad for the little one." Roni's voice softened, as did her eyes.

"Yeah," Mary agreed, "the poor child."

Suddenly Roni became awkward and businesslike, as though she'd just remembered Mary had lost her own child. She reddened and made her escape to fetch Mary's wine. Just then the door opened and Sam entered, making an immediate impression on the girl behind the counter. Mary's head was in her book. The girl blushed and stuttered a welcome. He pointed towards Mary to suggest he'd found his date. The girl seemed startled – as though it was impossible to imagine the living embodiment of Barbie's Ken eating with Mary of the Sorrows.

When he arrived at their table, Mary put down her book and smiled. He didn't lean in for a kiss and she hadn't expected him to. To an observer they would have seemed easy together, but after a glass of wine Mary was still not relaxed. She was glad that Sam had agreed to meet her but it soon became apparent that he was as tense as she was.

After her initial humiliation, she had come to realize it had actually been a good thing that Denis had arrived into her kitchen when he did. If he had not she would have jumped the man whose hand had electrified hers and whose close proximity had set some sort of fire in her – and that would have been bad, because she wasn't blind. During the time Sam had lived in her small town Mary had noticed the effect he had on women and she didn't want him to mistake her for another who would fall willingly at his feet. She wanted to know him because he was more than pretty. His eyes betrayed a troubled soul and possibly a fractured heart. Broken herself, she had the capacity to see it in others, despite their attempts to hide it. She was drawn to damaged souls like a moth to a flame. She wanted to help him. She didn't know how or why or even if she could, but something inside her told her to try. She also knew he wouldn't be around for much longer and that their time together would be short. Friendship had to be enough.

"I'm glad you called," he said, while he studied the menu.

"I'm thrilled you came. Besides, I wanted to apologize."

"You have nothing to be sorry for. I'm the one who invaded your space."

"Space invader," she mumbled, and laughed nervously at her own joke.

"That wasn't funny," he said, but his eyes gave him away.

"Frig off!"

"Can I ask you something?"

"What?"

"Well, I know what knickers are but what in the hell is a frig?"

"It's a replacement word for 'fuck'."

"Why not just say what you mean?"

"Well, I used to, until Nora Donnelly asked my three-year-old if he wanted an Ice Pop and he told her to go fuck herself."

He laughed and she laughed with him.

"I stopped swearing then."

For a minute or two they sat in silence over the menus. "You say, 'Are you kidding me?' at least once a day," Mary told him, out of nowhere.

"I do?"

"Yip."

"Does it bug you?" He grinned.

"A little bit."

He laughed. "I'll do my best to correct that."

"Don't. Nobody likes perfect."

They laughed together and any remaining ice thawed. He turned to look for a waitress, who appeared within a second at his side.

Later, over dessert, they talked about movies. Sam wasn't really into cinema but it was something to talk about that deflected from his misguided past.

"Robert and I saw *St Elmo's Fire* eight times." They had planned to move to America based on their love affair with that film.

Sam was amused. "You were going to move to the States because of one movie?"

"Well, that and a photography course in NYU." She sighed. "It would have been good."

"You could still do it."

"Yeah, right," she scoffed. "I'd fit in beautifully."

"You would."

"I was being sarcastic."

"And I was ignoring your sarcasm."

"What about you? Why didn't you follow your dream?" she asked.

"How do you know I didn't?" he asked.

"Do you play guitar for a living?"

"No."

"Well, then . . ."

"You're so sure that's what I wanted?"

"I am."

They were quiet for a moment. Then Mary asked, "Sam. What did you do?"

"I told you I was in management."

"Management of what?"

"Management of people."

"OK, don't tell me. But, whether you like it or not, you can't remain a mystery for ever."

"Just give me some time," he said.

Their night ended on her wall. They sat looking out onto a low tide of black water lit by sparse street-lights and uninhabited stranded boats.

"I've made so many mistakes," Sam said, taking Mary by surprise.

"We all make mistakes."

"Not like me."

"We all make mistakes," she repeated.

He said nothing.

"Are you free tomorrow?" she asked.

"For what?"

"If you can be mysterious, so can I."

*

Penny had spent two weeks locked indoors. She was working on her own assignments, picking up the slack from the Cork correspondent and investing the rest of her time on personal research. She had told Mary she wouldn't be around for a few weeks and Mary didn't question it – after all, she was often busy. All the same, her friend must have wondered what kept her off the phone. No matter how busy Penny had been before, she'd always made time for a quick chat, but Penny knew that, over the past while, she and her best pal had been drifting. This was her own fault – after Adam had left she had pushed Mary away. She wasn't sure why and she missed her but sometimes, despite the loneliness, it was easier to be alone. In those two weeks she spent more time working than drinking, managing to hand in her assignments on time and with little need for correction.

Each evening she would sit at her computer on Google. It was incredible how many times Sam's name came up. It was easy to find out he was in A&R. It was easy to trace the companies he'd worked for, and to find out how many famous acts he'd discovered. The relationship he had with Mia was not so simple to determine. Penny knew he had discovered and groomed her, but that picture suggested there had been more to it. But Google wasn't telling. Mia's relationship with Sam had never been made public so Penny was forced to dig a little deeper.

She started at the beginning. She spoke to Dave, the songwriter in Sam's second band Limbs, and he filled her in on Sam's arrogance and his propensity for violence. He spilled his bitterness, deriding Sam's contempt for the band's direction. Penny would later quote him in her article and yet, for the sake of credibility, she chose not to mention

"So you're telling me that Mia Johnson had a long-term relationship with a heroin addict?" she said, with glee.

"Excuse me?" he said, clearly alarmed by the change in her tone.

"You're right – I am from a small town in a small country, but it looks like I'm going to be the one to break Mia's sordid love story. Maybe you could pass on my number just in case she wants to comment. After all, these revelations can have a life of their own. If he was a junkie, maybe she was too. Maybe she drove him to drugs – or was she the angel who saved him?"

"You're swimming out of your depth," Leland warned.

"But I'm not the one sinking," she said, and hung up. She poured herself a glass of vodka with a shaking hand and pondered as to whether or not she would hear from the lady herself.

The sun was out and Sam had taken to playing his guitar in the back garden. He had woken with the idea for a melody that refused to go away so instead of fighting it he spent the morning working out the chords and, like the Pointer Sisters many years before, losing himself in music.

Mary popped up from behind the wall, scaring the crap out of him. "Nice song," she said. "What is it?"

"Nothing."

" 'Nothing'. I like it. It has a nice ring to it."

He laughed her off.

"Are you ready?" she asked. "For my surprise trip?"

He put the guitar down. "I'll meet you out front."

Once in the car they drove across the bridge and eight kilometres down a narrow, winding road. When they got out, they had to walk through a rain-soaked field of grazing cows. She refused to give him any indication of where they were or what they were doing until they reached what could only be described as the burned-out shell of a stone hut that housed two donkeys.

She stopped and took a photo.

"Well?" he said.

"This was your granny's family home." She smiled.

"You're kidding me?" he said, his voice laced with awe.

"Of course, it's buggered now, but I found an old map in the library and this article about the fire. I'm sorry about that." She nudged the map into his hand.

He was still staring at the remnants of his grandmother's house. "How did you know where to look?" he asked.

"You mentioned your granny's maiden name to Ivan who mentioned it to me. I spoke to my dad, who spoke to Jerry Letter, whose ancient ex-neighbour Dick Dogs had known your grandmother's brother David. I researched the rest in the local library."

"I didn't think there would be anything left," he said.

"I was pretty surprised myself," she admitted. "And look over here!" She walked towards a stand of tall trees.

He followed, wide-eyed.

"Someone thought to put up a plaque. It must have been your grand-uncle Tim, seeing as he was the only one to survive."

Sam read it.

AT THIS PLACE CALLED HOME SIOBHÁN AND COLM BRESLIN, MOTHER
AND FATHER TO FIVE, REST WITH THEIR SONS VINCENT, JACKIE AND
DAVID. THEY WILL BE FOR EVER MISSED BY TIM AND LENA.

A lot of text followed but it was in Gaelic.

"Lena was my grandmother's name," he said. "Can you translate?"

"I can. I had to look it up. I was always rubbish at Irish." She read the transcription: "'May God grant you always a sunbeam to warm you . . .'"

He joined in: "'. . . a moonbeam to charm you, a sheltering angel so nothing can harm you, laughter to cheer you, faithful friends near you. And whenever you pray, Heaven to hear you.'" He smiled. "It was a blessing my grandmother's father used to whisper to her each night before she fell asleep."

"A family blessing. That makes sense." She nodded as though something had clicked into place. "It's a bit of a weird prayer for the dead." She snapped a photograph.

"I can't believe you did this," he said, touched by all the trouble she'd gone to.

"Me neither. Usually I'm pretty lazy."

Later, walking to the car, he told her the story of how his great-grandparents and their three eldest sons had perished in a fire a year after his grandmother's father had waved goodbye to her. Tim had returned from a dance to find his family dead and his home destroyed. He'd left the town within weeks of the funerals. It was only when he'd died of pneumonia and his wife, a Cavan woman, had written to his grandmother that she had discovered the truth about the rest of her family. It turned out that for the six years after his parents' and brothers' deaths Tim had written to her in their names pretending all was well.

"My God," Mary had said, a little overwhelmed. "Why?"

"My grandmother used to say that her brother had thought it best to carry the pain of two."

When they got to the car, she said, "Let's open a bottle of wine when we get home."

"You celebrating?"

"No, but I think it's only fair to raise a glass to Tim."

"I'd like that."

# 17. I hate to say I told you so

Ivan went straight home as Sienna had promised she'd call in at the end of her shift. The place was a mess and he wanted to clear up before she arrived. He did it using the hiding and stuffing system he had perfected as a teenager. As long as Sienna didn't open any cupboard, she'd believe him to be a neater, and therefore better, soul than he was. He spent a maximum of two minutes dusting and banged the large rug against the back wall rather than hoovering. Mrs O'Connor of the O'Connor Murphys would be annoyed by his shoddy efforts to maintain her high stand-ard of cleanliness in her two-week absence. Although she would chastise him, much as his mother had done many years before, he was most definitely looking forward to her return.

He was sitting by the window, reading the paper and listening to Dave Fanning debate the hundred greatest rock stars on 2FM. A hot tea, an interesting article and ACDC's "Thunderstruck" suggested that a good night lay ahead. The phone rang as Brian Johnson was beginning the second verse. *Ah, Christ!*

He was surprised to hear his ex-wife on the line. Her tone was decidedly frost-free.

"Do you have a minute?"

"Of course," he said, a little alarmed – perhaps she was about to discuss his budding relationship with Sienna and, if so, a part of him prepared to be annoyed. After all, what right had she to talk to him about his relationships?

"The kids had such a good time this Easter," she said.

*Here we go.* But her voice sounded more relaxed than it had in months. She almost sounded like his wife.

"Justy's cheeks are still rosy. I'd forgotten what that looked like."

He found himself smiling. "She ate me out of house and home."

"She'd live on your mother's brown bread alone," she said, with warmth. "And Chris can't stop talking about that salmon he caught with you."

"It was a big one."

"I'm glad you've met someone," she said.

"Thanks," he replied.

"I'm really sorry about everything."

"Right," he said, which was stupid but he'd been unprepared for kindness.

She laughed, knowing him well. "I wish you both the best."

"Thanks," he said, but something in her tone made him consider asking if anything was wrong.

"I have to go," she said suddenly.

"Are you OK?" he asked, but she was gone.

It was a minute before he replaced the receiver. The conversation resonated as it was the first light one he'd had with his wife since she'd walked out on him, but he'd found it a little disturbing. *What the hell is going on over there?*

Sienna arrived a little after nine. They settled together on the sofa.

"What's on?" she asked.

"Me."

"I was talking about TV," she said, and blew her nose.

"I was talking about me."

"Will you still want to be with me when the first thing you don't want to do is jump me?"

"I can't see that happening."

Sienna punched him playfully. "It will."

"And I will," he said, which was a smoother response than she had anticipated.

His pants were around his ankles when the phone rang again.

The plane landed in Gatwick just after eight a.m. Ivan was up and out of his seat before the seatbelt light flickered off. Sienna grabbed his hand and squeezed it. "It's going to be fine," she said, trying to soothe him but instead tears of anger sprang to his eyes. He held them back with a giant effort of will and went about retrieving their hand luggage. He was exhausted – he hadn't slept a wink since that call. Sienna insisted on driving the hire car and he relented simply because he didn't have time to argue.

He called his daughter from the passenger seat. "Justy, are you all right, love?"

"I'm OK, Dad."

"Where's your brother?"

"Beside me."

"Put him on the phone, love."

"Hi, Dad."

"Hi, son. Are you all right?"

"We're fine."

"Your mother?"

"They said she's sleeping. I haven't seen her but I think it's bad, Dad." His voice broke.

"I'm on my way, Chris. I'm nearly there."

"OK, Dad."

He cancelled the call and looked at Sienna. "How could this happen?"

She didn't have the answer. Instead she told him to open the map so that they could take the right exit and get to the hospital as quickly as possible.

A momentary smile crossed his lips. He liked her no-nonsense approach to an emergency and would be for ever grateful for her help – he wasn't sure he would have coped as well alone.

They arrived at the hospital just over an hour later. Justine and Chris were in the family room, to which the nurse directed him. Sienna told him she'd get coffee and left him to go in alone. When he entered the small room Justine was lying across the couch, asleep. Chris had his back to him, staring at something in the middle distance.

"Chris!" he whispered, and his little boy turned to him, tears streaming down his cheeks.

"I'm here, son," he said, hugging him tightly. "I'm here now."

Justine woke. "Dad!" she said, rubbing her eyes.

"There she is!" he said, his voice light.

She smiled and Chris moved over so that she could share in their father's warmth. "I missed you, Dad. I really missed you."

"That's all over now," he replied, stroking her hair.

They were interrupted by a policeman who'd been assigned to the case. Ivan told his children to stay put and left the room to stand in the corridor and discuss his ex-wife's domestic disturbance. "What's happening?" he asked.

"By the time we got there your ex-wife had been badly beaten and, as you know, she was unconscious. Her boyfriend was gone, but with information provided to us by your son we tracked him down to his local pub. He's in custody. Obviously we can't hold him unless your ex-wife is willing to press charges."

"She's still my wife," Ivan mumbled.

"OK." The man nodded.

"Have you spoken to her?" Ivan asked.

"So far she's pretty uncommunicative. She's sleeping now but when she wakes maybe you could have a word."

Ivan doubted that anything he could say would assist but he promised to give it a try. The policeman walked away.

He spotted Sienna sitting in a chair, drinking coffee and reading the newspaper. He waved at her and she smiled, then shooed him away. He went back into the family room to his two hungry kids. They were in the canteen with Sienna, eating chips, sausages and beans, when the doctor tracked them down. Again, Ivan went into the corridor to talk to him.

"She's got three broken ribs, a broken arm and a cracked skull."

"Jesus Christ!"

"She's lucky to be alive."

"Can I see her?"

"She's very upset," the doctor warned.

"I'm sure she is. I'm only here to help."

"OK. Follow me."

Despite being apprised of her injuries, Ivan wasn't

prepared for the reality. His wife's face was reminiscent of a deflating purple balloon. Her left eye was swollen shut and her lower lip was bloody and stitched. Her arm wasn't in a cast: it was bandaged, with metal bars piercing her skin.

His hands went to his mouth. "Oh, Norma!"

His ex-wife's right eye started to leak and he wasn't sure if it was tears or blood. She tried to talk.

"Don't speak," he said. "You don't have to say anything."

She shook her head slightly. He pulled over a chair and sat close to her bed. He held her hand. "Mary warned me. I should have come to see you for myself. I was too busy with . . ."

Norma raised her good hand and placed a finger over her damaged lips.

"I'll murder him," he promised.

"He never laid a hand on the kids," she said, her words resonating with pain, both physical and mental.

"I know."

"I'm sorry," she whispered.

"I'm sorry too, love."

He stayed with her until she slept.

Ivan woke from a broken sleep at dawn. Sienna was sleeping soundly so he got up and moved across the room as quietly as he could. He managed to make it as far as the dressing-table and then he stubbed his toe – the yell was muted and he hopped just once.

"I'm awake," she said, eyes closed and a grin on her face.

"Sorry," he said, sitting down on the bed with his foot in his hand. "That feckin' hurt."

Sienna stretched, luxuriating in it like a comfortable cat.

"The bed's hard," she noted and Ivan agreed. "Have you checked on the kids?"

He confirmed that he'd looked in on them next door a number of times during the night.

"They'll be OK," she told him, hugging his waist.

"I know," he agreed, although anxiety was etched into his face. "I'll have to take them home."

"I know."

"I mean them all. Norma too."

"I know," she repeated.

"She can't stay here. She's got nothing here," he said, by way of explanation, but Sienna pressed a finger to his lips, much as his wife had to hers the previous evening.

"You don't have to explain."

"I don't love her any more," he said.

"Good." She glowed.

"Good," he said happily.

She lifted the covers. "Now get in here," she said, pointing, "and then get in *here*." Ivan, despite all his problems, was only too happy to oblige.

Sienna took Ivan's shell-shocked kids to the cinema so that Ivan could visit their mother. She seemed a little better than the previous day. Her lip was less swollen and her speech clearer. She wasn't in as much pain as the morphine had fully kicked in. Her mental state had improved too. She didn't appear to be constantly on the verge of tears. She'd even smiled at him, or so it appeared, but with the swelling and the stitches it was hard to tell. She told him how many times she had been beaten and why she hadn't confided in him. He didn't understand any

215

of the reasons she gave but he didn't say so because it was unnecessary and Ivan was never one to enter into an unnecessary argument. She reiterated that her boyfriend had never laid a hand on the kids. Ivan had soothed her when she became distressed while she was recounting her latest and most brutal ordeal. Later he brought in two coffees. He helped her to drink hers by holding it to the less damaged side of her mouth as her broken ribs and fractured arm prevented her doing it for herself. She gave up after a few sips.

"The doctor here says you'll be fit to travel in a week's time. I talked to Dr Macken and he said he can get you into the Regional in Cork for any follow-up appointments for your arm –"

She put up the good one to halt him. "Dr Macken? Ivan, I'm not going back to Ireland."

The shock on his face was clear to see.

"What made you think I'd go back to Kenmare?" she asked.

"I don't understand." He scratched invisible sea salt from his hair.

"Ivan, I won't be going back to that house, but we're staying in the UK." She tried to meet his eyes.

"Well, where will you live?" he asked, exasperated.

"That's my problem," she said.

"*What?*" he all but roared.

"We'll be fine," she said sternly.

"No, Norma, you won't be fine. You're in bits. You've nowhere to live. You've got some lunatic trying to kill you and you've got my kids." He was trying to be calm but his face had flushed.

"I'm tired," she said, when he sat down. "Please leave."

He got up. "This isn't over, Norma," he promised, and left her to her insane thoughts.

The kids were next door, playing with an Xbox he'd bought earlier that afternoon. Sienna sat cross-legged on the bed, listening intently to his rant and attempting from time to time to allay his increasing frustration.

"What the hell is wrong with her?" he said.

"Just give her time."

"To do what?" he shouted.

"She's had a shocking experience. You need to give her breathing space."

"I gave her breathing space and she nearly got herself killed," he said, lowering his tone.

"You're not her father. You can't just drag her home."

Ivan sat down on the bed beside Sienna and took her hand. "I know. But whatever she does," he said, with great resolve, "I'm taking the kids home."

"You've spoken to your solicitor?"

"In the car. They need to come home with or without their mother."

"Is that what you want? To take them without their mother?"

"Of course not. They've been through enough this year but she's leaving me with no choice."

"Talk to her," she said.

"I have!" he said, frustration building once more.

"No, you didn't. You presumed she was coming home and when she told you she wasn't you went mental. Going mental isn't talking."

"So what do you suggest?" he asked, burying his head in his hands.

"Look at the situation from her point of view."

"I am. She's fucked. Excuse my French. She needs to come home."

"She left her husband, her home town, her friends and her family for someone who ended up beating her and terrorizing her kids. If it was me I'd find it hard to face people." She shrugged – he'd noticed she did that when she was talking sense.

"You think she's afraid to come home?" Ivan mumbled, about to scratch his head.

"I think she just needs a little reassurance," Sienna said, taking his hand away from his hair.

She was right, of course. Norma did want to go home. While Sienna talked with Ivan, Norma lay in her hospital bed contemplating a bleak future. There was nothing but misery for her in the UK. She had wanted for months to go home – but how could she? How could she return to the home town that had watched her walk out on her husband for a man she barely knew? How could she return with her tail between her legs, beaten and broken by that same man? How could she ever walk through the streets of Kenmare with her head held high? People would say she was selfish. People would say she deserved what she'd got. People would say she was an unfit mother to have allowed her children to witness such violence. And all those people would be right.

Ivan took the kids with him for the evening visit. They were subdued in their mother's presence. They spoke quietly as though they were afraid that a loud noise would break her. They maintained a distance from the wires and protruding steel, but she smiled through her discomfort, insisting she was fine and that everything was going to be all right. Ivan sent the kids to the canteen so that he and their mother could talk, but first he offered to help his wife adjust an awkwardly positioned pillow. Norma accepted his assistance and was grateful for it. He had just placed his phone on her locker when it rang. Mary's name appeared. He silenced the call, noticing Norma's fearful expression. He realized it was a link to all those who judged her.

"It was Mary. She's been worried about you," he said.

It was obvious she didn't believe him.

"We weren't happy, were we?" he asked.

"No," she mumbled.

"No," he agreed, "but I would have stayed with you until the end."

She raised a hand as if to defend herself.

"You were right to walk away. I'm glad you did what you did. You knew something was wrong and you were brave enough to make a change." He smiled at her surprise. She hadn't expected gratitude. Norma's eyes sprang a leak. "Marriages break up, Norma. And no matter what is said or done, everyone knows there are two sides to every story." He tried to take her hand but she pulled it away.

"Easy for you to say. You're not the bitch who broke up her family!" Tears ran down her swollen face. "You're not the one who got what she deserved."

"My father always says a small town is like a big family. It doesn't matter what you do or where you go, you're always welcome home. People still care, Norma."

She remained silent. A minute or maybe two passed, then Ivan stood and put on his jacket. He leaned down to kiss the small area of undamaged forehead. Then he paused. "You have a lot of thinking to do," he said at last, "but you need to know this."

She looked at him quizzically.

"I'm taking the kids."

She nodded.

"I'm taking them home for good."

Her eyes filled.

"I didn't fight you before because I believed they were best off with you. I was wrong. If you choose to stay here, you'll be alone."

Tears slid down her face but she was in no shape to argue. "I thought it was all a little too good to be true," she muttered.

"I meant what I said. I'm glad you left. It nearly killed me but I'm glad. This isn't about punishing you. It's about our children. Deep down you know that to be true. You've been hurt enough, Norma. You're in a terrible place but you'll make your way back, and when you do we'll be waiting."

"Don't take them, Ivan!" she begged.

"I have to," he said, turned his back and walked away to the sound of her cries.

Outside he wiped away his own tears. *I'm so sorry, love.*

# 18. Beauty and the Beast

It was a beautiful spring day. The kind of day that instils a sense of wellbeing in even the most troubled soul – bright green grass, healthy brown bark and deep green leaves on branches that spread out against a translucent blue sky. Light shone down on the pretty town and with it came a heat that was more than the effect of global warming.

Sam had started his day with a walk down by the back of the pier. He lay on the grass and stared into the blue sky with a light heart. He had come to love this little place. He had come to feel a part of it. No journey would go uninterrupted by "Hello!" or "How are you?" No distance was travelled without a beep or a wave or a hat tipped in his direction. He was known. He was liked. And even though he hadn't made those around him aware of his past, he was no longer a stranger to the people of Kenmare. For the most part they didn't really care where he'd come from or who he used to be. They only cared about who he was now. Gossip mostly favours the present tense and he was grateful for that.

He had thought about coming clean with Mary. He figured she deserved to know the truth. She knew he was hiding and he knew it was only a matter of time before his past caught up with his present. The problem with enlightening her was a simple one. He had grown used to not hating himself and it felt good. That said, he was always on the verge of, and one memory away from, feeling sick. At home he was surrounded by those he had disappointed. They stood before him like mirrors reflecting his every flaw. Here it was different: he had a clean slate. If he told Mary the truth she would become another mirror he had to escape. He didn't want that. He couldn't bear the idea of losing sight of her – and not because he was foolish enough to believe in the possibility of a soul-mate. Neither was he stupid enough to think that because his skin tingled in her presence it meant anything more than physical attraction. His senses were often heightened in the presence of a woman he wished to invade. But he would never invade Mary. Instead he yearned to crawl inside her because someone unseen was whispering to him that in her he would find home.

It was such a beautiful spring day that Mary arranged a facial. Spring was a time for buds, lambing, blue skies and exfoliation. She was booked in for midday at Gemma's on Main Street. Of course she was fifteen minutes early, having miscalculated the time it would take to find parking.

Patty Winslow was sitting by the window, reading a well-worn copy of *The Canterbury Tales* while enjoying a complimentary cappuccino. "Hello, dear," she said, once she'd fixed her glasses on her nose.

"Hi, Patty."

"A little restoration?" Patty suggested.

"Something like that."

Patty dropped her book and sat back to look at her.

"What?" Mary asked, a little uncomfortable under scrutiny.

"You appear tired."

"I haven't been sleeping," Mary admitted.

"I haven't seen dark circles the like of that since Marianne Faithfull was a teenager in love."

"Well, I'm afraid it's not love keeping me up all night," Mary told her.

"And of that you're sure?"

She sighed. "We're just friends, Patty."

Patty chuckled to herself.

The Italian girl at the counter told Mary in broken English that the beautician was running a little late and asked if she would like coffee. Mary asked for a cappuccino. The girl looked at her in horror, shook her head incredulously, and made her way to the kitchen.

"Who is she?" Mary asked.

"Ah, the lovely Lucia!" Patty said, amused. "You see, it's nearly midday. You ordered what is essentially a breakfast drink, which upset the poor girl's sensibilities. Italians take coffee drinking very seriously."

"Really?" Mary mused.

"Oh, yes," Patty responded. "It really is a wonder how Italy isn't and never has been a superpower."

Mary laughed. She couldn't help but enjoy her upper-class British friend's acerbic wit.

Lucia arrived with the coffee. Mary introduced herself and welcomed the girl to Kenmare. Lucia melted and Mary's ignorance was forgiven. "I come to learn," she said.

"You're doing great."

Lucia raised an eyebrow. "Doing great?"

"Doing well," Mary amended.

"OK," said Lucia. "Yes." She smiled. "Nails?" She pointed to her own hand.

"No, but thanks."

"OK," she said, with a smile, and went back to the desk.

Patty grinned. "You have such a way with people."

Mary nudged her.

"So, how's Ivan?" Patty asked.

"He's fine – he's great, in fact. His kids are home and things seem to be going well with Sienna."

"Splendid."

"It is," Mary agreed.

"And Norma?"

"She's still in hospital and after that he doesn't know."

"Of course she'll come home," Patty said. "Where else would she go?"

"I don't know. Either way I hope she finds some peace."

"And you, my dear?"

"Me?"

"Have you found peace?"

"I haven't given up," Mary answered, with a lying smile.

"Any day now," Patty said, "any day now." She patted Mary's arm. "You just be careful not to miss out. Keep your eyes and heart wide open."

Enjoying Patty's honesty, Mary took a chance. "Patty?"

"Yes, dear."

"You and my dad – are you together?"

Patty smiled to herself. "If we are, then I'm certain neither of us would ever admit to it."

"Why?" Mary asked.

"Because, my dear, mystery is half the fun."

It was then that Gemma emerged from Room One with Penny trailing behind her. Gemma apologized to both ladies for the delay. She told Patty to make herself comfortable in Room Two while she took money from Penny. Tina would be taking care of Mary but she was just freshening up Room Three. Once payment was received, Gemma scurried into Room Two to Patty.

Penny sat beside Mary. "Well?" Penny said.

"Well?" Mary smiled – although she was shocked by Penny's appearance.

"Are you well?"

"I am."

"I've been so busy."

"I know."

"I've missed you," Penny said.

"Missed you too."

"Mary, I've been working on an article . . ." She didn't get to finish as Lucia returned, pointed at her cup and uttered, "Again?"

"No," Penny said sheepishly. She had already indulged in four of the strongest espressos in an attempt to disguise the smell of booze, which had seemed determined to seep from every pore.

Lucia left them alone.

"Are you free later?" Penny asked, having decided that the waiting area in a beauty parlour was not the ideal place to break news she needed to break.

"Sorry," Mary said. "I'm taking Sam to visit Dick Dogs."

Penny reeked of booze and now Mary acknowledged that her friend had a drinking problem. *What now? What can I do?*

"Dick Dogs?" Penny repeated.

"He used to be friends with Sam's grandmother's brother," Mary explained.

"Don't waste your time on him, Mary," Penny warned.

"Excuse me?"

"You don't know him."

Tina emerged from Room Three before Mary had time to respond. She didn't say goodbye to Penny – she was so hurt by Penny's cryptic words. Instead she just followed Tina into the small room filled with scented candles and soft music.

Penny left immediately, knowing Mary wouldn't be calling her and berating herself for not telling her friend why she had offered such advice. It was clear that the man had found his way through the armour that shielded Mary from most. It was even clearer that in exposing him Penny was risking her friendship. She didn't want to lose Mary, yet instinct told her to publish. The story was ready to go – she was just waiting on one thing. It was a long shot but still a possibility. Mia Johnson was scheduled to play at Wembley the following weekend. Then she had one day off before she played in Dublin. Penny was waiting to see if Mia would take the time to travel to a small town in Kerry to talk to the woman who was about to expose her errant boyfriend – or, indeed, face the man himself. After all, it would make an excellent ending, and if she didn't, well, that suggested another kind of ending. Either way, it was a story worth telling.

Mary needed to know who she was allowing to steal her heart. He was dangerous and hadn't the capacity to love, only to hurt. Mary had already been through hell and high water. Penny might lose her friend through exposing Sam for the selfish, weak bastard he was, but at least she would save her from grievous heartache. *She's suffered enough.*

Tina had lived in Kenmare for five years. She was a born-and-bred Dubliner and she didn't mind admitting to anyone who would listen that the transition from city to country was a bitch. She would never have dreamed of moving to a small town in Kerry had it not been that she'd met the love of her life in the Big Tree on Gardiner Street one Saturday night before an All Ireland final. At first she couldn't understand his thick culchie accent and he found her flat Dublinese as difficult, but by the end of that night, language had lost meaning and within five months they were engaged. She had settled in well, and even she would admit that, although Kenmare was full of culchies, two of whom were her children, and although she had to travel to find a branch of Next, the quality of life was far superior to what she had left behind. And although her extended family had spent a great deal of their time slagging her off about her move, it was all she could do to stop them visiting every chance they got. She enjoyed her job at the salon: it was a hub of activity and rarely did anything go on in the town that was not first discussed or revealed there.

While she was cleansing Mary's face she filled her in on her theory regarding the parentage of a local teenager's newborn.

"I didn't even know she was pregnant!"

"You and the rest of us, honey. Josie Riordan says she didn't know herself. She went into the hospital with suspected appendicitis."

"No!"

"Oh, you're way behind. It's bleedin' bizarre in this day and age not to know you're pregnant and it's not like the young one's mental."

"Maybe she was just scared to say anything," Mary surmised.

"That one? She's a cheeky mare. I don't know kids today. It wouldn't have happened in our time."

"Tina ..." Mary said, about to remind her that she herself had been a teenage mother.

"It was out before I thought. Jaysus, Mary, I'm sorry." Mary laughed.

After that Tina was silent, busy massaging Mary's face and shoulders. Her embarrassment made her work harder at relaxing her client. By the time she left her alone for fifteen minutes with a face-pack on, Mary was fast asleep.

Mary was standing on an empty street. She looked up and saw the red light glowing above her head, then at the ground where it was reflected in the rainwater pooling by the grate at the side of the road. *Oh, no. Not again.* The familiar teenage boy with a hood pulled tight over his face came around the corner. *Please let me go!* He was running as before and she could taste his panic. She watched him turn in time to see the boys following. *Run!* she screamed. *Run!* But she'd seen this movie before and, no matter how long or hard she called, the boy would be caught. *Please don't make me watch this!* she cried, into the night sky. *I don't want to be here!*

She turned away when one of the boys grabbed him. She heard the thud as the boy hit the ground. She heard him cry out as the blows connected. *I won't watch it!* she roared. *Do you hear me? I won't watch it!* She tried to flee the scene but every corner she turned brought her back. The boy leaning against the car was grinning sadistically, watching as the boy was kicked. Darkness seeped from his every pore. She wanted to hurt him. Violence welled inside her.

"Look, Topher's excited!" he sneered.

*Oh, no!*

"Give him a go!"

The boy-bear called Topher moved in and the others made way, leaving the hooded boy on the ground, too badly beaten to run. She felt his broken knuckles clutching at his face and saw his body curl into the foetal position.

*I'm so sorry! I'm so sorry!*

Gemma had finished Patty's pedicure and now had time to drink some coffee and berate Tina for not getting the scoop on whether Mary was getting it together with the cute American. Tina explained that she couldn't ask in the wake of her *faux pas*. Gemma laughed.

"Excuse me, I'm not from here – I can't remember every little bleedin' thing!" Tina snapped.

"There's definitely something." Gemma ignored her employee's outburst. "I mean, he was staying in her house for over a week."

"I heard she made him sleep on the floor," said Tina, conspiratorially.

"Dr Macken told her to!" Gemma informed her.

"My arse! My father's had a bad back for twenty years and I've never seen him lying on a floor."

"Have you seen Mary and the American tagging trees?" Gemma queried.

"That's so weird! I heard he's looking for something belonging to his granny."

"Excuse me?"

"That's the word on the street. Some say there's something buried under one."

"Jesus. It could be anything."

"I'd say it's jewellery," said Tina. "Obviously valuable or he wouldn't go to the trouble."

"And he visits that tree, the one where her little boy died. He's been seen there a number of times."

"Why would he do that?"

"I don't know. It's weird. They must be together."

"I'm not so sure – I always thought she was a lesbian."

"Sure, didn't we all? Herself and Penny made a lovely couple to most people's minds – until we found out that the bold Penny was servicing a married man all these years!" Gemma giggled. "People never fail to entertain."

"Speaking of which, she was reeking of wine this morning," Tina commented.

"Isn't she always? Brona in the off-licence maintains she's never out of the place."

It was at this point that they heard crying in Room Three. They stared at one another. Gemma was the first to move towards the door, with Tina following.

*"Run! Run!"*

"Is she saying 'run'?" Gemma asked Tina.

*"Please don't make me watch this!"*

"Wha' is she on?" Tina asked Gemma.

*"I don't want to be here! I won't watch it. Do you hear me? I won't watch it!"*

"She's crying," Gemma said, with her hand on the door, which she opened to reveal a sleeping Mary. It was clear she was very distressed – her face was wet with tears and her face-pack ruined.

*"I'm so sorry!"* she screamed, so loudly that Tina jumped.

It was then that Gemma gently took her client's hand and called her softly. "Mary! Wake up!"

"I'm so sorry!" Mary sobbed.

Tina started to cry. It was terribly upsetting to see such a strong woman crumble.

"It's all right, Mary, come back to us," Gemma said, squeezing her hand gently.

It was then that Mary woke to find her face a mess and an audience around her.

"You gave us a fright," Gemma said, but she didn't elaborate.

"Sorry – it was just a nightmare," Mary stammered.

"Let me fix your face," Tina said, wiping away her own tears, but Mary was too embarrassed – she just wanted to clean off the gunk and leave. Later she would hear bits and pieces of the story as to how Mary of the Sorrows lost it in Room Three.

# 19. People in glasshouses

At eighty-nine years of age, Dick Dogs was now a full-time resident of a local old folks' home. It perched on a hillock overlooking a spectacular and colourful view that, ironically, most of the residents were unable to see.

In the wake of her embarrassment in the local beauty parlour, and the headache brought on by having to watch a young man's agony, Mary had asked Ivan to accompany Sam in her place. He had brought a box of boiled sweets, which were immediately confiscated by Paula Dubury, who wondered aloud if he was intending to kill her residents. Sam had brought ice-cream, one of the few things his grandmother had enjoyed after her stroke. Paula smiled at him: not only had he presented the old man with a gift that wouldn't lodge in his windpipe but also he was a vision in jeans and a white T-shirt. Among friends, she'd later compare him to James Dean in *Rebel Without a Cause* – and mention that since Ivan had met Sienna he had definitely put on a little weight, not that she minded much. As one of his early conquests, she'd had a soft spot for him since before his marriage to Norma.

Dick was as blind as a bat and deaf in one ear. Paula directed Ivan to the old man's right side and Ivan reminded Dick of who he was before he introduced him to Sam.

"Sullivan, you say?" Dick shouted at Ivan.

"That's right," Ivan agreed.

"Which Sullivan?"

"He's not from around here. His granny was a Breslin."

"Ah, Lena!" he said immediately, and Sam's heart skipped a beat.

"That's right!" Sam roared.

"Ah, Lena," he repeated, "my good friend David's sister and the best-looking girl in the town!" He smiled, revealing a mouth empty of teeth. "She was a rare one."

Sam didn't know how to respond, but the old man was grinning madly at the memory of a young beauty.

"I'm glad she escaped," he said, after a moment. "That fire, what a terrible thing! No one survived. My good friend David – I hope he slept through it. 'Twas a terrible thing to see." The old man had tears in his eyes now. "The smell was the worst of it." He covered his nose as though he could smell it still. "I'm glad she escaped it." He paused. "They're all ghosts now. Laid to rest. They were lucky in their sleep." He laughed a little to himself.

Later, as Ivan and Sam walked down the pathway to their cars, under Paula's watchful eye, Sam admitted that maybe it was time he, too, laid his grandmother to rest. He hadn't found her inscription on the hundreds of trees he had tagged and now, on a bright spring day, the task seemed impossible. After all, his grandmother's graffito had been the work of a bored teenager and hardly a message from the grave to her adoring grandson. Ivan had patted Sam on the back and mentioned that perhaps when he'd arrived in Kenmare he'd needed a project to fill his time and now he'd enough to do without it. Sam nodded at his astute friend because he was right. It had occurred to him that during the hours he'd spent tagging trees he'd been able to work out many of the things he'd refused to touch in therapy. In the woods, he'd allowed his mind to wander into times gone by, and when Mary had joined him he'd rediscovered comfort in the company of another human being.

That afternoon, with the warmth of the sun on his back, he left Dick Dogs and the ghost of his grandmother in a home on a hillock sweeping towards green crystal water overlooked by a cartoon blue sky.

It had been a long day for Penny. First there had been her awkward encounter with Mary and then an unexpected and deeply unpleasant phone call with her editor, who had called to advise that he had sold the story on to a daily tabloid newspaper that would run it the very next day. Penny was appalled. Her editor informed her that the money they'd receive would pay her salary for the next two years and that they just didn't have the power to break such a story. He explained that the daily had enough contacts to check Penny's facts and a legal team behind them to fight any action Mia Johnson might wish to take.

"We're just too small," he said.

"You mean we've got no balls!" she had said angrily.

"You still get credited but not as the writer."

"So I'm the source? The sell-out, the fucking nark?"

"It's a tabloid story and we're not a tabloid."

"It was my story," she said, battling to hide the shake in her voice.

"Not any more," he said, and hung up.

And there it was. Penny's pet project had blown up in her face. Not only had she not told her best friend she was working on it but now it was being retold by another writer who, no doubt, would subvert every element so that only poison would emerge. Penny was not Sam's biggest fan but she wasn't stupid either and, despite her inexplicable distaste for the man, her better self had ensured that the second draft of her article had been balanced. Now the story was out of her hands and, worse, she would be credited. *Oh, God, Mary, please don't hate me!*

The phone rang just after eleven p.m., waking Penny from a drunken nap. The shrill voice hurt her sore head and it was a moment before she worked out who was speaking. Adam's wife's voice was distinctive with her Dutch accent. Penny was caught off-guard and the call had been a long time coming.

"You selfish bitch!" Alina correctly asserted.

Penny had known for a long time that putting her needs above those of Adam's wife and children was indeed selfish. She had no real answer to the accusation thrown at her.

"I'm sorry," she said, with her head in her hands.

"You're sorry?" came her adversary's disbelieving reply.

"I am. I'm sorry he married you when he was in love with me. I'm sorry I couldn't have loved someone else. I'm sorry your marriage is a joke and I'm sorry that I'm alone. I'm sorry for a lot of things – for you, for your kids, for me and for him. I spend most of my time being sorry."

For a moment there was silence at the end of the line and Penny wondered if her accuser would hang up.

"All you had to do was stay away," Adam's wife snapped.

"If only I could have." Tears escaped and raced down her cheeks.

"I hate you!"

"I hate you more," Penny replied. "And I'm sorry for that."

Then she hung up and threw the phone against the wall while she rocked and wailed, allowing all her pent-up pain to spill out.

It wasn't her broken phone that woke Penny the very next morning. Instead it was the incessant knocking and sustained ringing of the front-door bell. She dragged herself out of her bed and had barely unlatched the door when Mary stormed past her to the kitchen. Penny followed, mentally preparing herself for the onslaught. The newspaper was balled in her friend's hand and red-ringed eyes suggested that she was very upset.

"I'm sorry," Penny said, putting her hands in her pockets to conceal the shaking.

"I don't understand," Mary said, eyes filling. "How could you? How could you not even tell me?"

"I was going to. It wasn't supposed to come out until after Mia played Wembley next week. My editor sold it on. I swear I didn't know."

"You didn't know. *You* did this, Penny! *You* did it!" Mary slumped onto a chair.

"Have you spoken to him?"

"What would I say?"

Penny shook her head. "I know you're angry but I didn't mean for it to happen this way. It was a good story and I'm a journalist."

"That article is nothing but gossip-ridden tat. You think there's merit in destroying a person?"

"Your friend was the one who did the destroying," Penny defended herself.

"Really?" There was steel in Mary's voice.

"He's devastated everyone he's ever known. He was a heroin addict, for Jesus' sake – and, frankly, since he's come here he's been playing you for a fool. He's dangerous and not to be trusted."

"Why? Because he was an addict? That's rich coming from you!"

"What's that supposed to mean?"

"You want to know?" Mary asked, giving Penny a way out – but Penny didn't take it.

"Yeah, I want to know."

Mary went to the sitting room and returned with a few empty vodka bottles, which she placed in front of Penny. She went to the fridge and opened it. It was empty. She went to the bag that lay by the bin and untied the knot. White and red wine bottles and numerous cans spilled from it.

"How dare you?" Penny said, fighting tears.

"Is that it? How dare I? No excuses? No bullshit about an impromptu party or your editor and his wife coming to dinner or that it's been months since you've been to the bottle bank?"

"*Get out!*" Penny roared, so loudly that it was possible her neighbours heard.

"My pleasure." Mary grabbed her bag.

She made it to the car before she began to cry. It was ironic that she had intended to visit her friend to address her drinking problem that morning. Jerry Letter had called with a copy of the article. She had read it in disbelief. Hurt and shock had followed. Mostly she felt bitterly let down by both Sam and Penny. Penny had borne the brunt of it, but why wouldn't she? She was supposed to be Mary's best friend, not her worst enemy.

Penny was left shaking from her encounter with her best friend. She picked up the crumpled paper and straightened it on the table. The picture was of Mia. The story was about Mia. Sam was reduced to a footnote in the story of someone far more interesting to the public. He was merely the latest crisis that Mia had had to overcome: falling sales, a failing relationship with a man once her Svengali, then a junkie in her bed. A junkie whom she'd saved so that he could walk away from her. How Mia had suffered! How devastated she must be! How would this affect her new album? How would it affect her sell-out show at Wembley? A show that had previously been cancelled so that she could be at the side of her deadbeat boyfriend. Did his defection mean that the end of her career was in sight, or would she rise from the ashes, as the title of her first album, *Phoenix*, implied?

Penny realized now that the reason she hadn't lasted in the city was because she wasn't very good at her job. She had foolishly believed that because Sam Sullivan's life was interesting to her it would be interesting to others. How stupid of her! Of course Mia was the story. Who the fuck was Sam Sullivan? All this time she'd worried that Sam would make a fool of Mary but in the end the only fool was her. *You're such a loser.*

She cleared up the bottles. She walked around in circles, not sure what to do or what to think. Her best friend had turned on her. Mary had been venomous. She had humiliated and insulted her and, OK, she had been upset about the article but Penny hadn't done anything to deliberately hurt her while Mary had sought to destroy Penny, trying to make out that she was an alcoholic – and maybe she was. She knew she drank too much and maybe, if she tried, she'd find it difficult to stop – or maybe she wouldn't. Besides, Mary's intervention hadn't been prompted by concern: it had been an attack. She wouldn't allow herself to concentrate on Mary's accusations. She wouldn't allow herself to think about them – because Mary was right. She cleaned the house, even scrubbing the bathrooms in the hope that hard labour would silence her conscience. *I made a mistake. I didn't mean to hurt anyone. I don't need her. I don't need anybody.*

After Mary's ugly encounter with Penny, she drove first without direction but later found herself heading towards Cork. From her car, as Tina Turner blasted out "Proud Mary", which complemented Mary's hysteria beautifully, she called Ivan.

He was halfway through the article, which his mother had left for him to read. "Turn the music down," he ordered.

She switched it off.

"You've seen it," he said.

"A fascinating read." She laughed just enough to hint at the possibility of impending insanity.

"Are you OK?"

"I really cared about him." She'd given up on pretence.

" 'Care' . . . That's a funny word. I care about Mr Monkels."

"I don't know what to say."

"I thought I knew him. But how could I know him? I've had a longer relationship with an expensive night cream."

"It's a lot to take in but I'm not sure any of it changes who he is now."

"Yeah, maybe, but then again, maybe Penny's right – maybe he's made a fool of me."

"Then he's made a fool of all of us and I don't think that's true."

"Heroin," she murmured. "He told me he died once. He said he didn't see anything or believe in anything. How could he see anything when he was off his tits?"

"He came here to get better," Ivan reminded her.

"I always knew he wouldn't stay. I always knew there was something. So he gets better and I get worse!" Her laughter was fat with tears. "I was OK. I was content with my lot. I didn't care – I didn't want to."

"You can't go back. You've come alive again, Mary. Don't lament that," Ivan warned. "If you thank him for nothing, thank him for that."

"Heroin," she repeated, in disbelief. "The article refers to him as a pathetic junkie."

There was silence for a moment while Mary absorbed this new information. "And of all the frigging ex-girlfriends! What next? Demi Moore was his babysitter or Julia Roberts was his prom date?"

Ivan laughed a little but he didn't say anything. Mary didn't need to hear the hint of excitement his voice would betray. *Mia Johnson – that lucky bastard!*

It was Ivan who broke the news of Sam's exposure to him. He did so over the phone in a stilted manner that suggested his own hurt and hinted at a little anger. Sam was gracious and thanked his friend for the tip-off.

"So it's true?" Ivan asked.

"It's true I was a heroin addict. It's true I've done a lot of things I'm not proud of."

"You're clean?" Ivan asked.

"Yes."

"You're not the man I've just read about?"

"No, I'm not," Sam said, a little relieved that his friend was giving him the benefit of the doubt.

"You should have said something."

"I needed not to be that guy for a while. Does Mary know?"

"Yes."

"She hates me."

"I don't know."

"Where is she?"

"She's gone for a drive."

"I would have said something," Sam said, "eventually."

"I hope for your sake it isn't too late," Ivan said, and hung up.

Sam sat in his sitting room. The news had acted like some sort of anaesthetic that crept through him and left him paralysed. *It's over.*

Mary had called Adam from the road. "I need to see you."

"OK."

"Where?"

"The Gingerbread House."

"I'll be there in an hour. Twelve."

"I'll be waiting."

Adam was indeed waiting. He stood up to greet her. They hugged and sat down opposite each other. "I just got some coffee," he said, indicating the large cafetière in front of him. "It's still hot – I knew you of all people wouldn't be late!" He poured her a cup.

She drank some gratefully.

"It's good to see you."

"You too," she replied, taking his hand in hers. "How've you been?" She was concerned about her friend, whose grey face belied his carefully constructed happy-go-lucky façade.

"I'm fine." He was obviously lying.

"I've had enough crap for one day. Tell me the truth."

"Alina hates me. She's so angry all the time. I think she's planning on punishing me for the rest of my life." He dropped his head to hide his face. He took a series of deep breaths and Mary gave him the room he required to compose himself. "What about Penny?" he asked, after a few minutes.

"Not good," she disclosed, through gritted teeth.

"Drinking?"

"Heavily."

"She'll cut back – she always does."

"I think it's time we all faced the fact that Penny has a real problem."

"Jesus," he shook his head, "everything's such a fucking mess."

For a moment Mary looked as if she was about to cry.

"You know there's nothing we can do," he said, with resignation that came from a childhood spent watching his mother caretake an alcoholic grandfather.

"Right now I wonder if I even care," Mary admitted.

"I read the article. Whatever's going on, I know she didn't do it to hurt you."

"But she did," Mary said, welling up.

"It's my fault."

"You certainly didn't help."

"Good old Mary. I can always count on the truth from you. I should have been a better man. Your new friend isn't the only one to have made terrible mistakes."

"We all make mistakes," she whispered to herself.

"Do you think I should call her?" he asked, knowing it was the wrong thing to do.

"No," Mary advised, "it would only make things worse and I've already done that." She sighed.

"You made it worse?" He snorted. "I think we both know that any third-party responsibility for Penny's drinking is mine, not yours."

Mary shook her head. "I was hurt and said some things. I'm not sure there's a road back for us."

"Of course there is. She won't want to lose you."

"You think? If it comes down to me or booze, will I win?"

He looked into his cup and sighed. "Has it really got that bad?"

"I think it has," she said.

He put his hand to his forehead and rubbed it as though he was trying to erase this new information. "If things are that bad there's nothing any one of us can do. It's up to her now."

"She's too far gone."

"Then it's only a matter of time."

"Until?"

"Until she hits rock bottom," he said, biting his lower lip.

Later, over lunch, they realized they were more depressing

than a Dickens novel. Adam attempted to lighten the mood. "So you'll forgive the American his omission?"

"Pretty big omission," she said lightly. Adam could always make the worst situations seem perfectly normal.

"You're telling me!" He laughed. "Half the town was on the phone about it before nine this morning."

"That's comforting." She attempted a joke.

"Mia Johnson!"

"I was thinking about the heroin!" She laughed a little.

"Why would anyone turn to drugs with a girlfriend like Mia Johnson?"

"Do you want a slap?" she couldn't help but ask.

He laughed. "You'll forgive him."

"You're probably right," she admitted, a little disgusted with herself.

"He's definitely given up all that crap?"

"Yeah," she answered. She'd spent pretty much day and night with him for several weeks, and he wouldn't have been able to hide that particular addiction. "When he was staying with me I found a stash of his painkillers under the mattress. He was in agony but he wouldn't take the pills. I thought it was weird but I suppose it makes sense now."

"Did you say anything to him?"

"No. I ignored them for a while and then one day, just before he left, I had the impulse to bin them so I did. I didn't say anything and he didn't ask."

"How does he feel about you?" Adam was happy to concentrate on someone else's pathetic love life so that, for a while, he could escape his own.

"I don't know. I'm hardly Mia Shagging Johnson, am I?"

"No, you're not, but I guess he wasn't looking for Mia

Shagging Johnson." He raised an eyebrow. "The lunatic!"

She said nothing.

"Do you trust him?" he asked, after a moment or two had passed.

"I know he's hiding something," she answered, avoiding the question.

"You mean other than being a junkie?" Adam asked, intrigued: he was well aware that Mary was more intuitive than most.

"Why would a man who has the music world at his feet, millions in the bank and a rock star in his bed turn to heroin?" She swished the wine at the bottom of her glass.

"Well, I don't know, Hetty Wainthropp. What is it they say about rock-'n'-roll excess?"

"Cocaine is excess, heroin is desperation. But, then, what do I know? I'm just a country bumpkin with voice like a crow and a flat arse."

Adam remembered the rap-music video he'd seen a few days ago in which Mia Johnson had revealed her fabulously curvaceous arse in a tiny pink bikini. *Jesus, Mary, I love you but she's a hard act to follow.*

# 20. Facing up to those who would look down

Sam woke after eight. His sleep had been broken and a familiar weight had resumed its seat at the centre of his chest. Before he had turned in for the night he had watched Mary's house with the staying power of a stalker, but she had not come home. Earlier that evening he had wondered if Mr Monkels was OK. When he jumped the wall he found the dog asleep by the kitchen window, his bowls full of water and food. He was fine. *Good.* He had long ago forgiven the dog for his back injury – anyway, it had introduced him properly to his neighbour. Without it they might still have been passing acquaintances. *Please don't hate me.*

By midday he was desperate for food and, having imprisoned himself for one entire day, he felt it was time to face his public. He showered and changed, then paced a little and finally opened his front door. He met Mossy coming out of his house.

"Well, well," Mossy said, shaking his head, "you are a dark horse."

Sam didn't know what to say so he just stood there, nodding uncomfortably.

"Mia Johnson," Mossy was still shaking his head, "I wouldn't be able for you." He laughed. "Ha!" he called, as though to himself. "Mia Johnson and a side order of smack." He laughed again. "Jesus, boy, that stuff would kill you!" He nudged Sam and gave a little wink, then walked on, giggling to himself.

*OK. That was weird.* But it was Mossy. Still, if everyone was as easy as Mossy ... *It might be OK.* He took his time walking towards town. It was well after one when he entered the bar. It seemed to be buzzing with a little more energy than usual. However, as he materialized, the buzz subsided to a lull, which in turn descended into stark silence. All faces turned to him and it was difficult to ignore the collective inquisitive stare. His destination – a table on its own at the end of the room and near the toilets – seemed a million miles away but he couldn't turn back, not while the pack lay in wait. He sat down and took up his menu, which he quickly employed as a shield. Mary was nowhere to be seen, and neither was Jack nor Ivan. *Where the hell is everyone?*

Jessie emerged from the back and, pen and notebook in hand, strode over to take his order – as pleasant as always. "What do you want?"

"World peace!" he said, attempting an ice-breaking joke but she wasn't about to thaw.

"In the event that I cannot deliver on that order, is there something you'd like off the menu?" she asked, without cracking a smile.

"I'll have coffee, and a ham, cheese and onion toasted sandwich to go." His weary tone conceded defeat.

"We don't do 'to go'," she replied haughtily.

"To stay then." He sighed.

"Fine," she agreed, and strode back to base in the same military manner as she'd come over to him.

Now that she'd gone he realized that all eyes were averted and the buzz, although hushed, was returning. He wasn't close enough to hear his fellow diners' muted conversations but neither was he blind to the occasional eye cast upon him before a mouth was cupped and a head bent towards a companion.

Mary's father emerged from the kitchen with his coffee and sandwich. He took the chair opposite. "I thought you could stand to see a friendly face," he said, with a smile.

"Thanks, Jack. I appreciate that."

"You have the whole town talking," Jack said, absent-mindedly wiping the table.

"I get that."

"Ah, what harm?" He grinned widely enough to reveal a gold tooth. "Sure wouldn't it be worse if they weren't talking?"

"Not really. No."

"I suppose not. Still, it's something to pass the day and, after all, it's only talk and not the end of the world, now, is it?"

"I guess not," Sam conceded, trying hard not to sound like a teenager.

Jack nodded and got up.

"So Mary's not in today?" Sam said, hoping that any anxiety he felt was undetectable in his voice.

"She took a few days off."

Jack had demanded she get some rest, having been informed of his daughter's near-breakdown in Gemma Gibney's beauty shop.

"Oh. OK." Sam nodded. "Thanks."

"Son?"

"Yeah?"

"She comes across as tough as old boots but she's not. She's had it hard enough."

"Yes, sir," he heard himself say.

Jack left him to his coffee and unwanted toasted sandwich. Luckily lunchtime for the workers was approaching an end and the place was emptying out. He was sipping his coffee when he felt someone stand over him. He turned to see a woman whose face and name he recognized but with whom he had previously had no contact. Bridget the Bike.

"Hi, I'm Bridget Browne." She held out her hand and he took it. They shook. "Look, I just wanted to say that soon it will be somebody else's turn."

"You're so sure?" He almost laughed.

"I was the previous occupant of those boots you've just stepped into."

"Ah." He was enjoying her turn of phrase despite the circumstances.

"So, thanks for that." She smiled.

"You're welcome."

"It'll be OK. It always is."

At home that evening he attempted to watch a show from season two of *The West Wing*. Mary had presented him with the DVD box set on the day she'd helped him shop for a TV. He was finding it difficult to concentrate. Josh had just explained the super-string theory to Leo, and Toby seemed to be losing it with CJ but none of it was filtering through the haze that separated his visual cortex from his brainstem. *The West Wing* demanded the kind of attention that Sam couldn't commit to it so he switched it off and went into the garden. He sat on a plastic chair and took some deep breaths, focusing on the wall that separated his garden from his neighbour's.

He must have fallen asleep because the next thing he

knew he was cold, had a crick in his neck and his watch revealed it was after ten. Mary must have returned because Mr Monkels was in the back sniffing a bucket.

He went and knocked on her door but there was no response. He also peered through the window and called her name. He hoped she wasn't hiding from him but feared she might be.

He decided to go for a walk to clear his head. He found her sitting on the bench by the pier, looking out over the water and seemingly mesmerized by a bobbing red buoy. He sat down beside her. She remained still for a few moments, but then she switched off her Walkman and removed her earphones. "How does it feel to be the talk of the town?" she asked, without looking at him.

"I'm guessing you know."

"They'll get tired of it and soon enough the town spotlight will descend on somebody else," she said evenly.

"Bridget Browne was kind enough to tip me off."

"Well, she's certainly qualified to know," she said.

"She was kind," he muttered, and she faced him.

"Well, that's the thing about small towns. Everybody knows everybody else's business so sniggering and judgement usually follow, but when it's important all that fades away and what's left is solidarity. Maybe if you'd known that, you could have trusted us."

"I shouldn't have lied."

"Everybody lies," Mary replied, a little sadly.

"I should have told you about my past."

"So why didn't you?"

"I was afraid. I hadn't been a decent person for such a long time."

His eyes were dark and the melancholy she had seen in them that first night had returned. "And you're a better man now?" she asked.

"I'm trying to be," he said quietly, his eyes cast down.

"And your girlfriend?" she said, after a moment.

His eyes locked with hers and they shared a terrible sadness. "I didn't love her."

She turned back to the water.

After a few minutes she faced him again. "I need some space," she said.

"Because of my past?"

"No, because of mine. When I'm around you I feel like I'm falling. I need to stop before I smash into the ground."

"Are you always so honest?"

"No. Mostly I'm a liar like you."

"I don't want to lose you."

"But you won't be staying here."

"You don't know that," he mumbled.

"Yeah, I do," she said sadly, and stood up.

He grabbed her hand and held it until she pulled it away. Desolate now, he nodded. This was the first time either had shown their true feelings – and all at once it was over.

"I just need some time," she said, and left him with the bobbing red buoy for company.

*She knows. She knows I'm not worth it.*

On the day that the article was published about Mia Johnson, Penny began a week of self-induced oblivion. She'd requested a two-week leave of absence and because she rarely took holidays, her editor – the traitor – was happy to agree. She'd stocked up on booze and snacks in Killarney and, on returning home, she'd parked her car in her garage. Once inside she'd pulled out the plug on her home phone, switched off her mobile, locked the doors, closed the curtains and opened the first of many bottles, thus beginning a long descent to a place that Dante had termed *The Inferno*.

A few days had passed when she heard knocking. She wasn't sure how long Ivan had stayed there, interspersing the banging with calling her name, because she had drifted off to sleep in the middle. It might have been seconds or hours. *Just go away*. The second time she'd woken, all was quiet. The vodka bottle was nearly empty. She got up and went into the kitchen, opened the fridge and placed the near-empty bottle beside a fresh one, which was close to some eggs that she considered frying. Her stomach turned. She closed the fridge, then reconsidered. She opened the fridge again, took out the near-empty bottle and put it into the freezer. She switched on the oven timer for ten minutes, then sat on the floor and watched the countdown.

When the buzzer sounded, she opened the freezer, took out the bottle, downed the contents and spluttered. *This is the life*.

Four days into her binge, she had decided to open her laptop and write down why she felt she was a drunk. Even though she had drunk two bottles of vodka before midday she felt surprisingly lucid and it seemed a tremendous idea. She entitled the Word document "Why?" She took a drink from a fresh bottle of vodka, with a dash of lime. *Nice*. After a moment or two, with her muse coursing down her throat, she was ready to begin. She flexed her fingers and wiped the residual spittle from her lips.

She decided to title each paragraph and her diatribe went as follows:

# Why?

## Parents

My mother was on the pill, *ergo* my conception was as a result of a nasty case of the trots. Apparently my unlucky parents had decided against having children, even considering abortion, but then Catholic guilt set in and the fear of an angry God ensured that I would survive gestation to emerge into a world that didn't give a fuck. Were my parents cruel? Certainly not intentionally – but being cruel requires giving attention, which is something neither could afford. Do I wish I was aborted? Yes. It would have been kinder. Did my parents love me? How could they? I was fed and clothed. I was educated and then nothing. They don't even know me. I don't know them. Aren't parents supposed to know their kids? Aren't they supposed to care? So I wasn't abused. But was I neglected? Doesn't it mean something when you feel closer to your best friend's dad than you do to your own? Why didn't they care? Was it me? Why was it that when I was born the change that occurs in everyone else's parents didn't occur in mine? Where was my unconditional love? How is it that I could be so alone from such a young age? Why didn't they love me? Why didn't they love me? Why?

## Adam

He was my world. He promised me he would wait. He told me he loved me and I believed him. I believed him because he did love me. It was real, it just wasn't enough. He picked his wife over me. He picked his kids over me. Funny how the man I love and who loves me would choose his children and misery over me, and my father would choose his stupid job. Is it me? It must be. There is an emptiness in me that is noticeable. I couldn't make Adam happy. Just like his wife, I would be a letdown. That's why he left: deep down he knows there is nothing to me. How could there be? That night when we danced in the garden and when he said goodbye, I wanted to die. I desperately wanted to die. Why? What is wrong with me? Why can't I get over him? Why can't I just feel normal? Why won't he choose me? Why won't he choose me? Why?

*Mary*

She gave me hope. That first day on the train to Dublin she sat beside me and when she looked at me she made me feel like I was special. Together we were popular and she brought out all that was good and funny in me. Her encouragement ensured that I would strive to be the entertainer. Now I am the consummate entertainer but to be that I needed help. Why? I wanted to make her happy. I wanted to make her laugh. And now she judges me. She got pregnant and I was there for her. She nearly died and I nearly died with her. She lost her son and disappeared but I stayed with her because I loved her through it all. How hard is it to stay with someone so destroyed? Fucking hard. How hard is it to witness desperation? It's a nightmare. Watching the person you care about utterly decimated is tantamount to a knife cutting through bone. I didn't desert her. Has she deserted me? Worse, has she deserted me for some prick she doesn't even know? The girl who was once impenetrable now reduced to a sucker for an arsehole. Heroin is forgivable but alcohol is not? Why has she chosen him over me? Why has she deserted me? Why?

*Me*

I am nothing.

After that she stopped writing. She went to the fridge and pulled out a cold bottle of vodka, opened it and drank from the neck because she was thirsty, because she was desperate, but mostly because she wanted to vanish.

She lost track of time as the days blended into each other. She ignored the doorbell. One morning she woke to find a card on her mat. It was from Mary. She had written one word: *Sorry.* Penny tore it up, binned it, and then she cried until she was sure there was nothing left. A while later she began to feel hungry for something other than a bag of crisps, but she didn't want to stop drinking long enough to sober up so she called a taxi to take her to a little pub that served traditional fare just outside the town.

She found a quiet corner booth and hid there drinking while she picked at a plateful of cottage pie and salad. It was when she got up to go to the Ladies that she saw Ivan and Sam. However, she felt sure they didn't see her. She washed her face with cold water and cursed herself for leaving her coat in her seat. She hadn't paid either so she couldn't leave. She knew she could return to her table without them noticing her but she couldn't risk attracting the attention of the barman – and she'd been waiting for him to approach her for a while. She needed another drink. *Damn it.* She emerged from the Ladies and gingerly made her way back to her seat.

The men had their backs to her and were deep in conversation. She wished she was a fly on the wall – but of course she didn't need to overhear what Sam was saying. He was probably tearing her apart and Ivan had been nodding so he was probably agreeing. *Bastards.* She could hear them laughing. *At me?* Of course. She heard them get up so she pressed herself into her seat and they passed her without spotting her. *Thank God,* she thought, and ordered another drink.

Much later, when the same taxi man who had dropped her off had collected her and helped her inside, she flipped open her laptop and opened her document to add Ivan's name to the list of reasons she was finding for being a drunk.

*Ivan*
He's a backstabbing bastard.

She woke some time in the afternoon a week after the article had been published. Her head hurt, her breath stank and she was so dehydrated that her skin was flaking. She decided to clean up. Enough was enough. She couldn't go on as she had been. She accepted that she didn't want to. She even considered getting help. She poured the last of the booze stash down the drain. She showered and made herself some toast, which she barely nibbled. She opened her laptop and looked through her emails. All were work-related, even though her colleagues were well aware that she was on holiday. She opened up the document that blamed everyone and everything for her problems.

"Stupid girl," she heard herself say. She missed Mary and Ivan, but mostly she missed Adam. She watched an afternoon movie, but by seven she was pacing the floor with her head in her hands, her body screaming.

While Penny spent a week drinking, Mary was catching up on sleep and work. Sam played guitar, took long walks, ate late suppers in restaurants now busy with tourists. He had read, listened to music and once he'd even sat in the large empty church, soaking up the silence and contemplating his own Catholic upbringing. His mother was of Irish-Catholic descent, his father Irish-Polish Catholic. His mother had gone to a Catholic girls' school and his father had been taught by the Christian Brothers. They had met at a Catholic dance, aged seventeen and eighteen respectively. They were married at twenty-two and -three in a big traditional Catholic wedding. He had been baptized, he'd made his First Communion and was confirmed. For his first fifteen years he had sat in one of God's many houses on Sunday after Sunday and yet, aside from stillness, churches and Catholicism had nothing to offer him.

He looked around him at stone and tile, stained glass and candles. He could smell incense and hear the whispered prayer of a nun. He left unsurprised that, for him, it still held nothing. The nightmares had returned and no amount of guitar-playing, late suppers or even religion would make them go away.

Mid-week he'd met Ivan for a pint in a small bar a few miles outside town. Ivan had only an hour to spare as the kids had come home with him and he didn't like leaving them with a frazzled Sienna. He filled Sam in on how his ex-wife was coping and when she would be released from hospital. They discussed her indecision as to whether or not to press charges against her boyfriend and, more importantly, whether or not she would come home. Ivan was adamant that the bastard who had broken her deserved everything he got, but he was afraid she would go back to him.

Halfway through his pint, Ivan had mentioned another fear he'd harboured since he'd first seen his wife twisted and bloody. "You don't think he would have forced himself on her?" he'd asked, and Sam had nearly dropped his glass.

"Has she said anything?" he asked, recovering.

"No. And I can hardly ask her."

"I doubt it," Sam said, and finished his pint. "Just because he hits it doesn't mean he . . ." He didn't finish his sentence.

"You're right. But if I ever find out he did, I'll hunt him down and I'll kill him," Ivan said, with conviction.

"If you find he did, I'll be happy to help you," Sam said.

"You're a good friend," Ivan said. "For a junkie!" He laughed at his own wit.

Sam had become used to his past indiscretions being joked about, and he was smart enough to know that, although they teased, those around him would not tolerate his failure to remain clean. This worried him. Each night that passed made it harder, and all the more so now that he was being watched.

They talked a little bit about the aftermath of Penny's article. The furore hadn't been as considerable as it might have been. To Ivan and, indeed, most of the townspeople, the fact that Sam had got and stayed clean was a major achievement. The man described in the newspaper was far from the one he and his fellow townspeople had come to know, and when judgement was passed, it favoured their new resident, as Mary had expected it would.

Ivan had been sheepish when he broached the subject of Sam's famous ex but he couldn't help himself. "Give me something."

"Something?" Sam was playing with his new friend.

"Anything at all."

"OK." Sam sat back in his chair. Then he put his hand to his chin.

"Oh, come on!"

"It'll stay between you and me?" Sam asked.

"Absolutely," Ivan agreed, yet both men knew Ivan couldn't hold his water.

"Horror movies turn her on."

"What do you mean?"

"I mean horror gets her really hot." She'd jumped him midway through *Scream*. "The gorier the better."

"Really? I love horror films." Ivan seemed satisfied with the titbit he'd been given. "One last thing."

"What?"

"Did you ever do J-Lo?"

Ivan seemed lighter and happier since his kids had come home, Sam thought. They had wiped the gloom from his eyes. His smile was warmer and his laugh heartier. Neither mentioned Mary, and Ivan didn't say anything when he saw a dishevelled Penny sneak into a booth. *It's not the time. God save her!*

# 21. My, oh, Mia

It was one of those days that Ben would have called yellow – bright and sunny enough for summer. Mary had just returned from a shift at the bar and was busy fixing the remote controls in line with the corner of the coffee-table when the doorbell rang. She wasn't expecting company. Penny hadn't spoken to her for more than a week. Sam was giving her the space she had asked for. Ivan was busy with his kids. She answered it, expecting to see no one in particular.

The woman at the door was very beautiful. She also seemed familiar. It only took an instant for everything to click into place. *Frigging hell!*

"Hi. I'm Mia." The rock star put out her hand.

"Mary," she replied, embarrassed by her plain name. She shook the proffered hand.

"I was looking for Sam," Mia said, having been directed to Sam's cottage by the helpful hotel manager.

"Oh," was all Mary managed. "I'm not sure. I think he's on the water."

Mia raised her perfectly arched eyebrows. "Excuse me?"

"He usually fishes with my cousin on Sundays."

"Oh," Mia sighed, "I can't imagine him fishing."

"Would you like to come in?" Mary asked tentatively, not wishing to seem pushy.

"Sure, I'd love to," Mia said, and walked past her.

"Right, then," Mary said, closing the door and freaking

out a little. She turned off Alanis Morissette in case Mia had a problem with competition. Mia didn't seem to notice. Instead she sat on the kitchen chair Sam had occupied on the many evenings Mary had cooked for him.

Mary made a pot of coffee and placed it on the table between them.

"Nice place," Mia said, looking around.

"It's OK," Mary said.

"So, you and Sam are friends?" Mia asked, studying Mary's expression. She smiled when Mary nearly spilled the coffee she had begun to pour.

"We're giving each other a little space." She regained control of the coffee pot.

"Space?" Mia queried suspiciously.

Instantly Mary regretted her comment. *Shut your mouth, Mary!* "Are you here for long?" she asked, as breezily as possible.

"Not really. I was surprised to discover he was here. He never did like the countryside."

"People change."

"Not so much."

Mary wasn't enjoying her conversation with an international rock star. It was uncomfortable, as though the women were in some unspoken competition. It made her edgy, especially as, being so ordinary, she felt at a disadvantage. "Are you hungry?" she asked, for something to say rather than out of the desire to cater. Also, her auntie Sheila often said, "When in doubt, feed someone." It made sense now, especially as Mia's stomach refused to stop gurgling.

"No, I'm fine." But then her stomach grumbled again and Mary's face suggested that, unlike most, she didn't have the good grace to ignore it. "Well, actually, I'm a little hungry."

"Good. Do you like fish?"

"I love fish."

"Shellfish?"

"Yes, please."

"How about a warm scallop salad with home-made dressing and a round of fresh brown bread?"

"I'm sorry – I may dribble a little." Mia laughed.

Mary got her to work on chopping leaves for the salad, and it was while they were preparing dinner that both women relaxed.

"Do you like blues?" Mary asked.

"I should but I don't," Mia admitted.

Mary checked her CD player. Rufus Wainwright was loaded directly under Ms Morissette. "Rufus Wainwright?"

"Why not?" Mia said, taking off her jacket and shaking the salad dressing.

They were halfway through their scallop salads when Mia broached the subject of Mary's relationship with Sam. "I hope you don't mind me asking but are you two together?" she asked.

"Seriously, we've only ever been friends," Mary said.

"Yeah, that's what we said for the entire duration of our relationship."

"He's here to get better," said Mary, quickly, "nothing more."

"He got better at home."

"What about you – do you want him back?"

"Yes," Mia nodded, "but I'm not stupid enough to think it will ever happen. He's been here months and I didn't even get a phone call. I had to find out where he was through a damn tabloid. We didn't even officially end it. He wanted to but I begged." She was shamefaced. "Of course, deep down, I knew it was over."

"I'm sorry."

"Don't be. He didn't love me ... He didn't then, he doesn't now and won't in the future. It's just like I said: people don't change that much." She placed another forkful of salad in her mouth. "God, this is amazing!"

Mary smiled.

"You're wondering what I'm doing here," Mia said, when her mouth was empty.

"I suppose I am."

"My therapist says I need closure," Mia said, between bites.

"Oh. OK." *Americans!*

They were enjoying a glass of white wine, lying on deck-chairs placed at the edge of the pier, when Mary caught sight of Ivan's boat heading towards the shore. Ivan spotted his cousin at around the same time. His son was untangling a net.

"Chris, pass me the binoculars, son," he said, and Chris dutifully complied. "Christ in a canoe! It's Mia Johnson!" he yelled.

Chris grabbed the binoculars back. "Jesus!" he said, under his breath.

"Don't swear!" Ivan said automatically.

"Holy crap!" Chris was still staring at the rock star lounging beside his aunt.

"That's better." Ivan took the binoculars from the boy. "Sam!"

Sam emerged from below with Justine and a flask of coffee. "I heard you," he said, with a sigh.

Ivan had the boat tied off in record time. From their chairs, Mia and Mary watched Sam and his comrades walk the length of the pier. It was evident, despite his smile, that Sam was feeling the pressure for he was sweating excessively. Ivan was as dry as a bone and happy as a puppy, bounding towards the beautiful stranger to shake her hand and tell her how much he admired her. Mary wanted to slap him. Chris sat on the side of his aunt's chair to prevent his knees buckling in the aftermath of Mia's cheek-kiss. Justine held Sam's hand, uninterested in the woman. She liked Jamie Lynn Spears.

Sam was the last person to welcome her. It had been almost six months since he had nearly died of a heroin overdose and just over three months since he had ended his relationship with Mia, but now, seeing her face and feeling her arms wrapped around him, it felt like an entire lifetime had passed. She was a stranger with a tight grip. He pulled away and suggested he should take her back to her hotel but Mary and Ivan insisted she stayed, at least to finish her wine. They all went into the house, where Ivan found two more glasses and told the kids to watch TV in the sitting room. Then he joined Sam, Mary and Mia Johnson sitting around Mary's kitchen table sipping white wine. He was beaming like a kid at the circus.

"Mr Mockless?" Mia was saying, rubbing Mr M's back.

"Monkels," Mary corrected her.

"Weird name."

"Originally he was called Norman," Ivan said, still beaming.

"What changed?" Mia asked, intrigued.

"One day when my son was three years old he decided that Norman didn't work and Mr Monkels did."

Ivan laughed. "The strange thing is, the dog immediately responded to it."

"It was like he'd always been Mr Monkels," Mary added. "It just fitted."

"It's a cool name," said Mia. "Your son has good taste. So where is he?"

"He died," Mary said.

"Oh, I'm so sorry!" Mia was covered with embarrassment.

Sam stood up. It was obvious he was uncomfortable. "We should go."

"You don't have to," Mary said.

"No," Mia said, "Sam's right. I should go. It's been a long day. It was really good to meet you, Mary, and you, Ivan." She leaned over to shake his hand and he took the opportunity to kiss her cheek.

"You're a lady," he said to her, which seemed to please her.

Chris was too busy talking on his mobile phone, telling his friends about his encounter with a rock star, to say goodbye to her.

Justine waved at the window, with Mr Monkels at her side. Mary closed the door.

"Christ on a cruise ship!" Ivan said. "Stick a fork in me, Mare, I'm done."

She laughed, but she would have been lying if she'd said she wasn't a little jealous – not a lot jealous but definitely a little. *Frig it, why couldn't she have been a bitch?*

Mia returned to the old-world hotel she'd booked into earlier that day. Sam had agreed to meet her there for drinks at nine. She sat by her window, looking out at the grounds, which led to a little gate. She wondered what lay beyond it.

The suite was reminiscent of a bygone era, sumptuous and scattered with antiques and oil paintings. She hadn't expected such decadence and had thought Kenmare would be as hick as some of those places she had spent months in while touring the States. But, of course, that wasn't Sam's style – she was the hick, after all. She considered spending some time in the spa, impressed with the couple's day suite that offered seclusion, but then she remembered that she wouldn't be requiring a couple's day suite and there didn't seem to be a suite for one. No matter how many treatments, how beautiful the view, or how tranquil the spa pool, the empty chair would surely taunt her.

She lay on her bed for a while, opening a trouser button because she'd eaten too much brown bread.

She pondered on Sam's welcome. He'd put his arms around her and smiled, but deception was his strong suit. She had felt his warmth. He looked well and healthy. His friend Ivan seemed nice and the kids were cute. They were also a well-placed distraction. On the pier she had noticed Sam trying to catch Mary's eye. Mary wouldn't be drawn and she'd wondered, *What is it with those two?*

It was after eight when she showered, careful not to wet her hair, which had been styled in the UK that morning. She sat at her dressing-table to apply her makeup. The mirror was deceptively large and seemed to engulf her. *Mia, what are you really doing here?* She often stared at her own reflection with wonder, not because she was intoxicated by her beauty, as others were, and not because she saw herself as extraordinary: she stared at herself in the hope that her face might betray her origin. Mia didn't know where her beauty came from and she never would.

Declared an orphan, she'd been in the system since she'd been found sleeping in a cardboard box one hot morning in the car park of a K-Mart in Michigan. She was of mixed race and answered to Lola. In the late 1970s, mixed-race children had been difficult to place. Adoption agencies wanted a newborn, preferably one race, colour and creed. They didn't need the headache that came with a kid whose origin was in question and who was approaching two. Throughout her childhood she had been fostered over and over again and never quite found a family that fitted her. The other girls were jealous of her oval eyes and flawless caramel skin, while her height and grace had been an affront to her Plain Jane room-mates. The boys were always fighting for her attention, so much so that there was usually trouble. Her childhood and teenage years had been filled with insecurity, fear and disappointment.

One day a lady named Kiki Shaw, an ex-dancer and one of her many foster-parents, had complimented her singing voice. She only mentioned it once but that was all it had taken. After that day Mia had done nothing but sing, initially in the hope that her voice would attract the attention and praise she craved, but when neither was forthcoming she did it for herself. When she was fourteen she stole a guitar. She stalked the shop for a full week before she made her move. She knew exactly which one she wanted. It was blue and closest to the door. Usually there were two young guys behind the counter but on that day there was only one. He went into the back once in three hours, but when he did she darted inside, grabbed the guitar and ran away as fast as her legs could carry her, holding her newly acquired possession high in the air until she was far away from the scene of the crime.

She taught herself some chords from an old book she'd picked up second-hand. She wrote her first song aged fifteen. She left her last foster home at sixteen, got a job as a waitress and the owner let her live in the room above the diner. When she wasn't working she gigged in every dive that would have her. But as hard as she tried, six years later she was still a waitress and the dive above the diner was still home.

She was twenty-two when a beautiful man had come into her world and changed it utterly. He plucked her from obscurity. He dressed her. He styled her. He even named her. He believed in her and filled her with courage and hope. He had made her feel special and, for a long time, she'd thought he loved her.

Deep down, Mia had long believed herself to be Sam's creation. In him she had found her missing identity. He'd given her a family and her life, and she knew that, behind all his inexplicable fear and before heroin had stolen him, he *had* loved her. She knew this because once upon a time he'd been kinder to her than any other human being ever had. She couldn't let him go. She needed one last shot to get him back.

But then there was Caleb. She had lied to him, much as she had lied to Mary. Her therapist had not been involved in her decision to see Sam. In fact, he would have been wholly against the idea, and in any case, since Sam had left her she had become increasingly dependent on her bass player. Only the previous week he had declared his love for her in a beach house in Malibu. She had fallen into his willing arms, and this was something she didn't do lightly. She had never wanted Caleb to be her casualty as she was Sam's. And she cared for him: he made her laugh, he was kind, and he would even forgo a romp with an enthusiastic groupie in favour of winding down in a little café somewhere with her. If she did see him with someone, he would act as though he'd been caught out. She had spent last night with him in London, and had promised she would return the next day. Their relationship, if you could call it that, was new and she had made it clear she was very much on the rebound. He had told her he knew that. Then he had kissed her and said he'd wait for ever for her, which was sweet if unrealistic. She knew he was hurt by her insistence on the necessity of a final visit with Sam. She also knew he would forgive her. He always did.

Sam was talking to the barman as though they were old friends. "It's a warm night," he acknowledged.

"Warm? 'Tis almost hot."

"Well, it's nearly summer." Sam sipped his pint.

"Summer my arse!" the man said quietly, so that Mia had to strain to hear him from behind a well-placed antique plant pot. "We're being globally warmed as we speak. Sure if it keeps going as it is, in a few years we'll all be just stains on the street!"

Sam laughed. "Well, I guess you'd know better than I would."

"Oh, I would, Sam. I've been a connoisseur of Kerry weather for nigh on thirty-eight years now." He grinned. "So, you're here to see your lady-friend?"

Mia's heart missed a beat.

"Yeah."

"Well, I wish you the best of luck."

"Thanks, Henry," Sam said.

It was at this point that an elderly lady, who looked as if she might be a cousin of the Queen of England and smelt of roses, approached Mia's hiding-place. "Are you all right, dear?" she asked. "You seem a little lost."

"I'm fine. Thank you."

The old woman had attracted the attention of Sam and the bartender so Mia made her entrance. Sam immediately got off the bar stool. Henry followed with Sam's drink on a tray, his demeanour immediately changing from casual to professional. Once they were seated by the window overlooking the bay, he asked if Mia would like something to drink.

"I'll have a dry martini."

"Certainly, madam," he said, with a bow, and then they were alone.

"It's a beautiful place," she said, gazing out over the water. Sam nodded.

"Are you going to say anything?" Mia said, annoyed by his silence.

"What do you want me to say?" he asked, knowing he was being rude.

"You hate me that much?"

"I don't hate you. I just don't want to hurt you again."

"Is that what you've planned?"

"Why are you here?" he asked, as Henry appeared and placed Mia's drink on the table in front of her. Without a word, he was gone.

She looked from Sam to her drink and back to Sam. "I don't know," she answered honestly. "To say goodbye? To win you back?" She sighed.

He took her hand in his and kissed it. "Say goodbye."

She nodded. "The trouble is, I know I can get over losing

you as a lover but I don't think I'll ever recover from losing you as a friend."

"You don't have to," he said, unable to hide his relief.

"You've got my back?" she asked playfully.

"I've got your back," he said, with a grin.

Later, over dinner on the terrace, Mia told Sam about her burgeoning relationship with Caleb. "He's so good to me."

"Like you were to me. You deserve the very best, Mia. You just have to believe it."

"I shouldn't be here," she said.

"Probably not."

"Still, I'm glad I came."

"Me too," Sam said, and he meant it. "Are you in love with him?"

"Yes, I think I am. And are you in love with Mary?"

"Yeah, I think I am."

"She's lucky."

"No. She's pretty unlucky, actually."

"You're well matched, then."

"We're giving each other space."

"She told me. You know what I think?"

He shook his head.

"Space is for astronauts."

They laughed. He had missed his friend Mia and he was glad to have her back, even if just for one night. They made their way to the restaurant arm in arm, and after dinner they travelled down Memory Lane. She worried that her career would suffer without him. He reminded her that she was the talent and that every good student outgrows their mentor. She discussed her fears for the album. She knew it was good but it needed one more song, a signature tune, something she could hang the whole thing on. He agreed to listen to the rough cuts. She complained that she couldn't stay more than a day for fear that she'd put on weight, yet she was determined to finish her lobster. Over coffee he thanked her for saving his life and this time he meant it. At the end of their evening he kissed her goodbye. She hugged him and smiled. "Closure," she mumbled, before kissing him one last time. He waited while she walked up the staircase and she didn't look back.

"'Bye, Mia."

## 22. Holding on, letting go

Sam left Mia just after eleven. He was tempted to knock on Mary's door but her lights were off and he knew from Ivan that she had been having sleepless nights. He had also heard a greatly exaggerated account of her breakdown in Gemma's beauty shop. He wondered if she was having that terrible nightmare again. He worried for her as he knew how devastating nightmares could be. He had been haunted by them for as long as he could remember – but his were based in reality.

He fell asleep quickly. Minutes later the nightmare woke him. He was starting to panic – that terrible panic to which he had often succumbed in his past life. The panic that started in the pit of his stomach, then leaked into his system and threatened to debilitate him. The panic that had enticed him into messing around with drugs. Sam hadn't started with heroin – he'd tried pretty much everything else first: marijuana, mescaline, magic mushrooms, acid, china white, LSD, ketamine and cocaine to name a few, but nothing had come close to heroin. The others he could take or leave, but heroin had seduced him instantly and become his mistress. He had lost himself in her.

He made tea, trying to control the tremor in his hand. He sat at the kitchen table and tried to remember the breathing technique that Phones, his shrink, had taught him. He closed his eyes and attempted to visualize a calm day, but instead he saw a needle slipping into his vein, liquid slipping into his system and himself slipping into heaven. He shook his head vigorously to empty it. *No. No. Think of the sea or a cornfield or a park. Think of the sun, the moon or anything but that. Come on, man, you can do it. If only I could stop this damn tremor. Damn it, what's happening?* But he couldn't stop the memories of the almighty high flooding back.

When he was up, he was filled with colour. His body felt light and his mind free. He didn't need to be touched or loved. He didn't need to talk or listen. He could just be, wrapped up in his own heavenly bubble. He could almost feel the warmth. He stood up and walked around the room. *OK, you want to remember heroin, remember all of it. Remember the bad times. Remember the nightmare,* he told himself, as Danziger, his male nurse, had instructed. He closed his eyes and visualized coming down. It wasn't hard to relive the hell that always followed like a blinding light – his head aching, his ears and skin buzzing, his body screaming. He could see himself in a ball, cold and twisted. His only escape was to slip another needle into his vein. He opened his eyes. *I won't go back there. It's all OK. Everything is fine. I'm fine.*

It was the first time he'd really thought about using since rehab. *I'm OK. I'll be OK.* He needed to calm down so he took a hot bath. The techniques his shrink had taught him finally kicked in and the panic dissipated.

He was drying his hair when someone banged on the door. It was after two a.m. but he thought that maybe it was Mary.

He answered with a relief that was short-lived.

Caleb pushed past him. "You're a real fuckin' asshole, you know that?" He was holding a half-full bottle of Jack Daniel's. The rest was on his breath.

"I didn't ask her here," Sam said, closing the door.

"No, of course you didn't. Why would you? You don't give a damn about her!"

Caleb plonked himself on one of Sam's kitchen chairs. Sam took two glasses out of his cupboard and put them on the table. Caleb snorted at his presumption but poured them both some anyway.

"You're wrong," Sam said, after a sip of bourbon.

"Oh, yeah?"

"I do care about her. I just don't love her. Not like you." He drained his glass.

Caleb put his glass on the table in front of him. He began drumming his fingers. "She told you about us?"

"Yes." Sam poured another round.

"What's your hold over her, man?" Caleb asked, sounding defeated.

"She came to say goodbye," said Sam, "and that was what she did." He put his glass down without taking another sip. Instead he got up and switched on the kettle. "She was just looking for a clean slate."

"Easy for you to say," Caleb said, swirling the contents of his glass.

"Why?"

"Because I'm just holding on, man." He sighed.

"I know what you mean," Sam said, as he poured coffee grounds into a percolator. "So, where you staying?"

"Sheen Falls."

"She's at the Park."

"I always thought you were an asshole," Caleb said.

"You were right. I was – maybe I still am. It's a constant battle." He hid the reality of his statement. "She said she's in love with you."

"Don't fuck with me." Caleb looked as though he was about to cry.

"I'm not."

Caleb lowered his glass. "I've loved her since the first day I saw her. Do you think I should go to her?"

"Have some coffee first," Sam instructed.

"No, thanks. I must go." Caleb stood up. "You got a bathroom?"

Sam waited while Mia's bass player gargled with mouthwash. He emerged pumped up.

"Good luck," Sam said.

"Thanks." He walked outside and stopped dead. Sam deduced that he didn't have a clue where he was going. He'd probably come here in a taxi, which, of course, had gone when he'd paid it off.

"You couldn't drive me, could you?" Caleb wondered.

Sam smiled. "Get in the car."

Mary's day had been eventful. Although the glitterati often visited Kenmare, Mia Johnson was the first of the fraternity to have spent time in her home. By coincidence that evening she had invited Ivan and Sienna to dinner at Ivan's behest. He had confided in her that his relationship was suffering slightly under the strain of his children's homecoming. As their mother was at a rather unfortunate crossroads that she was taking her time to traverse, his new girlfriend could only wonder whether or not she had inherited another woman's kids. Of course, she hadn't said as much but she had become slightly snappy, if not downright sulky, especially after a long day's work. She was used to having Ivan to herself, and family life was way more difficult than *The*

*Brady Bunch* had suggested. Mary had agreed to distract his new girlfriend with her famous scallop salad, but unfortunately she had fed this to a ravenous rock star. Her father came to the rescue, providing her with fresh sole that she planned to serve with risotto. It hadn't been the dish requested but it was the best she could do.

Fortunately Sienna was partial to sole and it appeared that she was so glad to spend a night away from the kids that a two-litre bottle of cider and a park bench would have sufficed. Mary played an old Bonnie Raitt album, one of her favourites that she knew the hippie in Sienna would like. "I love Bonnie." Sienna sighed, and sipped some red wine.

Ivan sat at the kitchen table drinking beer and texting the baby-sitter.

"We've just left them, Ivan," she said, irritation in her voice.

"Sorry," he said, when he'd pressed *send*.

"Can I help?" Sienna asked Mary, who said she could manage fine.

Ivan took her hand. "Cheers!" he said. He and Sienna clinked glasses. "Any news from next door?" he asked.

"No."

"You're still giving each other space." His voice was laced with sarcasm.

"None of your business," said Mary.

"Well, I've some news on the subject," Sienna said. "An American booked into the hotel late this afternoon. He asked if his girlfriend was staying."

"Who is she?" Ivan asked.

"Mia Johnson." She smiled smugly.

"No!"

"Yes!"

"Did she mention a boyfriend to you?" he asked Mary.

"Hardly."

"Well, now the plot thickens," said Ivan.

"I wonder why she didn't stay in the Sheen?" Sienna said, as much to herself as anyone else.

During dinner Sienna revealed the strain she felt at having Ivan's kids around. He was talking about the great day by the sea that he, Sam and the kids had spent and said she should have come too. She told him it was hard enough for her to share a large house with them, never mind a small boat.

Bolstered by the presence of his cousin, he drew her on the subject. "They're not that bad, surely?"

"They hate me."

"They do not."

"Justine refuses to look at me when I talk to her. She doesn't respond when I call her. She won't eat what I give her, and instead of using my name she refers to me as 'the woman'." She drained her glass.

Mary was quick to replenish it.

"She's only a baby," Ivan said. "She's just getting used to the situation."

"Neither of them is a baby and Chris is as bad. He told me to fuck off the other day." Her voice had risen.

Mary poured her some water in a different glass. She ignored it.

"And I gave out to him," Ivan said, tired of the conversation.

"Not enough," she replied.

"Well, what should I have done? Beaten him?" he said, annoyed now.

"You're being ridiculous."

The meal pretty much finished in that vein. Ivan defended his children's behaviour and Sienna defended her reaction to a difficult situation. Mary opened a second bottle of red so that she could block out the bickering. The argument ended in stalemate so they sat in silence in front of the first episode of the second season of *Lost*. Mary and Sienna shared the bottle of wine, and Ivan got through a six-pack of beer.

They left at just after ten. Mary stood outside and waved them off. Sam's car was outside but she knew he was in the hotel with Mia. It was only up the road so he'd probably walked and his house was dark and still. She had drunk too much wine so she sat on her wall to watch the water. It was still so warm. She wondered if when Mia had said she needed closure she had been telling the truth. After all, why should she? Mary was a stranger. Then she wondered if Sienna was right and Mia was seeing someone else – and, if so, why had he followed her on a visit to an ex-boyfriend and why was he staying in another hotel. Mostly she wondered why she couldn't stop wondering about Sam Sullivan. *He's not yours, Mary.*

She went to bed early, hoping to sleep soundly, but woke to banging on her neighbour's door a little after two. She climbed halfway out of the window but she still couldn't see who was there so she convinced herself it was Mia. *He's not yours, Mary,* she reminded herself. *It's for the best,* she lied. "Closure," she muttered, and turned off the light.

Having deposited Caleb at his destination, Sam returned to bed. Now he had no distraction, he worried that he was slipping, and that although he had won a hard battle he was about to lose the war. He had come a long way in six months. Here, in this beautiful gentle place, he was further from his New York self than he could ever have imagined. And it wasn't just Mary who had encouraged the change: it had been the place and its people, but mostly it had been himself. For years he had desperately wanted to escape himself. He had known that the man he once was would have to die, and he had died one night six months and a lifetime ago, yet just below the surface that dead man's memories remained intact, haunting him as surely as a determined ghost.

Phones had tried to get him to talk about his past during his stay in rehab. He had employed every trick in the book to get his patient to reveal the depths of himself so that they could work through it. But he had failed.

Phones had certainly learned a lot, though. He discovered that Sam had been born an outsider. It became obvious early on that his patient's love of his grandmother, although not Oedipal, was certainly a form of idealization. And Phones's patient notes included his theory that the timing of her death at the cusp of his manhood ensured that her grandson would find it difficult to meet another woman, including his own mother, who could live up to the one his grandmother had become in his mind. A woman who, had she survived, would have revealed herself to be human and flawed, rather than the embodiment of a boy's idea of perfection. This theory was validated by Sam's inability to find lasting love but it did not explain the darkness that lay deep within his psyche. Something terrible had happened to him. Phones was sure that he had not suffered parental abuse, terrible poverty or, aside from an ill grandmother, loss. He'd never been at war and he seemed not to have been involved in an incident that would have precipitated post-traumatic stress. *What the hell happened to this guy?* Phones had circled his question twice while doodling on page fourteen of his notes, but Sam would never tell.

Much later that night, when Sam closed his eyes he dreamed of the woman only a wall away. Even as he luxuriated in her warm smile, chasing after her beckoning hand in a world full of colour and light, she descended to the depths of darkness and a place in which, again, she saw the hooded teenage boy curled into a bloodied ball.

Suddenly the boy was staring at her. "Save me!" he begged.

# 23. Sacrificed

Mary was just outside the Kerry border when smoke began to pour out from under the car's bonnet. Within moments she had pulled over to the side of the road with a car full of whiskey and what appeared to be a clapped-out engine. She called the AA and was told the wait would be at least an hour. The guy joked that she should get comfortable, which annoyed rather than entertained her. She cursed herself for having forgotten her all-important travel CD collection.

It was after she'd grown tired of flicking through radio stations that she phoned Ivan. He picked up without much delay.

"You're not going to believe where I am," she said.

"Where?"

"On the side of the road in a clapped-out car waiting for the AA," she said.

"You're not going to believe where I am," he countered.

"Where?"

"Kerry airport."

"Norma!" she gasped.

"She's coming home," he said, clearly relieved.

"Oh, that's fantastic! Where's she staying?"

"With me and the kids," he said happily.

"Have you lost your mind?"

"Excuse me?"

"Your relationship with Sienna is on dangerous enough ground already," Mary reminded him.

"But now that Norma's home it'll get better."

"Not if she's living in your house, Ivan! God almighty!"

"All right, calm down. I'll work something out."

"You do that," she said, and hung up.

It was just after seven in the evening, and as the tow truck appeared to be light years away she made sure that her hazard lights were on, locked her doors and settled down for a snooze.

Ivan drove out of the airport with his wife in the passenger seat, the kids buzzing in the back. Norma had made a remarkable recovery. She looked fresh and happy, and was grateful for the lift.

"Don't be soft – we were hardly going to let you get a taxi," he said.

The kids laughed at the notion.

"The woman's put flowers in the spare room for you," Justine announced.

"Her name is Sienna," Ivan said.

"That's nice of her," Norma said politely.

"Chris says they look gay," Justine noted.

"Well, he shouldn't," Ivan told her. "Your uncle Barry is gay."

"I know," Chris replied. "That's why I call him Uncle Gay." He grinned at his mother, who had turned to laugh with him.

"Sorry," she said, in response to Ivan's dirty look.

He grinned.

*Just like the old days.*

\*

Penny's dry spell didn't last as long as she'd hoped and, as she'd tipped most of her booze down the drain, she needed to stock up. Luckily she'd located a bottle of vodka in an old suitcase, having conducted a large-scale search operation. Once it was empty she was forced to go to the off-licence so she fixed her makeup, brushed her hair and straightened herself up generally before she got into the car to drive to town. She picked up a basket and, as she did so, she noticed, from the corner of her eye, that one of the two young Murphy girls behind the counter was pointing at her and making a glugging gesture, then mimicking a drunken walk. The other had a hand over her mouth to smother a snigger.

Penny dropped the basket and walked out.

*Stupid little bitches!* She vowed she wouldn't return to that shop ever again. Instead, she decided to go to Killarney for her booze. It was a good twenty miles away from the local gossips and, besides, she could do with the drive.

In the car she started to panic. Her heart was racing and she felt so hot that she had to turn on the air-conditioning – usually she reserved it for stifling days. Beads of sweat rolled from the nape of her neck down her spine. *What the hell am I doing? What the hell is wrong with me?* Her hands were shaking on the steering-wheel so she pulled into the side of the road and stopped. She briefly wondered why she had come over the mountain and supposed it was just habit. No one else was around, just her sitting in the car, the grey rock towering over her and cascading below. She got out, needing to breathe fresh air, and stood by the small railing that separated her from the glassy lake below.

And it was there on the mountain that she admitted to herself what she'd long hidden in the deepest recess of her mind. *I am an alcoholic.* Tears swelled in her eyes and tumbled. Mary's words and the Murphy girl's imitation ran through her mind. *Oh, God help me!* She spent just over thirty minutes crying, then returned to the car. She cleaned her face with an old tissue she found in the glove-box and reapplied her eyeliner and some lipstick. Then she drove on to Killarney to purchase much-needed alcohol.

After all, alcoholics drank alcohol.

Mary didn't get home until after ten p.m. Mr Monkels was scratching to get in and she opened the back door to discover the clothes-line on the ground, with the washing still attached to it. "Reaching for the stars or the birds?" she asked her dog, whose lowered head and disappearing tail were evidence enough to suggest that this mini-disaster was of his making. She was picking up her muddy clothing when she heard Sam's door open. She had an armful of clothes when he peered over the wall.

"Hey." He looked tired.

"Hey," she reciprocated.

"Have you had enough space?" he asked candidly.

"Are you OK?" she asked, grabbing at a wayward sock.

"Not really," he confessed.

"Come inside," she offered.

He made his way over the wall.

"You could have used the front door."

"This way is quicker."

He followed her into the kitchen. She put the clothes back into the washing-machine and offered him coffee. He didn't have time to answer before the phone rang.

Seconds into the call Mary's face changed. Sam knew

that something terrible had happened. When she hung up he demanded, "What?"

"I need your car." She went straight to the door, grabbing her handbag and jacket on the way.

"Excuse me?" he said, following her outside.

"It's Penny. She's been in an accident." Her voice was trembling.

"Is she hurt?"

"Yes."

"How bad?"

"I don't know."

"Where is she?"

"The mountain," she replied, in a strangled whisper.

He headed into his house to pick up his keys. "I'll drive," he said, when he got back to her.

He sat into the driver's seat and she strapped herself in beside him.

"Don't worry, the emergency services will take care of everything," he said, putting the car into gear.

"We *are* the emergency services."

"I don't understand."

"We can't call anyone – she's drunk," she said, and bit her lip.

"Is this wise?"

"I don't know, but she's my friend."

Sam drove onto the mountain while Mary talked to Ivan, who agreed to meet them at the accident site. She hung up and tried Penny's phone, but five minutes previously Penny had warned her that it was running out of juice. Her speech had been slurred and Mary wasn't sure if it was from alcohol or a head injury. *We need to get there.*

Sam saw Mary's fear – she was gripping her phone so tightly that her knuckles were white. "Calm down," he soothed.

"Can't," she replied, staring straight ahead. *I hate this fucking mountain.*

"She's fine."

"We don't know that."

"She can talk – that's a good sign," he said.

"She's crying. She says she's bleeding." The thought of her best friend abandoned and hurt made her well up. "She's really scared." *I should have been there for her. I should have seen this coming.*

"You couldn't have seen this coming," he said, and she wondered if she had voiced the thought without realizing it.

"Is this rock bottom?" she asked, remembering Adam's words.

Sam seemed to understand what she meant. "Only time will tell," he said.

"We really need to get there."

Minutes later they came across Penny's car, smashed into the side of the mountain. The front was crumpled against a dying deer impaled on sharp rocks. Blood leaked from its mouth and Penny was crumpled beside it. Mary was out of the car as soon as Sam had pressed the brake. It was the first time since her accident that she had actually set foot on the mountain, and her proximity to the edge of a steep cliff across the road wasn't far from her mind. *Breathe.* She made her way to her friend who had passed out. Mary was scared to turn her over, afraid of spinal injury. She was scared to touch her at all.

"Penny! Penny! Wake up!" *This is insane.* "Christ, we need to get someone here who knows what they're doing!" she cried, battling encroaching vertigo.

Sam placed his hand on Penny's wrist. "She's got a strong pulse," he said, then went back to the car and pulled out his and Mary's jackets. "We need to cover her." He laid them over her.

A second or two passed before she moved.

"Don't move!" Mary barked.

Penny ignored her and turned over. "I'm OK," she slurred, as blood streamed from a cut on her forehead. The gash was deep and fleshy. The current of blood masked broken teeth, a split lip and a badly broken nose, but when Penny moved her head, the damage became all too apparent.

"Oh, Jesus!" Mary gasped. Her friend's face was pulverized.

Sam took off his shirt and handed it to Penny who, until then, hadn't noticed him. She took it from him and buried her face in it.

When Ivan arrived, the deer was breathing its last.

Penny lifted her hand to its head and stroked it gently as its eyes lost all expression. "I'm so sorry!" she cried, spitting broken teeth. "I'm so, so sorry!"

Ivan took over. His previous incarnation as a commercial diver had ensured he had sufficient first-aid skills to confirm that his friend had no bone or spinal injuries. Her face concerned him most. He carried her to his car and laid her on the back seat. He wrapped her in Sam's and Mary's jackets and rested her head on a Barbie pillow from the boot that Justine had insisted on bringing home, only to forget about it when they arrived. He took ice from the cooler he had filled before he set off – he often used it when he was fishing. He wrapped some in a towel and handed it to her. "It'll slow the blood flow and curb the swelling," he said.

"What about shock?" Mary asked.

"She's drunk enough for shock not to be our biggest problem."

He closed the door on Penny, who was mumbling something about killing Bambi. He went back to his car and got out the jack. He returned to Penny's car and, with one blow, smashed the glass on the driver's side.

"What the hell are you doing?" Sam asked.

"We need to make it look like the car was stolen. That, or Penny goes down for drink-driving. Not to mention that the red deer she killed is a protected species."

"Oh," Sam said.

Mary was mesmerized by the dead animal, horrified by the suffering it had endured. Her nose was running. She wiped it with her hand. She felt faint.

"Follow me," Ivan said.

"Where are we going?" Mary asked, wondering what the hell her cousin was doing.

"Cork. Adam's meeting us in the Regional."

Sam and Mary went to their car, Sam supporting Mary who had now succumbed to a combination of vertigo and fright. Ivan took off, with Sam following. Mary tried to control her breathing as Sam sped around the bend that had once nearly claimed her.

"We'll be OK," he said.

"I know."

"I'm a good driver."

"I wouldn't go that far."

Even when she was struggling with terror Mary could make him smile. Once they were off the mountain and driving on the Cork road, Mary took several deep breaths. She called Ivan on her mobile – she knew he had a hands-free set in his car – and he assured her that their friend was OK. At one point she'd actually attempted to sing the chorus of Phil Collins's "Against All Odds".

Mary hung up and Sam asked how Penny was.

"She's singing."

"Anything I'd like?"

"Phil Collins."

"'Can't Hurry Love'?"

"'Against All Odds.'"

"Apt," he said and, despite the desperate situation, they burst into laughter.

A few minutes passed in silence.

Mary couldn't help herself. "Did you have a good night with Mia?"

"Yeah." He nodded. "It was nice."

"Right," she said, a little put out.

"It was just dinner. Actually, her boyfriend had followed her but I'm guessing you heard that."

"It was mentioned."

"He came to see me."

"Really?"

"Oh, you remember!"

"What?" she asked innocently.

"When you nearly fell out the window trying to get a look?"

"That's the last time I tell Ivan anything."

\*

Adam was waiting at the front doors of the hospital. Ivan and Sam carried Penny between them, with Mary following. He gasped at her injuries, and Penny started to cry as soon as she saw him.

He took her in his arms. "It's all right," he said. "Everything's going to be all right." Penny didn't seem certain of that. She pulled away from his embrace and tried to shield her injured face with a hand. Once they were inside and a woman behind a glass window had taken down her details, a nurse escorted her to a cubicle so that her injuries could be assessed. "How much have you had to drink?" she asked.

"I don't know – a lot," Penny admitted.

"What happened to you?"

"I fell."

"Some fall," the woman said, unconvinced.

After testing Penny's responses the nurse determined that she was not critical, and although she had facial lacerations they weren't considered serious enough to merit her skipping the large queue in the waiting area. Penny returned to her friends and sat down.

"Well?" Adam said.

"I wait."

"But your face is a mess."

"Thanks."

"This is ridiculous," he said, and stormed across to the reception desk.

Mary, Sam, Ivan and Penny watched him argue a case for his mistress skipping a long queue. The woman behind the window was unmoved. He returned to them, disgusted. "You'd find a better health system in the third world," he said.

"It's OK," Penny said.

"I'll get coffee," Mary offered.

"No, you go home," Adam said. "I'll stay with Penny. It looks like it's going to be a long wait."

"Can I talk to you over here for a minute?" Mary asked him. She stood up and walked towards the door. An old woman in her eighties lying on a trolley was pushed past them by ambulance men. She was complaining that she couldn't leave the dog at home alone; her weary daughter reminded her that the dog had died in 1987.

"I thought it was your father died in 1987," the old lady said.

"No, Mother, he died in 1977."

"Time flies," the old lady said. "Still, I really do need to get home to the dog."

Adam smiled at the daughter, who smiled back. Mary punched his arm. "What are you doing?" she asked.

"What do you mean?" he responded in surprise. "I just smiled at her – it looked like she could do with cheering up."

"Yeah, you're a real humanitarian. I'm not talking about her, I'm talking about your marriage."

"I'm not leaving Penny in that state."

"I'm here," she said. "It's late at night and you have a wife to go home to."

"I'm not leaving."

"OK," she said, shrugging her shoulders, "have it your way."

"Mary –"

"Grow up, Adam," she said, and went back to the others.

After that they debated whether or not it was a better idea to stay in Cork or go home. Eventually, after much negotiation, Sam, Mary and Ivan decided to leave. Mary felt bad to be contemplating deserting her best friend, but there wasn't enough room in the waiting area for the actual patients, never mind the people accompanying them. Penny insisted she was fine and happy to be left alone, but Adam insisted on staying: like Margaret Thatcher, he said, he was not for turning. Ivan laughed, but Mary glared at him. He grinned and gave her the fingers. She couldn't help but smile. Something about an adult giving another that gesture never failed to amuse her.

They left Penny and Adam sitting in the Regional Hospital.

"You shouldn't be here," Penny said.

"I've already been through this with Mary." He got up from his chair. "I'm getting us some coffee."

"You shouldn't be here," Penny repeated, but Adam was already halfway down the corridor.

Ivan, Mary and Sam sat in a hotel bar. Ivan and Mary debated their next move while Sam drank a ginger ale. Once her injuries were sorted Ivan suggested moving Penny to a drying-out facility in Dublin. It was well respected and a man he knew, who had been a fall-down-in-the-street drunk, had passed a spell with the lads in there and returned a pillar of the community; he had since acquired a golfing handicap of four. Mary wondered if Penny would agree to go there but Ivan wasn't to be swayed. "Christ, Mare, she's just killed one of God's most majestic creatures and nearly herself! Surely to God she can fall no further," he said, then finished his pint.

Sam hoped that Ivan was right. He was painfully aware that sometimes it took more than a car crash to hit bottom.

Ivan headed into his hotel room so that he could talk to Norma, who was spending her first night back in Kenmare alone but was happy watching over her sleeping children. He phoned Sienna and left a message on her voicemail since she was most likely asleep – either that or she was pissed off that he was housing his ex-wife.

Sam and Mary stayed in the late-night bar, neither wishing to be alone.

"When we were kids Penny was terrified of the dark," Mary said.

"Yeah?" Sam encouraged her.

"She was convinced it would swallow her," she remembered. "She could get in trouble for this," she added.

"She'll be fine."

"You shouldn't have to deal with it. I'm sorry. I should never have asked you to come."

"I want to be here."

"Why?"

"You're here."

"Jesus," she sighed, "some day soon you'll get sense and then we'll both be very disappointed."

"Not a chance."

"Tart!" She got up. "Goodnight."

He watched her walk away.

Some time after eight a.m. Penny was finally seen by a doctor. The long wait had sobered her so a surgeon could repair the damage to her face. Three hours later she lay on cold steel under glaring lights and beside buzzing machines. The anaesthetist slipped a needle into her arm, and in her head Phil Collins sang "Against All Odds" on repeat.

When Penny woke her nose had been set, her lip, cheek and forehead were stitched and she had the mother of all hangovers. Her teeth were sharp in her mouth and as she ran her tongue over them she discovered that the four front ones were badly damaged. She dreaded looking in the mirror, having felt the bandages on her cheek and forehead. Her nose felt bigger than her entire head. She cried because she'd remembered Mary and Adam's gasp at the sight of her and guessed she'd been disfigured. She cried because she had watched a beautiful animal die a slow and terrible death. She cried because she really had wanted to stop drinking but she couldn't.

It was just after nine when Adam made his way to his own front door. He wasn't sure what he would say to his wife. At least the kids were at school. Maybe he'd be lucky and she'd be out. Maybe she hadn't noticed he'd been out all night. She was often asleep when he got home from the restaurant, and on delivery days he'd be up and out of the house before the alarm rang. He was too tired for an argument. He hoped that the separate lives they'd been living since his arrival to Cork would work in his favour.

Unfortunately for him this was not to be. As soon as he opened the door he saw suitcases packed at the foot of the stairs. Alina was on the upstairs landing. She made her way downstairs to meet him in the hall.

"Are you going somewhere?" he asked.

"No," she said. "You are."

"Alina!"

"I don't want to hear it, Adam."

"Alina –"

"Leave."

"No."

"Leave."

"I can explain."

"I don't care."

"It's not what you think."

"You were out all night, Adam."

"I know, but –"

"You were with her," she said.

"Yes, but it's not what you think."

She walked away from him and into the kitchen.

He followed her. "She was in trouble. She needed me."

Alina fought the urge to shove his head through the glass patio door. "Our marriage is over," she said.

"Just like that?" He was shocked.

"You've got your wish, Adam. You're free."

"And the kids?"

"They've settled in Cork. We're happy here. We'll stay and you can go back to Kenmare. You win."

"I never wanted this."

"Yes, Adam, you did."

"Why now?"

"Because I can't stop hating you. I wanted to for the kids' sake but I can't. I look at you and I want to gut you. It's not healthy." A tear rolled down her face. "I really do hate you."

"I'm sorry," he said.

"Go home," she said. "Go on – get out."

He stood there trying to process what she'd said.

"Get out!" Alina roared, angered by his failure even to pretend to fight for her, but he didn't move. She ran at him.

"Get out of my house!" She shoved him into the hallway. She opened the front door and threw his suitcases into the garden. He followed them and turned to her.

"When the kids ask why their dad doesn't live here any more, I'm going to tell them," she said. "There've been enough lies in this house."

The door slammed, and Adam was alone.

*What have I done?*

Mary, Sam and Ivan were halfway through breakfast when Adam arrived with his suitcases. He dropped them by the table and sat in beside Sam, facing Mary and Ivan.

"What's this?" Ivan asked.

"She threw me out."

"About time," Mary said.

"OK, rub it in."

"Maybe if one of us had said something a little earlier, your marriage wouldn't be in such a bloody mess and Penny wouldn't be an alcoholic."

"That's all I need! First my wife and now you! Anyone else want to jump into the ring?"

"She's right," Ivan said. "It was only a matter of time before it all ended in misery."

"Jesus." Adam sighed. "Have you anything to say?" he asked Sam.

"Your friends have summed the situation up perfectly."

"I've been a selfish arsehole," Adam realized.

"Yes, you have," Mary agreed.

"I'm sorry," he said, and began to cry.

Mary escorted Adam to her room so that he could

compose himself in private. While he took a shower she called the hospital to check on Penny. She was told that if there were no complications she'd be discharged the next day. She ordered some breakfast for Adam, which arrived just after he emerged from the bathroom.

"Thanks," he said.

"Are you all right?" she asked. All trace of animosity had disappeared.

"I'm fine," he said. "I'll let things settle and call the kids tomorrow – or do you think tomorrow is too soon?" For the first time in his life Adam seemed unsure.

"I think tomorrow would be fine."

"OK."

Ivan had phoned his friend who had been to the drying-out facility in Dublin. Now he had a contact name and number. He made the call and Lorraine Ryan explained that they would be happy to admit his friend but only if she was a willing patient. He told her he'd ring her back. An hour later he met up with the others in the hotel lobby.

"Do you think she'll agree?" he said worriedly.

"I'll talk to her," Adam said.

"She needs to hear it from all of you," Sam said.

"He's right," Mary said.

"OK, so today we go home and tomorrow we come back and talk to her," Ivan said.

"I'll stay here," Adam said. "She'll be awake later."

"Are you going to tell her about Alina?" Mary asked.

"No," he said, "this isn't about me. It's about Penny."

"At last he sees the light," Ivan said.

Adam agreed to phone them that night with an update

298

and, all going well, they agreed to meet back at the hotel the next morning. Adam walked them to the door and Mary hugged him, assuring him that everything would be all right. *It's a little late for that,* he thought.

Garda Sheehan was on Mary's doorstep just in time for afternoon tea. She made a pot and put out some sandwiches. He patted his belly and mentioned that he shouldn't indulge, but of course he did. He was munching his third before he brought up the subject of Penny's car. He took out a pen and notepad. "And you're sure she left it here?" he asked, referring to the brief details with which she had provided him over the phone.

"I rang her from the road. She said she'd drop it over. Mine is in the garage and she was going to Dublin anyway," she said, lying through her teeth.

"So you never actually saw it?"

"No. It was gone when I got home. I was waiting for the AA for ever."

"And you're sure she left it here?"

"I'm sure."

"Did she phone you and tell you she'd left it?"

"No."

"Then if you didn't see it, how do you know she left it?"

*Crap, I should have said yes.* "My neighbour saw it."

"Well, why didn't you say so in the first place?"

After that Sam was summoned into Mary's home to answer the charge that he had witnessed Penny's car parked outside.

"What time?" Garda Sheehan asked.

Sam pretended to think for a minute. "Six or seven."

"Mary, you said you rang Penny around six, didn't you?" Garda Sheehan said, referring to his notes.

"It must have been seven, then." Sam smiled.

"Right," he said, scribbling. His phone rang and he excused himself to take the call, leaving Mary and Sam alone.

"Do you think he believes us?" Mary whispered.

Sam shrugged. He didn't want to panic Mary but guilt was written all over her face.

Garda Sheehan returned. "Did I mention that the car's been found? It was reported as crashed on the mountain."

"No, you didn't. Is it damaged?" Sam said.

"Any casualties?" Mary chimed in.

"A red deer," Garda Sheehan said, "and, yes, the car is a write-off."

"Right," Sam said.

"Well," Garda Sheehan pocketed his notebook, "it looks like we're all done here."

"OK, then," Mary said, smiling.

Garda Sheehan made his way to the front door. "One last thing."

"Yes?" Mary said.

"It would appear that Penny didn't make it to Dublin last night," he said, reminding her of Columbo just before he revealed a poisonous plot.

"No?" she said, her heart racing.

"No. It appears she only got as far as the Regional Hospital in Cork."

"Right," Mary said, nodding in a way that suggested she knew the game was up.

"She could have killed someone."

"I know."

"She was drunk?"

Mary nodded again.

"I should arrest you for aiding and abetting. Not to mention attempting to take me for a fool."

"Sorry."

"Is she going to get help?"

"Yes."

"You see that she does," he said.

"I will," she said. "Thanks."

"Don't thank me, Mary. I don't know what I'm going to do about this yet," he warned her.

"OK." She opened the front door.

"And, Mary?"

"Yes?"

"You really are a pathetic liar."

"I know that too."

He left.

She sat on the sofa, where Sam joined her. "I'm not sure what happened there," he said. "Did we get away with it or not?"

"Yes and no."

"It's been a hell of a week."

Sam was tired. He hadn't slept well in the hotel and he was weary of drama. He made his way to the door.

"Sam!"

"Yeah?" he replied.

"Will you come with me tomorrow?"

"I doubt Penny would be happy about that."

"I know what she did to you but she didn't mean it. She's not like that when she's well."

"I'm sure you're right but I don't belong there."

"It's an intervention. Isn't that the correct term?"

"Yeah."

"Well, who better to intervene than someone who knows what they're talking about?"

He was silent for a moment or two. His head hurt. He really needed to sleep. "I'll do it."

He was gone before she could thank him.

# 24. Clean up, clean out

Sam, Mary and Ivan were waiting in Adam's hotel room when Adam opened the door to usher in a bandaged Penny. She surveyed those in front of her and knew there could be only one reason for the meeting. Feeling weak, she sat on a chair against the wall, facing the jury of her peers.

Adam gave her two painkillers and a glass of water.

"D Day," she said. Her friends remained silent.

"We're going to get you some help," Adam said, but she chose to ignore him in favour of concentrating on Sam.

"Is this how rehab happened for you, Sam? Oh, no, I forgot. You were brought in on a stretcher."

"Penny," Mary growled.

"It's OK," he said to Mary. "You're right. I went in on my back and, if memory serves, I was also strapped down. You want to go in like that, I'm sure it can be arranged."

"Fuck you!" she spat. Her hands had been trembling all morning. She felt sick and badly needed a drink.

"Do you know why you don't like me, Penny?" he asked.

"Enlighten me."

"You look at me and see yourself."

"Bullshit!" she said, touching the bandage on her forehead.

"I'm an addict and you are too." He leaned towards her so that she was forced to look at him. "I know how hard it is. I know the agony of saying no. I know that if you don't you'll die." He pitied her with every ounce of him.

Tears rolled down her face, which she tried to hide with trembling hands. "I don't think I can do it," she whispered.

"I know you can," he said.

"I don't want to be like this any more."

"You don't have to be."

Penny and Adam found themselves on the ten thirty a.m. train to Dublin. They sat in the dining section, Adam tucking into a full Irish breakfast and Penny playing with the foil wrapping of her painkillers. She had been silent since she had said her goodbyes at the hotel. Mary had cried and Penny had felt like an arsehole, remembering the stupid document in which she had spurted venom at the very people who were helping her.

When her tremor became so severe that Adam feared she might seize, he made the executive decision to allow her a shot of vodka. While she attempted to sip it he called the clinic to ask if he was doing the right thing.

Eventually the tremor subsided. "What have you told Alina?" Penny asked.

"I lied," he lied.

"It's still that easy?" she said.

"It was never easy."

They looked out of the window at the fields and grazing animals, the towns and houses, all passing them at speed.

"I want another drink," she said.

"I know."

"Thanks for being here."

"It was the very least I could do."

*

The taxi pulled up outside the clinic and Penny sat pinned to the back seat, looking much like the deer she had destroyed.

Adam paid the driver, then reached for her hand. "Time to go," he said.

"I can't."

"You can."

Fresh tears spilled. "I don't want to."

"Yes, you do."

"I'm really scared."

"It's OK to be scared."

He helped her out of the car and the taxi drove away. He guided her towards the door. A nurse emerged with a clipboard and stood there, waiting. Penny stalled. Adam put his hand on her waist and she snuggled into him. He spun her around and suddenly they were dancing as they had on the night he'd said goodbye. In her head she could hear Sinéad singing about sacrifice. He kissed her cheek and held her close to him, and all the while the nurse watched and waited.

"You're always leaving me."

"I never want to."

He wasn't allowed past the front door. The nurse took her new patient by the hand and Penny smiled through her tears and waved goodbye to the love of her life, who waited for her to disappear behind the white doors.

*I'll always love you, Penny Walsh.*

Mary sat on the sofa alone that night, Mr Monkels having fallen asleep on the window-seat. She was drinking tea and listening to Snow Patrol. For some reason she felt like crying. The boy in her dream was haunting her. She didn't have to sleep for him to find her now. At any given moment he would appear, staring at her with the most terrible expression on his face. She had seen things before, but they had all been so vague and about people she knew in the here and now. Nothing had ever manifested itself as this had – and what was it telling her? What part of the story was missing? And why, suddenly, did the boy seem familiar? Who the hell was he?

Emotion welled inside her, like untapped oil ready to burst through solid rock, and she wondered if she was having her tenth breakdown in that month. But then, of course, it had been so long since she had felt anything. When her child had died a part of her had stopped, like a broken clock, stuck for ever in the past. She had become Miss Havisham minus the wedding dress and the cruel streak. Until a stranger had appeared and something inside her had begun to tick . . .

Sam sat in his kitchen sipping a glass of Jack Daniel's from the bottle Caleb had left behind. He hadn't slept properly in a week and earlier had succumbed to the shakes, like he used to when he was without control. Penny's intervention had hit him harder than he'd expected. For some reason it had projected his mind to another place. A place in the past when he had been a shit-scared teenager, running with all his might. *Oh, God, no!*

And then he was somewhere else, in another time, a time when he was older and successful and an addict. He was in a communal bathroom in a bad area, kicking the shit out of another junkie much larger than himself. He was beating him with all his strength, both mental and physical, even though he was coming down and needed a fix so badly.

The junkie was crying and begging, "Don't, man! I'm sorry. You don't know!"

But Sam did know. He knew he wanted the fucker dead.

"I've paid for it – I've paid for it a hundred times!" the junkie cried.

"Not enough." Sam kicked him so hard in the nuts that the guy vomited.

"I'm a dealer! I can sort you out – I can keep you going, man," the junkie shrieked, and Sam stopped kicking him.

Just like that.

Ivan was sitting on the sofa with his daughter asleep on his lap. Chris was on the chair and they were watching a show about football. Norma was in the kitchen, making the kids' favourite biscuit cake. The doorbell rang and Chris got up.

Seconds later Sienna was in front of Ivan. He stood up, forgetting that his daughter's head was resting on his lap. "Dad!" she cried, rubbing her eyes.

"Sorry, Button."

He hugged Sienna, who seemed a little stiff. Later, when the kids were in bed and Norma had made herself scarce, they sat in the kitchen together.

"I haven't heard from you," she said.

"We keep missing one another."

"We never used to."

"It's been chaotic. I'm trying to find Norma a place with the kids, there's been madness with Penny and it's just –" He stopped.

"Maybe we should cool things for a while," she said.

"I don't want to."

"You've got your family back, Ivan," she said sadly.

"But I want you," he said, and she rested her head on his chest.

"I know, but I think this is a case of bad timing. Maybe when things settle down . . ." Then she added, "You're a good father, Ivan, and a good man."

"I'll work it all out," he promised.

"I know."

"I love you."

"I hope so," she said.

He walked her to the door and watched her leave.

*You can't have it all.*

# 25. To know you is to love you

The funeral was lovely. Dick Dogs had been one of Kenmare's best-loved. His greyhounds had won many a race and those who'd backed them had profited time and time again. In his early years he'd been a fixture in many a local pub. He had always enjoyed a pint but, unlike some, he'd known when it was time to go home. He was kind too, always having time for those less fortunate than himself. He'd never married, which was a pity because most would say he'd have made a good husband. Everyone agreed that it was his time, though. He was the last of his generation to go. His friends had led the way and he had said openly that he was looking forward to seeing them again. He had died early in the morning just before the sun rose. He hadn't suffered, just stopped. Paula Dubury had found him, cold but with a smile on his face.

"What were you dreaming, sweet man?" she'd asked. If his corpse had had the power of speech he would have told her that, just before he left this world, he had relived a time when he was a young man and he and his best friend David Breslin were standing at the back of a dancehall watching the girls line up in their Sunday best, their hair fresh out of curlers.

Dick had winked at Lena, who shook her head and wagged a finger.

David had laughed at his high ambition. "She'll never be yours," he said.

"But she could be," Dick had responded.

"She's leaving," David whispered.

"And where would she be going?" Dick had queried.

"We're sending her away."

"Away?" Dick repeated.

"My mother's got it in her head that she'll marry Joseph Dunne."

"But what about me?" Dick asked.

"What about you?" David responded. "She wants something else and what Lena wants Lena gets. She doesn't know it yet but she's leaving tomorrow."

"You're killing me," Dick said, and his friend had laughed.

"Take your dance. It'll be your last," David said, not knowing how prophetic his words were. Halfway through it, the old man reliving the memory breathed his last.

The funeral was held two weeks after Norma's homecoming. She had kept a low profile and Dick Dogs's funeral would be her reintroduction into Kenmare society. She didn't feel ready, still bruised and broken, yet she had always been fond of the old man. She wanted to pay her respects and her ex-husband encouraged her to do so. She was worried about how she would be viewed, yet her fondness for the man who had dedicated his life to caring for animals ensured that she was there.

The church was packed, which was odd for a man of Dick's age, especially as he'd had no family of his own. Ivan stood beside Norma, and the rest of the congregation didn't seem to notice her presence. All heads were bowed in remembrance of an old friend.

When the time came during the service for them to shake

hands as a sign of peace, people went out of their way to shake her good one. It was only when she saw men and women, with a perfect right to judge her, walk towards her smiling with hands outstretched . . . It was only when she heard . . . "Glad to have you home."

"Everything will work out."

"You don't have to worry any more."

"God bless you."

It was only when she stood in front of those she'd been convinced would hate her that she discovered what it meant to be forgiven.

*Thank God I'm home.*

Mary had spotted Sam standing at the back of the church. She had been with Ivan and Norma during the service. She had had a particularly bad migraine over the previous five days and he had called every day to make sure she was OK, seeing her at her worst and seeming not to care. The injections Dr Macken gave her meant that the week was full of holes but she did remember Sam holding her hand, wiping her brow and whispering to her. If only she could remember what he'd said. She'd continued to have the nightmare, always the same, always unfinished. The lack of progress was frustrating but she knew that sooner rather than later the curtain would rise.

She noticed that Sam had attempted to leave the church unseen but Paula Dubury had nabbed him in the church-yard. She wanted him to know how much Dick had enjoyed his visit, reliving his affection for Sam's grandmother. He had talked of it often in the past few weeks. She wanted him to know, too, how glad Dick had been that he'd taken the time to call in and that the old man had thoroughly enjoyed his gift of ice-cream. Sam thanked her, but she wasn't finished. She wondered if he was seeing anyone. He told her he wasn't. She giggled girlishly, and asked if he wanted to see someone. Despite her curves, her shining black hair and her pretty face, he told her his heart lay elsewhere.

"Pity," she said.

"Sorry."

"Can't win them all," she said cheerfully. "Is Ivan still seeing that hotel girl?"

"No."

"Right," she said. "Well, watch this space! After all, every dog has his day!" She laughed uproariously. She waved and she was gone.

He turned away to find Mary standing behind him. "You shouldn't be here," he told her.

"I'm going straight home to bed." She still felt weak.

"How's Penny? Any word?"

"She's still hanging in there but they won't let me talk to her."

"It's not unusual. It'll work out."

"I know I've seen you but I miss you," she said.

"I miss you too." He looked sad.

"Maybe you could come for your dinner tomorrow?"

"We'll see how you are."

He seemed distant and she didn't want to push it. "OK," she agreed, and then she, like Paula, was gone.

Penny was allowed to make one phone call at the end of a very long week. It had begun with urine and blood tests that revealed Penny hadn't a moderate dependence but was a high risk for delirium tremens. She didn't know what the doctor was saying – it was all Greek to her.

"The DTs," he explained, and went on to outline what she might be in for over the next three to four days. He mentioned confusion.

*I think I'm already there.*

Agitation was also possible.

*Stop drumming your fingers, Penn.*

Disturbances of memory came next.

*Not necessarily a bad thing.*

Hallucinations. He ticked his page again.

*Just another Saturday night.*

Fever appeared on the list.

*You give me fever.*

The doctor informed her that she might experience high blood pressure and/or seizures.

"My grandmother died of a stroke," she said.

"We'll be keeping a close eye on you," he promised.

The headache started on day two, and it was worse than any hangover she'd ever had. The fever kicked in that afternoon. Her heart-rate increased and she felt nauseous and dizzy.

"You're doing really well," the nurse said.

"Easy for you to say," she said, to both of the woman's heads.

Day three was even tougher. She lost track of time. Her eyes leaked something that felt like pus and her body shook. The seizure took hold that evening but Penny was so out of it she had to be told about the incident rather than having any memory of it. By day four she was over the

313

worst. She still had the symptoms but they were milder and the IV fluids and tranquillizers were helping. She had been allowed out of her bed on days four, five and six.

Now, a week on, she sat in a hospital corridor dialling a number she hadn't dialled in a long time. She figured she'd have to leave a message and was quite surprised when her mother answered. "Hello," she'd said breezily, as though she'd expected a call.

"Mum," Penny said, "it's me, Penny."

"Penny! It's been an age, darling. How are you?"

"Fine," she said.

"Good," her mother replied. "Your father was only talking about you last week, saying we should all get together soon. There's a Law Society function in a few weeks and we've got a spare ticket." She laughed. "There's a few tasty treats attending, I don't mind saying!"

"I'm not looking for a man," Penny said.

"Of course not – let them look for you. Right? How's all in Kenmare? I really am sorry we got rid of the house but who knew then that bloody prices would soar?"

"Mum."

"Yes, dear?"

"I'm an alcoholic," Penny said, for the third time that day.

"What?" Her normally unflappable mother sounded a little flustered.

"I'm in a hospital in Dublin."

"Good God!"

"Mum?"

"Yes?"

"Do you love me?"

Her mother took a moment to answer. As a solicitor, she

was trained to absorb all the information in a case before she responded. "Is this our fault?" she asked.

"No. It's mine. I just want to know."

"Of course I do. You're my child. I may not be Mary Poppins but I love you with everything in me."

"Mum?"

"Yes."

"Can we try to talk more?"

"Absolutely." Her mother sounded a little shell-shocked.

"Good," Penny said, relieved.

"Do you want us to come and see you?"

"No, but thanks for asking." She smiled to herself.

"I love you. Your father loves you."

"Thanks, Mum," Penny said. She put down the phone and went back to her room.

In the short time Norma had been home she had slipped back into the centre of Ivan's life, ably assisted by her children. Her intention was not to get in the way – on the contrary – but her mere presence had already ended his burgeoning relationship with Sienna. Norma had been upset by this news but he had told her it had nothing to do with her homecoming: the relationship had simply run its course. He had known that Norma living under his roof, roaming the corridors in a nightgown and making breakfast while his new girlfriend was ringing the bell, like a kid wanting a friend to come out and play, was never going to work. But he had asked his wife to stay because that was best for his kids.

His mother watched Ivan's wife entwine herself into the fabric of his life and worried for her son. She asked Norma to join her for a coffee in Jam on the pretext of catching up. Norma was no fool and prepared herself for her mother-in-law's interrogation over tea and scones.

"I see you're doing his washing now?" Sheila said, having witnessed Norma separating Ivan's dark from white smalls.

"Well, I might as well, seeing as I'm doing my own and the kids'."

"He'll miss that when you go."

"I'm sure he'll cope." Norma smiled.

"I wish I was. He had a nice thing going with Sienna."

"He said it had run its course."

"He lied," his mother said. "Norma?"

"Yes?"

"He has strong feelings for that girl. He might even love her but he would still take you back in the morning."

"You're so sure?"

"He'll do what he thinks is best for his family. I'm his mother, and I know."

"What do you want me to say?" Norma asked, taken aback.

"Say you'll do nothing to hurt him. The first time I'll forgive, the second I won't," Sheila said, and smiled at a passer-by.

"I won't hurt him," Norma promised.

"Good. I'll hold you to that."

Mossy was frying steak and onions when the bell rang. Sam stood at the front door, nervous and a little shaky.

"You look like a dead man," Mossy said, without concern.

The door swung open and Sam followed him inside. "I'm wondering if you have anything to buy," he said.

Mossy lit a cigarette and resumed cooking. "Be specific."

"Drugs."

"I thought you were clean," Mossy said, turning to stare at him.

Sam's legs were threatening to give way. He sat down on a hard chair with his head in his hands. "I am. I just haven't been sleeping. I need to sleep," he said, in a voice that almost begged.

"I don't sell," Mossy said.

"Please," Sam muttered.

Mossy took his pan off the heat. He ran his fingers through his hair, taking time to scratch his head. "All I've ever done is hash," he said.

"OK," Sam said.

"I don't feel good about this."

"It's just hash. I want to sleep."

"I'll give you enough for two joints and then you're on your own."

"Thanks."

Mossy cut a small piece from his stash, took out some papers and two cigarettes. "I suppose you know how to roll?"

"Yes."

"Right so," Mossy said. He handed Sam the contraband.

"Thank you."

"Don't thank me," Mossy said. "We both know you're fucking yourself up."

Sam left without another word.

Mary lay on the sofa with Mr Monkels's head on her lap. She had drifted into sleep during *That '70s Show* but woke an hour later with panic rising. Everything within her told her to go next door. She lifted Mr Monkels off her legs. He moaned and moved to take up the entire sofa.

She knocked on Sam's door but received no answer. She knocked on the window and still nothing. She knew Sam was inside and every fibre of her screamed that something was wrong. She went back into her own home. In the kitchen she opened the french windows. She fetched a chair and dragged it outside. She placed it against the wall and levered herself over and into her neighbour's garden. The back door was open. She slipped into the empty kitchen. She went to the sitting room but he was not there. Upstairs, his bedroom door was open, but the room was empty. The bathroom door was closed. She tried to open it, but it was locked.

"Sam!" she called.

"Go away."

"No!"

"Please go away!"

"Come out!" she said.

"I can't," he said. She heard him flick a lighter.

"Sam, please don't give up!"

"I'm not strong like you."

"I'm not strong like me! Please come out!" She sensed his terror – and that he wanted to tell her something desperately but didn't know where to start. She sat on the floor, leaning against the door. "Just tell me," she said, after the longest time.

"I can't," he said, as though he'd been expecting the question.

"Why?"

"Because you'll hate me."

"I've never told anyone this." She took a deep breath. "I wanted to have an abortion," she said. "That night on the mountain I told Robert I was pregnant and I wanted an abortion. He wanted to keep it. We argued and he died. When I woke up full of baby, I hated it. I wished it would die. Every day in that hospital and through rehab and right up until he was born I wished my son would die." Tears streamed from her eyes. "And then he did die . . . Do you hate me?" she asked.

"No. That wasn't your fault."

"Maybe. Maybe not. Sometimes it's hard to tell."

Sam was silent for a minute or two, but Mary waited and her patience paid off. "It was the night I overdosed," he said.

She sat perfectly still, afraid that the slightest stir would stall the tale.

"There was this dealer, a guy I knew from school. I'd bumped into him a few weeks before. He was a junkie too. He sold to feed his own habit. He was a *loser*! He'd said he'd fix me up if I ever got stuck. My guy had been lying low. I didn't want to use him. I fucking hated him but I was desperate. I went to his place. He lived in some shithole in the Bronx on the third floor. It took a while to make the stairs. I hadn't banged up in a while."

Sam was talking to Mary from the bathroom floor in a little cottage in Ireland but right then he was in a dank apartment block on 233rd Street. He was walking up the stairs, his legs aching. The damn lift was broken, which was typical. He had an abscess on his foot at the point where he injected. It burst on the second floor. *Fuck!* He got to the third and smelt piss. He felt sick but he knew if he could make it to 56C he'd be

319

OK. He knocked on the door, but there was no answer. He was pissed as the asshole had sworn he'd be waiting. He knocked again, harder and with urgency. He would have broken the door down but suddenly it swung open.

He entered a room. The kitchen merged with the bedroom, which was also the sitting room. The bathroom was a tiny cubicle off the kitchen. He knew it was the bathroom because of the shit stench coming from it. The guy was sitting on the sofa with his back to him. Sam called from the door. He noticed the paint peeling down the walls and the frayed furniture from a different era, which didn't meld with the large-screen TV and hi-fi system in the corner. He called again but the guy just sat there. He closed the door behind him. He was annoyed that the fucker thought it OK to ignore him.

Then he was facing him. The guy's skin was a translucent blue against deep purple lips. A needle was stuck in his arm, which was bent and ready to receive. The elastic was tight around his forearm. His eyes were open and he was hunched as though the end had come in a second.

Sam took a chair and sat close to absorb every detail, as though the dead man was some sort of macabre museum piece.

"Oh, my God!" Sam heard Mary say. He hadn't spared her the graphic details. Why should he? He wanted her to know. She needed to know what a rotten degenerate he really was. She deserved a fair chance to run.

"After that I robbed him of his stash. I closed the door good and tight and left him to rot." *No more than he deserved.*

"Jesus!" he heard her mumble.

"But just as I was leaving I heard something. I could have sworn I heard him take a breath. It was barely audible and there was no movement when I stared back at him – but I was sure I heard something. An hour or two later I was choking on my own vomit in my Manhattan penthouse." He spoke as though the story had ended.

"I don't understand."

"I lived. He died. What's not to understand?"

"Why didn't you call an ambulance?" she asked.

He laughed as though she'd told a joke. "Why would I?" he asked bitterly.

"But if he was still breathing?"

"Maybe he was, maybe he wasn't." A tear slipped down his face.

"Why didn't you call the police?"

"I was a drug addict in a dealer's apartment."

"Why did you leave him to rot?"

"Because that's what he deserved!" he shouted.

"Why?"

"*Because I wanted him dead!*"

"Why?"

"I despised him." He got up and walked to the bathroom door.

"Why?"

He leaned against the door.

"Why?" she repeated.

He opened the door and she fell back a little. "You know what the worst thing is?"

"No," she whispered.

"When I left him I had a fucking smile on my face." He walked past her and into his bedroom.

"Why?" she called. *Tell me!*

He turned to her. "You don't understand. I'm so full of hate, Mary, I rattle with it. Fucking Topher!" He mumbled the last words and fell onto his bed.

She flushed the joint and pocketed the lighter. She sat on the floor at the end of his bed.

"Go home."

"No," she said, and she listened to him cry until at last he fell asleep.

Later, alone and in the half-light, she sat in her sitting room with her sleeping dog at her side. She recalled every aspect of his story up to the final mumbled "Fucking Topher!" She closed her eyes. She no longer needed sleep to see the boys circle the kid in the hood. She heard, "Look, Topher's excited!" She saw the kid, and the ring-leader leering. She heard him direct the other boys: "Give Topher a go!" She saw the boy-bear called Topher move towards the kid lying on the ground. *Oh, Sam, what did they do to you?*

# 26. Down but not out

It was six the following evening before Sam saw Mary again. He had spent most of the day in bed with a headache that stubbornly refused to go away. In trying to sleep he employed every trick in the book, but counting sheep, hot milk, herbal remedies and even a sleeping tablet didn't help. His mind refused to comply – it was too busy picking apart the previous night's revelation. Part of him had wanted to finish the tale – perhaps if he confided in Mary he would finally be free of that which gnawed at his insides. Part of him wanted her to know everything but the rest stopped the words in his head pouring out of his mouth. He just couldn't do it. And now, worse, he feared he couldn't bring himself to face her. *I've lost her. I deserve to lose her. She's better off without me. Oh, God, I can't stand it!*

He was in the kitchen taking two painkillers when the bell rang. The door had been on the latch since Jerry Letter had dropped in a parcel that Sam hadn't bothered to open. Mary didn't wait for him to answer: she walked into the kitchen with her car keys in hand. "Let's go," she said, turning on her heel.

"What?"

"You heard me. Let's go." She stopped. "I'm waiting."

"I'm not going anywhere. I'm in my sweats, for God's sake!" He looked down at his unsightly navy sweatpants in an attempt to avoid eye contact.

"We're going," she said, with a look that meant business.

"I have nothing more to say."

"There is nothing more I want to hear," she replied.

"You drive me crazy," he said, following her to the car.

"You were always crazy. I just highlight it."

She smiled at him and he felt like crying. *I've disappointed everyone who has ever cared about me.*

They drove in silence for at least twenty minutes before he asked about their destination. "You'll see when you get there," she said, and turned up the volume on her CD player so that Marilyn Manson's ode to "Beautiful People" filled the car. He turned it down and looked at her but she continued to stare straight ahead.

"What is this?" he asked.

"An ending," she said.

"An ending?"

"Everything has to end. You need peace. I need to give it to you."

"And you think you can?" He snorted.

"I don't know, but there's no harm in trying." Her eyes were fixed on the road. "And then we'll say goodbye."

"I never wanted to hurt you."

"I never wanted to be hurt."

"I'm damaged goods." He sighed.

"We're all damaged."

He fell silent. *Not like me.*

It was close to eight o'clock when they arrived at the small strand. Mary parked the car on the hill and handed a flask of coffee to Sam. She pointed at a spiral sandy pathway that led to the beach below. "Follow the path," she said.

"What about you?"

"This isn't about me." She smiled.

He opened the door, but before he could step out onto the cold sand, she grasped his arm. He faced her with a quizzical look.

"It's going to be OK," she said, pulled him to her and kissed his forehead. "Everything's going to be fine." She hugged him tight, as a mother would a child. Then, without another word, she released him and pointed again to the pathway.

The glistening water captured him. The tide was high and pink under the last of the evening sun. The beach was empty save for a woman and her dog, and a lonely figure sitting close to the lapping tide. He stood for a moment breathing in the salty air.

The man turned and Sam saw it was Mary's father. He smiled at Sam and beckoned to him. Sam approached and Jack patted the sand beside him. "Sit," he said.

He complied. "Jack?" *What the hell was going on?*

"In the flesh," Jack replied.

"I'm not sure what this is," Sam said.

"Me neither," Jack replied, with a sigh, "but Mary has a way of getting people to carry out her will. She's just like her mother that way."

"What is it she wants?"

"She wants me to tell you a story," Jack replied softly.

"A story?" Sam asked, perplexed.

"I've only ever shared it with one human being and that was my daughter, and only because after Ben died I had an inkling she'd try to follow him. I needed her to know that a lifetime of happiness can't be destroyed in one moment, no matter how terrible or what is lost in that moment." He sniffed the sea air. "Did you bring the coffee?" he asked.

Sam lifted the flask.

"Good." Jack took it and poured a cup for Sam. Then he pulled a plastic mug from his pocket and poured for himself. "She makes great coffee."

Sam drank half of his in one gulp, then balanced his cup on a rock. He looked back towards the hill, and could barely make out Mary's car. Jack took a slug and began.

"It was the summer of 1957 and I had just turned sixteen. My father had a friend with a farm who offered to pay me half nothing to help him clear out an old stable that needed fixing. I'd been working three days before he came near me and I was exhausted from lifting and hauling. The place was in a terrible state. He brought me a lemonade drink his wife had made. Jesus, I can still taste the sugar – it was thick with it. I sat down to drink it. He sat beside me. The next thing I know his hands were in my hair. I thought maybe there was straw but then his other hand was in my crotch."

Sam wanted to stand but his legs failed him. "I can't," he said. He put his hands to his ears, but Jack gently removed them.

"I tried to push him away but he was a strong man. It didn't take much to knock me out, just one clatter of his hand and I was a goner. I wasn't out for long, though. Only long enough for him to have my pants off."

Suddenly Sam was crying, tears streaming down his face. He was shaking the way he did when the anger took over.

"I understand that kind of hate," said Jack. "I know how it can infect your entire being. I know how it can destroy a soul. I know how you feel, son."

Sam was sobbing and Jack stayed quiet. He focused on the tide turning and the birds calling until Sam had collected himself enough to speak.

Mary sat in the car. It had become clear now – she had seen it all. She saw him rehearsing above an old launderette. She watched him say goodbye to the others and turn onto a street marked 7th. She saw him pass those boys. They were calling out, *Loser, hey, loser, where ya going, loser?* He gave them the fingers. They started running. He started running with everything he had in him. Again she felt the concrete under his feet and heard the steam emitting from a grating. She could hear the car screeching to a halt and the horn beeping. She could feel the steel bumper against his thigh as he brushed past it. She could hear them coming and the thud of eight feet moving closer and closer. She could feel his chest tighten and his breath shorten. They were closer now, the hairs on the back of his neck standing to attention, warning him of danger. He tried to speed up but his legs weighed heavily. He slowed by a fraction but it was enough.

Seconds later they had caught up. The kicking and punching started. He was on the ground, his hood pulled tight around his face and his hands attempting to protect himself from their blows. There was the big guy Topher, the one they called Bear. He was standing there with a bottle in one hand. He was jumping up and down and laughing.

"Topher's excited. Give Topher a go! Go on, Bear, give it to him! Give it to him!"

Sitting in that car she was lost, lost in another time when a boy was about to be raped. *"Do it! Do it! Do it!"* The words resonated in her head. She closed her eyes but she heard Topher release his buckle and unzip while two of the others held the boy down. She heard them tearing at his jeans. She felt one unzip him, then the cold air strike him, as though he'd sat on ice.

*"Do it! Do it! Do it!"* the boys chanted.

"Get him on all fours!" their twisted leader called, but he was barely audible.

She saw them pulling him to his knees. He wanted to call out but his voice was gone. He wanted to kick and punch and make them all bleed, but he couldn't. He just wanted to run. It felt like he was tearing inside. It felt like he was burning and every invasion burned deeper and deeper until time meant nothing. The moment froze. Then, suddenly, he was alone, covered with blood, shit and piss, and still he couldn't scream, so instead the rage simmered until it infected every part of him.

Mary returned to the present, sobbing and wiping the never-ending stream from her eyes and nose.

*"Save me!"* the boy had called to her.

"Even if it means losing you," she said to her empty car, then put it into reverse and drove away.

"If I hadn't given them the fingers!" Sam groaned.

Jack nodded. "If I hadn't agreed to the lemonade."

"If I'd run faster," Sam said.

"If I'd grabbed the pitchfork by the stable wall," Jack replied.

"If I'd been stronger."

"If I'd been stronger," Jack repeated.

Sam turned to him and Jack smiled as best he could. "If

328

'if' was a donkey we'd all have a ride," he said. "Time to let go." He waved towards the sea. "Time to turn it around."

Sam watched the tide lap away. "Is that possible?" he asked.

"I'm proof of it," Jack said.

"What if I can't?"

"Then you've allowed those bullies on that night to wage a war that would last a lifetime. Don't let them win, son."

They sat in silence until the tide was far away and the evening chill had set in. Then they walked together to Jack's car.

"I have to go home," Sam said.

"No more running away," Jack stated.

Sam nodded. "Mary."

"Maybe in another time and place," Jack said, with a sad smile.

"Maybe," and Sam was crying again.

Mary returned home to Mr Monkels, who was waiting for her, his tail wagging. She sat on the floor and hugged him. Earlier that day when she had asked Jessie and Pierre to watch over the bar so that she and her dad could talk, they had sat in Jack's apartment and she had told him what she suspected about Sam's past. He had agreed to talk to Sam, as difficult as it was for him.

Before she left, he offered a warning. "If you're right, he might never forgive you for knowing," he said.

"I know. Just help him."

"He might never be able to look you in the face again."

"I know."

"No, love, you don't. So many times I wanted to tell your mother but I couldn't."

"He needs help."

"You could lose him."

"He was never mine to keep."

Van Morrison was playing in the day room. Penny looked up from one of the books Mary had sent and marked the page. The phone was free and had been for at least half an hour. She couldn't delay making the call any longer so, after she'd helped Eileen from Ward Five to find the remote control, she dialled Adam's number.

"Hello?" she said. "It's me."

"Penny." He sounded relieved to hear her voice. "Are you OK? I've been worried sick. Why haven't you let me visit you?"

"I needed time."

"Fair enough. I'm just happy to hear from you now."

"Adam," she began, "I know you're back in Kenmare."

"I made Mary promise to say nothing," he said, a little annoyed.

"Don't blame her. I asked about you and, well, you know what she's like. She tried to cover but failed miserably." She laughed a little. "How are you getting on in the restaurant and with your dad?"

"We're fit to kill one another. Still, it's not too bad. We just hired a new chef and he's a pain in the arse but excellent."

"Good. I'm sorry about you and Alina."

"You are?"

"Yeah. I am."

"The kids are OK. I'm going to have them every second weekend. It's hard but they'll adjust and they definitely don't miss the arguing."

"That's good."

"When are you coming home?" he asked.

"That's what I'm calling about."

"You want me to pick you up?"

"No."

"Oh, OK, what can I do?"

"Nothing."

"I don't understand."

Penny remained silent just long enough for Adam to worry. Eventually she said, "You told me once about the first time you ever saw me."

"You were wearing blue shoes."

"That's right. I was alone and you said you saw me cry."

"And all I wanted to do was save you."

"Yeah," she said. "Well, you can."

"How?"

"Let me go."

"I don't understand," he said, sounding panicked.

"I've been such a mess and for so long. I need to be a different person. I need to move on."

"Is that your doctor or you talking?"

"It's the right thing to do."

"No, Penny – please."

"I'm so sorry." She hung up.

Eileen from Ward Five was waiting to give her a hug. "It's hard to let go," she said.

Penny nodded and dried her eyes. "Come on, let's see if we can find an episode of *CSI*," she suggested.

"My favourite." Eileen smiled.

Mary made it home a little after eight, exhaustion threatening to shut her mind down. Mr Monkels was waiting by the window. She watched him stretch in anticipation of her key turning. He approached, tail wagging. She rubbed his head and together they walked upstairs. She fell onto her bed and he flopped beside her. Within minutes they were sleeping soundly.

She didn't wake until mid-afternoon the following day. Her eyes opened to the sound of Mr Monkels licking himself with the enthusiasm he usually reserved for prohibited foodstuffs. She sat up and looked out of the small square window. The sky resembled a perfect light blue silk and was cloudless. She stood up and went to look outside. Below, a woman walked past wearing sunglasses and pushing a pram with a parasol protecting a little face from the hot sun. Ivan was varnishing the deck of his boat, which he'd been promising to do all year. Chris emerged from the water and hauled himself aboard – his father pushed him back in, to Justine's glee. The little girl threw her head back, laughing, perched on the side, swinging her legs. Mossy sat in his front garden, smoking a cigarette and cutting his toenails. His battered old radio was dangling by its cord from the window and from it Van Morrison sang to her about the water and the rain.

Before she noticed the absence of Sam's car, she knew he was gone.

# 27. Those left behind

It was a warm September evening. Mary drove home, anticipating a walk in the woods with Mr Monkels. She was determined to make the most of the weather and her time before it changed and she left. She'd stop at the plaque that bore her son's name and walk through the trees with her camera in hand. Since Penny had returned, she had often joined Mary and Mr M and, while Mr M investigated the undergrowth, they'd gossip and laugh about all manner of subjects.

It was during one such walk some weeks earlier that Mary had confided she had been accepted into a photography course in London.

"You're joking?"

"No."

"Congratulations, you deserve it."

Mary was grinning from ear to ear.

"When?" Penny asked.

"Next month."

"I can take Mr Monkels," Penny offered. "I'd love to help."

"Dad's having him, but thanks."

"Good for you," Penny said, and they stopped to watch the sun dance on the water.

"You'll come and visit?" Mary asked.

"Absolutely." Her friend hooked her arm through Mary's. "Any excuse to shop in London."

"You'll be OK?"

"I will." Penny smiled. "It's all changed. It was the same for so long and now it's not."

"It's better?"

"It's much better."

But this evening Penny wouldn't be joining them on their walk – she was going to her cooking class.

Mary got home a little after six and called to Mr Monkels. He didn't come out of the kitchen or down the stairs. He wasn't stretched out on the sofa or by the window. He wasn't in the garden because earlier he had made it very clear that he had no wish to go out, despite the warm weather. She made her way upstairs.

"Mr Monkels!" she called. "Where are you, boy?"

She found him on her bed but this time he wouldn't wake. She knew instantly that he was gone. She sat beside him, kissed his furry face and then called the vet.

After he'd left Mossy helped her carry her dog downstairs.

"He wouldn't stay to see you leave, Mare," Mossy said.

"Yeah," she agreed, blowing her nose.

"It's for the best."

"I know," she said, with a sob. "I'll really miss him, Mossy."

"Of course you will," Mossy said, patting her back. "Mr Monkels was a fine dog, loving and faithful and –"

"Mossy."

"Yeah?"

"Shut up."

"Right."

Mossy made tea while Mary sat stroking Mr Monkels. Ivan was the first to arrive, with Sienna trailing behind.

Their separation hadn't lasted long. In fact they had only managed a week apart when Norma had announced she'd found a job and a new place to live. Once Ivan had approved the house as fit for his wife and children, he insisted on paying the rent. Norma and the kids moved out and, one long conversation and a romantic trip to Paris later, Sienna moved in.

Despite the late hour, Ivan and Sienna had managed to secure a wreath in the flower shop before it closed. The card read: *Mr Monkels, we love you*. The thought was so nice it made Mary's nose and eyes run. All the crying was starting to get to Mossy, who took their arrival as an opportune moment to make his getaway.

Adam arrived with a couple of spades and a large box. This, too, made Mary cry, so Sienna comforted her while Ivan and Adam dug a hole in her back garden. Penny arrived last, having received the text message at the end of her cooking class. She had shared Mary's news with the entire class, who had all donated their lamb and vegetable stew and lemon tarts so that Mary wouldn't have to cook for a week.

"It's just like a real funeral," Sienna said to Ivan, who took a break from digging to get a glass of water.

"It *is* a real funeral."

"It's a dog," she reminded him.

"It's more than a dog. It's Mr Monkels," he said.

When the hole was dug and Mary was ready to say goodbye, Ivan placed Mr Monkels in the box and, with Adam's help, they lowered it into the earth.

"Do you want to say anything?" Ivan asked.

"I think the wreath says it all." Mary gave a little sob.

The scene was so sad that Penny and Sienna joined in

with the sob, as did Mossy, who was standing on a beer crate and peering over his wall.

In the absence of anything else to do or say, the lads filled in the grave and placed the wreath on top of the fresh earth. *Rest in peace, Mr M.* Afterwards an impromptu party was held. Jack arrived with a crate of booze, closely followed by friends Patty and Con, each bearing boxes of soft drinks and mixers.

Pierre followed with some leftovers from the day's trading. When Mary made a face, he chastised her: "This is perfectly good food, Marie. You Irish are so wasteful."

"You're giving out to me at my dog's funeral?" she asked, managing to hide a smile.

"Say you're sorry," Jessie said, giving him a slap as she passed him.

"You are right, Marie, today is not the day but as *la belle* Scarlett once said, 'Tomorrow is another day.'"

Jessie laughed. "I could listen to that man all day but it's an awful shame I have to look at him."

"There's something weird with those two," Penny said.

"You're right," Mary agreed.

"What?" Penny asked, mouth agape.

Mary winked.

"They did not?" Penny said, eyes wide.

Mary said nothing.

"Jesus, you think you know people!"

Penny walked off into the sitting room where Mossy was playing the only song he knew on guitar and Ivan was heckling.

Mary watched her pass Adam, who was talking to Norma – she'd arrived with the kids who were outside placing flowers they'd stolen from a neighbour's garden on Mr Monkels's new place of rest. The birds above them were quiet.

Adam called to Penny, who came back to join in their conversation.

Their relationship was being redefined and it was hard on them both but, watching from her kitchen, Mary guessed that they would be all right.

Steven and Barry arrived – without Pluto, as a mark of respect. "We didn't want to rub it in, Mare," Steven said. "After all, Pluto is incredibly cute and alive."

Mary smiled at him. "Thanks, Steve, you really know what to say."

Tin arrived into the kitchen looking for a bin. "Mare, sorry about the dog dying but still and all you're looking great on it!" he said.

Before long her house was filled with family, friends, neighbours, well-wishers and music.

It was after twelve and the party was still going strong. Mary sat in her garden beside the mound covering Mr Monkels. Penny came out to join her. "Do you want some company?" she asked, handing her a freshly made coffee.

"Only yours." Mary smiled.

"You're being really brave," Penny said, nudging her.

"I know he was a dog and not a person but . . ."

"But every time you said his name it brought back Ben," Penny said.

"Yeah," Mary nodded, "it did."

"Everything was the same for so long." Penny repeated the words she had said in the wood.

"But it's all changed now," Mary replied.

"And as hard as it is to let go . . ."

". . . it's for the best," Mary said sadly. Then she said, while watching Tin and Mossy attempt a two-hand reel through her kitchen window, "I received a copy of Mia Johnson's third album today."

"Sam?" Penny asked.

"No, Mia." Mary smiled. "She sent a card."

"Such a nice woman. I still feel like such an arsehole," Penny mumbled. "What did she say?"

"She said that Sam was well and asked how I'd managed to get him into therapy. Apparently it was something she could never do. She said he was happy and healthy."

"What did happen between you two?" Penny asked.

"Nothing," Mary said, with a smile. "Nothing at all."

"OK, you don't have to tell me – tonight." A moment or two passed. "So, what's the album like?"

"It's good. I especially like the track Sam wrote."

"He wrote a song for Mia?"

"He wrote the music. Mia wrote the lyrics. She's a very intuitive woman," Mary said.

"Did she mention me?" Penny asked, laughing, and Mary joined in.

# Epilogue

It was a cold morning in New York City. Sam stood in the centre of the room taking a long look at the white walls and white-painted wooden floor. It reminded him of rehab and the man he used to be, if only for a moment. This room was much bigger than the one he had emerged from three years previously.

Mia pushed him from behind. "Come on or we'll be late."

"I still don't know what we're doing here."

"You're so impatient," she said, looking at the other people milling around. She pointed to a room off the one in which they were standing, which contained plants and a table of white and red wine. "Do you want a drink before we go in?" she asked.

"No, I want to go home. Don't you have a husband to do this stuff with?"

"He's in the studio."

"Oh, yeah? Who with?"

"Does it matter?" she asked, pushing him towards the door.

"OK, what about you? Shouldn't you be resting?"

"I'm pregnant, not ill. Come on!" She took him by the hand. "You'll like it."

Sam stood in the middle of another white room. Black-and-white photos lined the walls. Mia pulled him to take a closer look. They were all gravesides or memorials, each instilled with a sadness that seemed familiar. He couldn't explain it – you had to see the photos to be able to understand. He was lost in a photo of a young girl cleaning a broken headstone. She looked East European; she wore a scarf over her head and couldn't have been more than ten. The headstone listed four names and their deaths were all dated for the same day. He wondered who they were and what they were to her. Was it her family or had she even known them? Maybe it was a summer job, but that didn't explain the girl's sadness.

Mia pulled him along. He passed a photo of an empty goal with flowers intertwining the net and an empty bench in memory of a woman called Emily.

"What do you think of this one?" she asked, stopping in front of another. " 'We love you, Mr Monkels'," he read. "There's only one Mr Monkels."

"Yes, there is, or sadly was – the photo testifies that he's no longer with us," Mary said, from behind him.

He turned. "I can't believe you're here."

"I was going to phone, but it's been so long."

"I was going to write. I just didn't know what to say."

"You're both as bad as each other," Mia told them. "It's a good thing I like to read the arts section."

They were staring into each other's eyes.

"I'm going home," Mia said. "My feet are killing me."

Mary and Sam said goodbye to her, then turned to one another. It had been a long time and yet no time at all.

"I have one photo I think you'll like," Mary said, and he followed where she led. She stood in front of a picture of a tree. Light streamed down from the sky above and rain poured down the bark, running into and past the carving.

*I WILL GO*
*MY ♡ WILL STAY*
*LB 1930*

"LB – Lena Breslin! You found it! I can't believe you found it!"

"It took a while," she smiled, "but I had some time after you left."

"It's a beautiful exhibition," he said, gesticulating at the photos of ghosts that lined the walls.

"Yeah, well, what else would you expect from Mary of the Sorrows?" She grinned.

"I'm guessing you haven't been that for a long time."

"You're right."

"Would you like to catch up over dinner?"

"Very much."

"And, if you're free, maybe afterwards we could get married."

She laughed. "Let's just have a shag first and see how it goes."

And in a moment reminiscent of the closing credits of a Hollywood romance or a French drama, Sam and Mary stood in the middle of a white room. It would have been obvious to anyone who cared to look that all they could see was each other. And if that person was given to fantasy they might have expected them to live happily ever after.

# Acknowledgements

Thanks to my family: Mary and Tony O'Shea for being my aunt, my uncle, my mum, my dad, and all things during times good and bad; Denis, Siobhan, Brenda, Caroline and Aisling for taking me into your home and making me feel like I was a part of it; their significant others, Lisa, Paul, Mark, Ger and Dave, for all that you are to the people I love. Mary and Kevin Flood, for being my home away from home, and to Mary for being the eternal reminder that my mum once lived here; their sons Eoin, Dara, Cónal & Ruaraí for the eighties, and for being the people who never failed to make me laugh; Paudie McSwiney, for your friendship, which I hold dear; the McSwineys of Kenmare for being the first family in Ireland to buy a copy of *Pack Up the Moon*; my grandparents, Bertie and Nora McSwiney, no longer living but still in all our hearts – we loved you then and we love you now; Claire McSwiney, my half-sister and some would say better half, thank you for your kindness; Claire's mother Mary – you were and always will be a lady; Don and Terry McPartlin for your enduring support, help and friendship.

To my husband, who fell in love with me even though I had a God-awful perm and a penchant for wearing polka dots – like Dolly P once said, "I will always love you", and the day you bother to read one of my books is the day you'll get a dedication.

To my friends: Valerie K – to me you will always be my

Hallie and no one makes me laugh the way you do; Fergus E, I love you like a fat kid loves cake; Enda B, did you ever know that you're my hero? Sing it with me now – you're everything I wish I could be. Tracy K, I'd jig naked just to hear you laugh; Edel and Noel S and Lucy and Darren W, you're sensible, forthright, intelligent, irreverent, funny and I'm glad I met you; Joanne C, you are me in a parallel universe except you get to be blonde and have better dress sense but I love our weird ways; John G, how can I not love a guy who married the blonde, better-looking and better-dressed me? Martin C, the first time I met you I was wearing baggy pants and bunny slippers and you didn't hold it against me – you are and will always be one of my best friends; to Trish C for making me fill out forms on an Easter Monday – I know I moaned but without you we'd still be renting; Graham D, for those nights when the band was courting record companies in Reynard's or Lillie's and I was bored stupid – you always knew what to say – and to your wife Bernice D for becoming a great friend; Angela D, the ultimate punk rocker with flowers in her hair; to Lisa and Warren: Lisa sings, Warren supports, and you can't beat that.

To my friends from Kenmare: Leonie K, we laughed, we cried, people died, we survived and through it all I love you; Dermot K, I love you, your wife and your kids; Cliff M, you're the only person in the whole world I would watch a gardening show with; Gareth T, you get me on a whole different level; Mark L, thank you for being the first person to tell me a joke after Mum died – I'll love you for ever for that; Nina B, for being one of the kindest and best people I've ever known; Bernice and Rosita, the C twins, for our friendship through all those years.

To the buyers and sellers in Easons, Hughes and Hughes, Dubray and Tesco: your support has been overwhelming and much appreciated, thank you, thank you, thank you.

To Paula Campbell, Poolbeg's publisher – you have the hardest job of all. You find talent where others don't. Without you many of the writers in this country wouldn't have been heard of. Thank you.

To all at Penguin in Ireland and the UK: Michael O'Loughlin, Patricia Deevy. Thank you.

To my agent Faith O'Grady, I'm scattered and you're coping, to you and all at Lisa Richards, thank you.

And finally to the people of Kenmare, thank you.

# He just wanted a decent book to read ...

Not too much to ask, is it? It was in 1935 when Allen Lane, Managing Director of Bodley Head Publishers, stood on a platform at Exeter railway station looking for something good to read on his journey back to London. His choice was limited to popular magazines and poor-quality paperbacks – the same choice faced every day by the vast majority of readers, few of whom could afford hardbacks. Lane's disappointment and subsequent anger at the range of books generally available led him to found a company – and change the world.

*'We believed in the existence in this country of a vast reading public for intelligent books at a low price, and staked everything on it'*
**Sir Allen Lane, 1902–1970, founder of Penguin Books**

The quality paperback had arrived – and not just in bookshops. Lane was adamant that his Penguins should appear in chain stores and tobacconists, and should cost no more than a packet of cigarettes.

Reading habits (and cigarette prices) have changed since 1935, but Penguin still believes in publishing the best books for everybody to enjoy. We still believe that good design costs no more than bad design, and we still believe that quality books published passionately and responsibly make the world a better place.

So wherever you see the little bird – whether it's on a piece of prize-winning literary fiction or a celebrity autobiography, political tour de force or historical masterpiece, a serial-killer thriller, reference book, world classic or a piece of pure escapism – you can bet that it represents the very best that the genre has to offer.

**Whatever you like to read – trust Penguin.**

# No Way to Say Goodbye

ANNA McPARTLIN

PENGUIN BOOKS

PENGUIN BOOKS

Published by the Penguin Group
Penguin Books Ltd, 80 Strand, London WC2R ORL, England
Penguin Group (USA) Inc., 375 Hudson Street, New York, New York 10014, USA
Penguin Group (Canada), 90 Eglinton Avenue East, Suite 700, Toronto, Ontario, Canada M4P 2Y3
(a division of Pearson Penguin Canada Inc.)
Penguin Ireland, 25 St Stephen's Green, Dublin 2, Ireland (a division of Penguin Books Ltd)
Penguin Group (Australia), 250 Camberwell Road, Camberwell, Victoria 3124, Australia
(a division of Pearson Australia Group Pty Ltd)
Penguin Books India Pvt Ltd, 11 Community Centre, Panchsheel Park, New Delhi – 110 017, India
Penguin Group (NZ), 67 Apollo Drive, Rosedale, North Shore 0632, New Zealand
(a division of Pearson New Zealand Ltd)
Penguin Books (South Africa) (Pty) Ltd, 24 Sturdee Avenue, Rosebank,
Johannesburg 2196, South Africa

Penguin Books Ltd, Registered Offices: 80 Strand, London WC2R ORL, England

www.penguin.com

First published in Ireland as *Apart from the Crowd* by Poolbeg Press 2006
This edition published in Penguin Books 2010

2

Set in Garamond MT Std 12.5/14.75pt
Typeset by Palimpsest Book Production Limited, Grangemouth, Stirlingshire
Printed in England by Clays Ltd, St Ives plc

ISBN: 978-1-844-88189-5

www.greenpenguin.co.uk

Penguin Books is committed to a sustainable future
for our business, our readers and our planet.
The book in your hands is made from paper
certified by the Forest Stewardship Council.